CL

Rescuing
Rose

ALSO BY NICOLA MARSH

Saving Sara

Rescuing
Rose

NICOLA MARSH

LAKE UNION
PUBLISHING

Published by Lake Union Publishing, Seattle
www.apub.com

Amazon, the Amazon logo, and Lake Union Publishing are trademarks of Amazon.com, Inc., or its affiliates.

ISBN-13: 9781503936577
ISBN-10: 1503936570

Cover design by Lisa Horton

Printed in the United States of America

For Sammia and Katie.
Thanks for your editorial insight,
enthusiasm and general all-round awesomeness!
Working with you is a pleasure.

PROLOGUE

Rose Mathieson had done some dumb things in her twenty-six years. But nothing came close to her stupidity today. Forgetting to pick up her precious six-year-old son from school because she'd been on a self-pitying bender last night trumped all the other dumbass things she'd ever done.

Because Olly was her everything. Her reason for living. And she'd never forgive herself if anything happened to him because of her selfishness.

"Mommy, I made you dinner."

She felt a hand tug on her sleeve and she cranked her eyelids open with difficulty. Even now, eighteen hours after she'd consumed three-quarters of a bottle of vodka, her eyes felt gritty, her eyelids heavy.

She stared at the peanut butter sandwich Olly had jammed together in a messy squish and was holding out to her like a prized offering. Her stomach roiled and she swallowed back the nausea.

"I'm not hungry," she snapped, instantly regretting her terse response when his eyes filled with tears and his lower lip wobbled.

Damn.

She reached for him, wishing the persistent jackhammering behind her eyeballs would ease. "Sorry, baby—"

"It's okay," he said, so softly she barely heard him as he hung his head.

But it wasn't okay, because when Olly raised his eyes again to meet hers, she saw something that served to kick her in the guts, sobering her like nothing else would.

Fear.

An invisible weight compressed her chest, making breathing difficult. She knew fear. Had lived with it her entire childhood. A constant companion that ate away at her innocence and eroded her self-esteem. Now, staring at her son's wide-eyed, wary gaze as he took a step back, she knew she'd hit rock bottom.

Olly's palpable fear rattled her down to her soul, for she was in danger of becoming the one person she'd vowed never to be.

Her father.

"Come here, sweetie." Rose patted the sofa cushion beside her and held out her arms. "I'm sorry for being so grumpy."

Olly hesitated, and that long second made Rose want to bawl. He sized her up before he dumped the sandwich on the makeshift coffee table and flung himself into her arms. "Are you tired, Mom? Is that why you're so sad and you don't feel like eating and why you forgot me at school today?"

Guilt stabbed Rose in the heart as she cuddled Olly. "Yeah, I'm really tired, sweetheart. I fell asleep this afternoon and that's why I was late picking you up, but it'll never happen again."

She'd make sure of it.

The downward spiral had to stop. She had to make a stand before she lost the most important person in her life.

"I was okay," he said, snuggling into the crook between her neck and shoulder. "But I did get scared."

He wasn't the only one. When her cell had rung, raising her from her stupor, and she'd seen the school's number flash on the screen, her heart had stopped.

"Oh, sweetie, I'll always be here for you." She hugged him tighter, knowing her promise would be an empty one unless she broke the patterns of the past. "But I might have to go away for a while, so I'm not so tired anymore."

She eased back a little, placed a finger under his chin and tipped it up. "Would you like to stay with Uncle Jake?"

Concern clouded Olly's big brown eyes but he nodded. "He's cool, so that'd be okay, I guess."

"It won't be for long—just 'til I feel better." She kissed the top of his head. "I love you, beautiful boy."

"Love you too, Mom." His little arms reached around her and squeezed tight. "But come back soon."

Rose intended to. Nothing could keep her away from Olly, but unless she faced her demons, she couldn't be the mom he deserved.

And he deserved the best. She'd make sure of it.

She never wanted to see that fear in his eyes ever again.

1.

FOUR MONTHS LATER

Rose hated packing. It reinforced what she knew and despised: that her life was transient. That she had nothing to show for her time on the planet.

This was not entirely true, though . . . Her gaze fell on a framed photo of Olly at his adorable best, tilting his face to the sun and laughing.

Her cheeky, rambunctious six-year-old son was the only good thing in her life and she'd do anything for him, including moving from New York City to backwater Redemption.

Life in a small Connecticut town promised to be her worst nightmare, with her every move scrutinized and found lacking. But Olly had been living there for the last few months while Rose had been in the recovery center, and he was thriving. Her brother Jake had been looking after Olly, and staying with their Aunt Cilla had been a masterstroke. Her pragmatic aunt had convinced Rose to stay with them too once she left the center.

Rose had to make the move. Didn't mean she had to like it.

She surveyed the small studio apartment she'd tried to make home for her and Olly over the last year or so. No matter how many homey touches she'd tried, like plastering the walls with

Olly's artwork or hanging cheery daffodil curtains, the place was still a dive.

But it had been hers, the first tangible thing that was proof she was doing it on her own. Sure, she'd worked manic hours cooking at a local restaurant to pay rent and bills, but she'd been independent for the first time in her life and proud of it.

When she'd been fired that fateful night a few months ago, she'd hit the bottle in a big way, determined to drive away the demons of the past. Demons like her father's voice insisting she was no good and worthless no matter how hard she tried. It bugged the crap out of her that even from beyond the grave, he held power over her.

When she'd forgotten to pick up Olly from school the next day because she'd been on a bender drowning her sorrows, she'd rung Jake in desperation and handed her precious son into his care while she straightened out at the New York Recovery Center. Jake had come through for her in a big way. Despite battling his own issues after a commercial liner he'd serviced as an aircraft mechanic had crashed, killing eighty-nine passengers, he'd agreed to care for Olly while she'd been in the center and had finally bonded with his nephew. Throw in the fact he'd also moved to Redemption to be with his new girlfriend and it was a no brainer.

She'd used every last cent of her savings for Olly's college fund to attend the holistic wellness center she'd seen on TV, which considered overall health as well as treating addictions. Technically, she wasn't an alcoholic like dear old dad, but she had realized a stint in a rehab facility would give her the time to get her head together. And it had.

She'd told the counselors about her lousy childhood. Purging all the crap she'd bottled up for so long had been cathartic. She'd attended group therapy sessions, done dawn yoga daily, swum laps until her muscles ached and cooked alongside kitchen staff when they discovered her passion for food.

She had only one more secret to divulge, and she hoped when she met Jake in an hour that he'd understand.

Meanwhile, she couldn't wait to be reunited with Olly, although she couldn't ignore a niggle of apprehension about how her son would react, considering her absence had been longer than anticipated. While she'd missed him dreadfully, attending the recovery center had been the best thing she could've done. Staying there had done more for her beyond the therapeutic benefits.

It had given her self-belief again.

She could do this. Be the mother Olly deserved, determined to break the habits of the past and forge a new future.

Smiling at her mental pep talk, she made up the last box and rummaged through the final cupboard. So far, she'd filled a meager six boxes. Four contained Olly's toys and clothes; two contained her stuff. Her limited wardrobe was in one, her precious cookbooks in the other.

Nothing grounded her better than flipping through those books, mentally rehearsing the procedure for concocting a difficult soufflé or a tricky *tatin*. For getting the crispy skin on pork belly just right. For calculating the correct time to slow-braise lamb wrapped in smoked eggplant. For imagining a personal twist on elderflower sorbet, rhubarb semifreddo and caramel infused with mandarin curd. The pages of those books fired her imagination and soothed her soul.

While her soul could always do with some soothing, she didn't have the time to wallow, and she emptied the last cupboard.

The contents were sparse: an old plastic bowl and plate set Olly had used as a toddler, a ball of string, a glue stick and a shoebox covered in sparkly blue glitter.

Her heart fluttered as she eased the lid off the box, knowing the contents would make her teary.

Memories, poignant and softened by time, floated all around her like dust motes. Impossible to grasp and hold onto, but there all the same.

As she sifted through the newspaper clippings featuring Olly's father, Dyson Patrice, a lump swelled in her throat. She'd been young and naïve, falling for him. Even if he hadn't died in tragic circumstances, she doubted they'd be together today. He hadn't been a long-term kind of guy. While she occasionally lamented the demise of their relationship, she'd never regret it. Thanks to the bold, brash celebrity chef who'd died too young, she had Olly.

Tears blinded her as she shoved the clippings back into the box. As she did, a few photos wedged into the side of the box tumbled free and she glanced at them.

There hadn't been many happy times in her childhood. Her mom had died from a heart attack when she was four and her dad had taken it out on her and Jake. He hadn't bothered with photos, but Aunt Cilla had, and the few Rose owned had been taken during occasional visits to Redemption.

Uncle Vernon had been as mean as her dad, but Aunt Cilla had been lovely. Still was, as far as Rose could tell from Cilla's visit to the recovery center with Olly. Cilla had hovered in the doorway, giving Olly time to run into her room and squeeze her tight, her steady gaze fixed on Rose, filled with understanding. There'd been the sheen of tears too, mirrored in Rose's eyes. And when Olly had eventually disengaged, Cilla had breezed into her room and enveloped her in a bear hug, just like she used to when Rose had visited her as a kid.

Rose had clung to Cilla, battling tears, letting her aunt's warmth infuse her. Releasing her when Olly tugged on the hem of her top to draw her attention to the present they'd brought, a care package filled with her aunt's fabulous baking. Brownies, oatmeal cookies, lemon cake, all Rose's favorites, and she'd fought the urge to blubber anew.

They'd chatted, small talk mostly, but for the sixty minutes Cilla had visited, Rose felt more relaxed than she had in ages. When her aunt had invited her to come and stay when she left the center, Rose found herself agreeing.

Her son obviously adored Cilla too, the way he continually grinned at her or deferred to her, and providing Olly with a stable family life was the main reason Rose was moving to Redemption.

There were six photos in total, of her and Jake playing in Cilla's garden. Those times at her aunt's had been the only bright spot in her miserable childhood and she knew Cilla's attentiveness, home cooking and mothering would be the perfect way to ease back into her life after being cloistered away for four months.

Buoyed by the thought of getting to know her aunt again, Rose slipped the photos back inside the shoebox, covered it and placed the keepsakes into the last packing box before sealing it. She was about to close the cupboard when she spied a brown paper bag tucked into the farthest corner. Dread made her hand shake as she reached for it.

Her secret stash.

Her go-to bottle in case of emergencies.

Rose had never craved alcohol, but for the last six months before she'd checked into the recovery center, she'd found herself increasingly relying on it for comfort.

It had started innocently enough. A glass of wine from a bottle her neighbor Mrs. Petrovsky had brought over one evening to toast the delivery of her tenth grandchild. That one glass had made Rose giggly and carefree in a way she hadn't felt in a long time. So she'd had another and slept better that night than she had in years.

From then on, whenever she'd had a particularly rough day, Rose would have a glass of wine to unwind. Never more than that, because she was terrified her father's DNA would suddenly ignite and turn her into a raging alcoholic.

Unfortunately, no matter how hard she worked at the restaurant, she was still overlooked for promotions and pay raises. It became harder to save for Olly's college fund and that made her frustrated. Rent and bills gobbled her wages faster than she could earn them. Then the restaurant changed ownership and her struggles multiplied tenfold: less time off to spend with Olly because she had to pick up extra shifts to impress the new boss. A grouchy new head chef who demanded perfection when he could barely boil an egg. And a relentless head of house that groped female staff more than he seated customers.

One glass of wine became two, and she discovered a taste for vodka. More precisely, its lack of taste, which made it the perfect addition to juices. A splash into cranberry juice, a dash into OJ. Taking the edge off without the guilt.

The night she'd been fired had been the proverbial last straw. She'd been five minutes late for her shift because Mrs. Petrovsky had fallen in her apartment. Rose couldn't leave the old woman in pain, considering she helped mind Olly whenever Rose needed her, so she'd tended her injury—nothing more than a twisted ankle, thank goodness—and rushed to work.

The boss had yelled at her and fired her on the spot.

The thing was, her boss's irate tirade in front of the staff hadn't bothered her as much as the realization that she'd fallen into a familiar pattern: doing whatever it took to please people but ending up taking crap regardless.

So she'd headed home, drunk three-quarters of a bottle of vodka and ended up with the hangover to end all hangovers the next day. The kind of hangover that made her forget to pick up Olly from school. The kind of hangover that had prompted her to seek help, more for her addictive do-gooder behavior than her alcohol consumption.

She opened the paper bag and pulled out the vodka. Baffled as to why she hadn't simply tipped the alcohol down the sink, she unscrewed the cap and inhaled.

It did nothing for her. But as she swirled the vodka around, she wondered what it would taste like now as a shot, if it would still give her a buzz.

Despite how far she'd come at the recovery center, she was tempted for a moment. Tempted to relive that wonderful floaty feeling when all her problems faded away.

She lifted the bottle to her mouth. Caught a glimpse of herself in a mirror. Recoiled.

This wasn't her. Wasn't the person she'd striven so hard to become in the last four months.

With a strangled cry, she leapt to her feet, ran to the bathroom and poured the vodka down the drain. Hands shaking, she recapped the bottle, marched to the kitchen and deposited it in the recyclable waste.

Leaning against a cupboard, she wrapped her arms around her middle and took several deep breaths. Counting each one. Calming.

Time to start her new life in Redemption.

The sooner the better.

2.

With the importance of what Rose had to divulge to Jake, she chose the one place that had provided comfort and given her a much needed confidence boost as a child. Alicia's Bakehouse felt like the home she had never had. Cooking had ultimately saved her, and the kitchen in the heart of Brooklyn that had kick-started her foodie love affair had always been a safe haven.

Parking was always at a premium, with people flocking to the iconic bakery for brunch, but for once fate had to be smiling on her because she found a parking spot within two blocks. As she strolled the sidewalk and passed familiar sights like the shoe repairman, the electronics store still firmly stuck in the nineties, the Chinese take-out and a state-of-the-art laundromat, she hoped the bakery hadn't changed.

She hadn't visited in over a year, and before that her bi-annual visits had gradually petered out as she juggled manic motherhood with long work hours. During her time off, she'd taken Olly to Central Park rather than to a bakery in Brooklyn that he didn't appreciate.

She'd taken him to the bakery once, when he'd been three, and he'd spent the entire time wriggling in his seat or running along the length of the display cabinet, disturbing other patrons. Besides, it wasn't the same since Alicia, the Polish immigrant who'd been like a mother to her, had died. Rose knew the attraction of the place had had as much to do with its eccentric owner as with the incredible pastries and breads on offer.

Rose had barely mourned her father's death. She'd cried for a week after Alicia had died of an aneurysm.

As she reached the bakery's thick wooden double door and the first waft of rich yeast hit her nostrils, she knew she'd chosen the right place to meet Jake.

She needed confidence to tell him the truth about their father's death.

So she'd come home.

She pushed through the door and an instant calm enveloped her as the tempting aromas of freshly baked bread and sugary good-ies infused her senses.

Aesthetically, the place hadn't changed in sixteen years. The same long wooden tables framed by benches. The same massive counter with display cases brimming with items baked fresh daily. The same chalkboard behind the cabinets, with prices and specials of the day. The same exposed rough-hewn brick walls and steel-slung ceilings.

It had always reminded her of a big barn, filled with warmth and friendship and food. She loved it as much now as she had the first day she'd set foot in the place, a hungry ten-year-old eager for a treat to fill her aching belly because her father had spent the grocery money on beer.

Thankfully, her favorite table was free, a small table for two tucked away near the kitchen, a place patrons rarely frequented because they preferred the longer wooden benches and looking out on the street.

She'd spent many a Sunday perched at her table, poring over cookbooks Alicia would stack in front of her, alongside a steaming mug of hot cocoa and a slab of apple cake.

That had been the beginning for her, when she'd flick those pages and absorb the recipes like she was cramming for an exam. Memorizing easy stuff to begin with: homemade raspberry jelly, chocolate cake, cornbread, blueberry pancakes. Becoming more engrossed in the creative process of assembling ingredients, following a method and producing a quality, edible end product. Bouncing ideas off Alicia. Brainstorming. Moving on to more complex dishes like creamy potato salad with bacon, meatloaf, hamburgers, fried chicken, peach cobbler.

Jake had been blown away by what she'd concocted as a kid. Her father hadn't given a damn. He rarely ate anyway, preferring to stick to a liquid diet.

Later, she'd taken those recipes and improvised, putting her spin on the classics to create her own signature dishes. She'd never be a famous chef or have her own TV show or publish her own cookbook, but none of that mattered. Because when she cooked, it made her feel good. She didn't need the validation of others. She'd learned long ago that no matter how much she did to please people, they never appreciated her efforts. She knew she produced quality food and as long as she was happy doing it and her work provided a roof for her child, that's all that mattered.

She looked around and realized that she didn't recognize any of the staff. And the window to the kitchen had been replaced by a fancy chrome backsplash so she couldn't see if any of the familiar faces were still working behind the scenes. So she ordered a cocoa and a red velvet cupcake, picked up a glossy magazine from the stand near the register, and waited for Jake.

She idly flipped the pages, not really registering the latest fashion trends or celebrity gossip, content to let the soothing ambience of Alicia's Bakehouse wash over her.

Whenever thoughts of what she had to tell Jake intruded, she pushed them aside, focusing on the many hours she'd spent here in the past. Each precious moment rotated through her mind like the slow-moving reel of an old movie.

Alicia scolding her for sucking lemon frosting off a spoon and then using it again to mix another batter.

The first loaf of sourdough Rose had made from scratch being taken out of the oven and presented to her like a crown.

The time she'd slipped on flour, landed on her butt and burst into tears because she'd dropped a batch of chocolate chip cookies, the pain of a broken coccyx nothing compared to her precious creations lying crumbled around her on the floor.

The memories made her smile. Made her dab her eyes. Made her wish for a simpler time when the biggest decision she had to make was whether to have the strawberry shortcake or pineapple upside-down cake for breakfast.

As she glanced at the crooked portrait of a rosy-cheeked Alicia hanging over the doorway, she saw Jake enter, immediately home in on her favorite table and wave.

Her stomach clenched with nerves but she returned his wave and focused on her breathing, like they'd taught her in the meditation classes. By the time he'd wound his way through the tables and bent down to kiss her cheek, she felt more in control.

"Hey there," she said, returning his hug, relieved he looked less harrowed than the last time she'd seen him.

Then again, that probably had to do with the fact she'd summoned him to the recovery center ASAP after freaking out following her visit from Cilla and Olly, when her son had appeared healthier and happier than ever, making her residual low self-esteem blossom. Now, she couldn't believe she'd considered asking Jake to take custody of Olly. That was the thing about secrets left to fester: they messed with her head. Which is why she had to get this last one off her chest before she made the move to Redemption.

"You look great," he said, taking the seat opposite. "I'm so proud of you, Rosey-Posey."

She hoped he still felt that way when she revealed the truth.

"Thanks." She smiled and pointed to the specials board. "What are you having? My treat."

He patted his belly and groaned. "Cilla force-fed me a massive breakfast before I hit the road so I'm good for now."

Rose could imagine their aunt doing that. She'd always been caring, and far more nurturing than their dad. "She's amazing. When she came to visit me, I couldn't believe how little she'd changed."

He nodded, tenderness making his eyes gleam. "She's the best. It'll be good for you to let her spoil you with some TLC for a while."

Rose had never been spoilt by anyone in her life, and the thought of her aunt taking care of her while she found a job and got her life back on track sounded pretty darn appealing.

"Aunt Cilla and Redemption sure have done a number on you," she said. "Or has your love-fest for the place got more to do with *Sara*?"

She drew out his girlfriend's name and ended on a smooch sound, laughing when Jake blushed. "Wow, you really do have it bad."

"I never thought I'd meet anyone like her, let alone be open to a relationship, when I first visited Cilla to coerce her into helping me with Olly." His bashful expression made her want to hug him again.

"She's incredible, and I can't wait for you to meet her," Jake said, his goofy grin proclaiming exactly how in love he was, because Rose had never seen him like this, ever. "Which makes me wonder what's so important we had to meet here to talk rather than us catching up when you arrive in Redemption?"

Busted.

She should've known Jake would move past the small talk fast and focus on the real reason behind her request to meet before she left the city.

"Can't a sister enlist the help of her brother to move a few boxes?"

He snorted. "If that were the case, we'd have met at your apartment."

"True." She clasped her fingers together and rested her forearms on the table. "You've never let me get away with anything."

"You're still avoiding my question," he said, astute as always. "And this was always your go-to place, so the fact we're meeting here means whatever you have to say is big."

Increasingly nervous, she stalled for time. "Remember when you came down here to interrogate Alicia and make sure I wasn't a ten-year-old getting embroiled in anything nefarious?"

He nodded. "She took one look at me, said I was too skinny, and insisted I eat a croissant, cannoli and a sticky bun."

Rose chuckled. "Those early Sunday mornings I spent here, covered in flour and sugar, surrounded by the bakers' chatter, kept me sane."

"I know," Jake said. "When you started spending more time here, popping in after school, doing prep work, I was glad." He glanced away, sadness darkening his eyes. "It kept you away from Dad."

Jake had given her the perfect opening to reveal her secret and she blew out a breath.

"I hated how he lashed out at me for the most mundane things, like buying him the wrong brand of toothpaste or putting pepper on his veggies rather than salt." She wrinkled her nose. "He terrified me."

"He was a prick." Jake scowled. "Nothing either of us did was good enough. We cooked the meals. Cleaned the house. Grocery shopped. Did our homework. Got good grades. Yet he drank more and took it out on us."

She nodded. "I talked through a lot of my issues with the psychologists at the recovery center. Told them stuff about the past. Told them about my constant need to people-please to gain affection and approval. My craving for recognition in whatever I did."

She inhaled a deep breath, released it. "I blabbed it all. How I'd pandered to him in the hope of gaining a scrap of affection. How I got knocked up as a teen. How I'd dealt with my shit lately . . ." She shook her head. "But rehashing our crappy childhood isn't why I called you here." Her fingers clenched tighter. "I need to tell you something. Part of the new me, getting everything out in the open so I can move on. Much healthier than bottling it all up."

Concern creased his brow. "Go on."

Rose had mentally rehearsed how she'd tell Jake the truth many times during her stint at the recovery center. Had visualized this moment to help her muster the courage to tell him. But now that the moment had arrived, she couldn't formulate a single word.

"You're scaring me, Sis." He reached out to touch her arm. "Whatever's bugging you, you know you can tell me anything and I'll always be here for you."

"I know." She took another deep breath and let it out, hoping it would release some of her tension. It didn't help. "There's something I have to tell you about Dad."

Anger darkened his eyes, before he eradicated it with a blink. "What is it?"

She had to blab the truth all in one go before she lost her nerve. "That day Dad fell down the stairs? I startled him. I'd had a gutful after preparing that meal especially for him. Came out of my room to tell him off for the first time ever. He must've thought I was downstairs because he was so surprised to see me charging out, he lost his balance and fell."

To her surprise, Jake chuckled and the tension bracketing his mouth eased. "And all these years, I blamed myself for his death."

Shock rendered her speechless for a moment, before she could form an articulate response. "Why?"

Jake's eyes glazed slightly, as if he were lost in memories of the past. "We'd had a massive argument a minute or two earlier. He'd stormed out of my room, and the next thing I know I heard the thud at the bottom of the stairs and he was dead." Jake rubbed the back of his neck. "I thought he must've lost concentration because of that argument and that's why he fell."

"Wow, I didn't know," Rose said, a small part of her relieved that maybe she wasn't solely responsible for her father's death. A larger part was relieved that Jake didn't think she was some kind of monster for contributing to it. "I should've told you earlier."

"Yeah, you should've." He shrugged. "But we've both dealt with his death in our own way." He sniggered. "We should've thrown a massive party."

Rose wanted to rebuke Jake for speaking ill of the dead, but she couldn't bring herself to do it. Her upbringing at the hands of that man had tainted everything she'd done since. Every bad decision she'd made. Every friend she'd deliberately alienated to ensure no one got too close. Every stupid night she'd cried herself to sleep because she didn't feel good enough to cook for a living, let alone hold down a job as a chef. It was all because of *him*.

She hated him for that alone.

"I still blame him for so much . . ." She shook her head, needing to savor her relief rather than dwell on the crappy things in her life because a monster had shaped her. "But at least I feel better finally telling you about that night."

"Quit worrying about it, Squirt." He reached across the table and tugged on her ponytail like he used to do when she was a kid. "Looks like we've both wasted enough time blaming ourselves for the past. When we have a hell of a lot of living to do now." He leaned back. "I appreciate you telling me, but let's keep the past in the past and concentrate on the future, okay?" He gestured at the window. "Which includes us leaving this place behind and heading to Connecticut."

"Okay," Rose said, feeling lighter than she had in years. "So fill me in. What's it like living at Cilla's?"

"Interesting," he said, his eyes crinkling with amusement. "She's got a new boyfriend and he's eighteen years younger than her."

"Wow." Rose grinned. "Good for her."

"That's what I said. The guy, Bryce Madden, is a doctor. Used to be a friend of Tamsin's when they were younger. Came back to town recently to locum and pursued Cilla relentlessly." He rested his forearms on the table and leaned forward, as if about to impart a juicy piece of gossip. "Turns out Bryce had a crush on Cilla all those years ago. But that's not the best bit."

Rose vaguely remembered her cousin Tamsin as an older teen who had disinterest down pat. But she couldn't remember ever meeting Bryce. "Come on, spill. I want to hear it all."

"Bryce is moving in."

Surprise made Rose drop the menu she'd been fiddling with. "But with the rest of us there, won't it be crowded? And won't Olly and I cramp her style?"

Jake shrugged. "I think we take each day as it comes. Cilla's really looking forward to having you stay, and she dotes on Olly."

He paused, deep in thought. "Apparently Tamsin never comes home and they speak infrequently. From what I can gather, they've had a fraught relationship since Tamsin was a kid. Maybe Cilla feels like she missed out on mothering so she's thriving, having a child to take care of."

"Olly's lucky to have her. She was always so good to us." Though Bryce moving in with Cilla changed things: as much as Rose needed a bit of TLC right now, she had no intention of being a third wheel in her aunt's relationship and would start looking for a new place as soon as she arrived. "So what's the lowdown with you and Sara?"

Jake glanced at his watch and grinned. "As much as I'd like to fill you in, I've got an appointment I need to rush to. Rain check?"

Rose smiled. "Don't think I'm going to let you off that easily. Though I guess I'll see for myself why you're so smitten when I arrive in Redemption."

"That town will be good for you, kid." He stood and dropped a kiss on her forehead. "You'll see."

Rose certainly hoped so. She could do with a change of luck. With a renewed purpose.

A new future in Redemption sounded pretty damn good.

3.

Caden hated gardening. He'd much rather be inside on a gaming console or video-conferencing college buddies about the latest accounting software than mowing grass or pruning.

The only reason he maintained the garden was to keep his parents off his back. He might have bought the family home from them years ago, when they'd moved into a new house in town, but that didn't stop them having an opinion about his upkeep of the place.

In fact, his parents continued to have strong opinions about most aspects of his life, something he tolerated out of respect but did his best to avoid where possible.

His cell vibrated in his back pocket and he fished it out, his heart sinking when he saw his mom's number on the screen. His thumb hovered over the "divert" button before his conscience got the better of him and he hit "answer."

"Hey, Mom."

"Caden, where are you?"

"Home on a Sunday like most sane people," he responded, waiting for the inevitable advice his mom would offer to the contrary. He never should've let her railroad him into joining the election a year ago. Her constant interference was his reward.

She tsked. "The mayoral race is gaining momentum. You can't afford to have time off."

"And here I was, thinking Sunday was a day of rest."

His sarcasm fell on deaf ears as she continued. "Even now that your father's retired from preaching, he continues to work unfailingly on the local council." She scoffed in annoyance. "You should be in town today. Campaigning. Mingling at the barbecue in the town square. Talking up your chances."

He refrained from saying that ever since he'd agreed to run for mayor, her meddling had magnified tenfold. "Mom, my team has a clear strategy to follow. We're doing okay."

"The polls are too close to call," she said, sounding miffed. "You need to ram home every advantage."

No. He needed to ram home the fact that he'd been floundering after the tragedy a year ago and still hadn't recovered completely. This campaign was a distraction, nothing more.

"Thanks for the advice, Mom, but I have to go."

"You know I'm right, Caden. Just like I was right about that hippie woman who lied to you and used you and broke your heart—"

"'Bye, Mom."

He hung up, belatedly realizing he was clenching the cell so tight it might break. Loosening his grip, he slipped it back into his pocket, hating his mother's constant interference, abhorring the fact that she'd been right about Effie all along.

He resumed pruning a rose bush with particular viciousness, glimpsing an old Ford pulling into his neighbor's drive and parking under an elm tree near the carport.

He didn't have much to do with Priscilla Prescott, beyond a courteous head nod or wave if he glimpsed the widow. But lately, there'd been a lot happening on this private back road of Redemption.

According to his mother, who thrived on local gossip, old lady Issy, Cilla's other neighbor, had died four months ago and her grand-daughter Sara had moved in. Then Cilla's nephew Jake had moved into her place, with a young boy assumed to be his son.

Caden didn't give a flying fig about the goings-on of his neigh-bors, as long as they left him the hell alone. He had a thriving accountancy business to run and an electoral campaign that took up most of his time. Twelve- to fourteen-hour workdays weren't uncommon lately—just the way he liked it. He liked to keep busy and stay focused. Less time to dwell on the past and torture himself with maudlin memories.

He grasped the pruning shears tighter, ready to resume his trimming, when a woman stepped from the car. She looked vaguely familiar, her natural beauty eye-catching at a distance . . . petite, with a heart-shaped face, silky, wavy hair the color of burnt toffee cascading past her shoulders and big brown eyes fringed in long lashes. Her wary gaze darted around, as if she expected to be accosted by a bogeyman.

That's when he recognized her. Rose Mathieson. His childhood friend. One of few he'd had back then, considering he'd been the dorky only child of the town's preacher.

She'd had that same guardedness as a kid, approaching every situation with circumspection. Cautious to a fault, she hadn't wanted to befriend him until he'd shown her his secret hiding spot in his backyard. She'd liked him after that, had spent many hours hiding there with him when she visited her aunt.

Until the night he'd discovered the reason for her caginess and she'd withdrawn her friendship as swiftly as she'd given it. He'd missed her after that but knew why she'd done it. On that fate-ful night he'd been privy to her horrible family life and what she tolerated with her father. An invasion of privacy she couldn't stand, even as Caden tried to support her.

He hadn't heard from her since.

As she continued to glance around, as if looking at the place for the first time, Caden wondered if she'd remember him. And if so, would she manage a fair Usain Bolt impersonation and sprint as fast as she could in the opposite direction from him?

Rose's gaze landed on him at that moment and he nodded in acknowledgement. Her eyes narrowed, coolly assessing, her reserved stare blank before she returned his nod and turned away.

Guess that answered the question of whether she remembered him or not.

Oddly disgruntled, he turned his back on her and resumed pruning. Though it took him a good few minutes to realize he'd done more hacking than trimming and had butchered the bush.

Rose had no idea who the cute guy staring at her over the fence was, so she gave him her best disinterested stare. She had zero interest in dating, especially not since she might only be in town for a limited time. Then again, she'd forgotten that friendliness and over-familiarity were as much a part of small-town life as the requisite town hall and fast-traveling gossip grapevine.

Hoping she hadn't offended a friend of Cilla's, she popped the trunk open and bent over to hoist the first box.

"Let me help," a deep voice said from over her shoulder, and she straightened, surprised to be confronted by a second sexy male in as many minutes.

Maybe she should've returned to Redemption years ago.

The guy was tall, broad-shouldered and had a George Clooney thing going on.

"I'm Bryce." He smiled and held out his hand. "We've been expecting you."

"Rose," she said, and shook his hand, mentally making a note to commend her aunt on her stellar taste in boyfriends. Bryce was seriously hot for an older guy.

Flustered when his grin widened, she blurted, "Jake told me you're living here now?"

He nodded. "Hope that's not going to be a problem?"

"Maybe for you," she said, and screwed up her nose. "Can't be much fun moving in with your girlfriend to discover she's invited her niece and great-nephew to stay too."

"I'll be honest and say it's not quite what I had in mind when Cilla asked me to move in." He shrugged. "But you're Cilla's family, and reconnecting with you and Jake has made her incredibly happy."

He paused, tenderness darkening his chocolate eyes. "And anything that makes Cilla happy, I'm all for."

Bryce's lack of BS ensured he went up another notch or ten in Rose's estimation. "She deserves it," Rose said, wondering how much Bryce knew of her aunt's past.

"After what she put up with from that bastard Vernon, absolutely." Bryce's vehemence was touching and Rose found herself warming to him even further. "I don't blame her for making me sweat before she actually agreed to date me."

Rose had heard the basics about Cilla's new man from Jake, and while she didn't feel comfortable prying, she needed to know more about Bryce for the simple fact she'd be living in her aunt's house alongside him.

"She made you sweat?"

"Yeah, big time." He laughed and she joined in. "Tried to push me away using every excuse she could come up with, from our age difference to me missing out on having kids, but I wore her down."

"I'm glad, because when she came to visit me in the recovery center, I'd never seen her look so happy."

It was the truth, but Rose had another reason for slipping that into the conversation. She wanted to be upfront about where she'd come from, not hide behind the past and what she'd been through because of it.

Bryce leaned against the car, like they had all the time in the world to chat, when in fact Rose had almost reached her limits of polite small talk and was desperate to head inside and see her son.

"Cilla told me where you've been the last few months. That center is one of the best."

"Certainly got my head screwed on right," she said, sounding flippant, when in fact she was feeling increasingly uncomfortable because her aunt had probably filled Bryce in on her sordid past and how she'd ended up in the recovery center.

As if sensing her discomfiture, he straightened and gestured to the boxes. "Let me give you a hand with these."

"Thanks. That'd be great."

As she hoisted one of the smaller boxes into her arms and Bryce lifted two, he paused, his foot on the bumper bar so he could balance the boxes in his arms.

"Your being here means a lot to your aunt," he said, his expression somber. "And from the little I know of your background, I think it'll be good for you too."

She smiled, grateful for his circumspection. "I do too."

As they headed for the house in companionable silence, Rose couldn't help but think if her aunt could find a great guy like Bryce at her age, maybe there was hope for her yet.

Bryce propped the boxes inside the front door and went back to Rose's car for the rest.

She'd barely set foot inside when Cilla appeared in the living room doorway and opened her arms in welcome. Rose flung herself into them, stifling the urge to cry.

"I'm so glad you're here to stay," Cilla said, squeezing her so hard all the air whooshed out of Rose's lungs. "Come on in."

"Thanks," Rose said, sniffling a little as she disengaged and glanced around with open curiosity.

While there weren't major changes to the structure of the house she hadn't seen in eighteen years, the decor now radiated a cozy warmth that had been absent back then. Shaggy rugs in autumnal colors adorned the floors, plump crimson cushions lay scattered on the ochre suede sofas and local landscapes dotted the walls.

"The place looks lovely," Rose said. "And I'm surprised it's still in one piece, with my cheeky little monkey living here. Is he around?"

Cilla squeezed her arm. "He's with Jake at Sara's place next door, making you a welcome home surprise."

"That's sweet," she said, hoping her aunt didn't pick up on her disappointment. She'd envisaged her reunion with Olly, had expected him to rush out to the car to greet her and hold on to her like he'd never let go. The fact he was with Jake and his girlfriend shouldn't have irked her, but it did and she wished she could march over there, drag her little boy into her arms and hug him tight.

"They should be back any minute." Cilla ushered her into the kitchen. "Coffee or tea?"

"Chamomile tea would be great if you have it."

Cilla nodded. "Take a seat."

As Rose sat at the kitchen table and Cilla placed a plate piled high with oatmeal and lavender cookies in front of her, the aroma catapulted her back in time to doing this very thing every time they visited.

Back then her dad would join Uncle Vernon on the veranda the moment they arrived, ignoring his children in favor of a beer as usual. Rose would run around after him like she did at home, until Cilla insisted she relax. Then Cilla would fuss over her and Jake, plying them with homemade treats until they could hardly move.

She'd bring out a board game or a stack of comics and leave them to unwind before tucking them into bed.

Rose had treasured her times in this house, had loved her aunt for caring. Had been heartbroken when her dad had cut off all ties after Uncle Vernon died. She could've re-established contact with her aunt once her father had died, but so much time had lapsed that Rose felt awkward. Now, sitting here in the warmth from the sun's rays streaming through the high-set windows, Rose wished she'd made more of an effort.

"Olly's been sleeping in your old room upstairs so I've given you the room next to him," Cilla said, bustling around like she used to. "It's rather small, though, so I hope it's okay."

"It'll be fine," Rose said, "and I can't thank you enough for looking after Olly the way you have and for letting me stay now."

"It's been a pleasure." Cilla placed two cups and a porcelain kettle decorated in hand-painted violets between them. "I missed having kids around."

Rose did a quick mental calculation and figured her cousin Tamsin must be in her early forties. Which meant she either had a brood that rarely visited or no kids at all.

Treading carefully, Rose poured them both a steaming cup of chamomile. "How's Tamsin?"

"Good," Cilla answered, a little too quickly, and hid behind her cup.

"Does she get home very often?"

"Try never," Cilla said, with a heartfelt sigh. "Tam returned for her father's funeral and that was it. She's a high-flying corporate lawyer in New York and we don't get to see each other very often."

Rose heard the pain in her aunt's voice and knew now wasn't the time to push for answers to satisfy her curiosity.

"New York has that effect on people. Everyone rushing around in a hurry to get places."

Cilla studied her over the rim of her cup. "Will you miss it?"

A question Rose had asked herself a million times before making the decision to move here. She loved the hustle and bustle of the big city, but the thought of finding another job in one of the endless cafés or restaurants, then fighting for a flexible schedule so she could also be home for Olly, had been a battle she hadn't been looking forward to.

Here, she could find a job in town and lean on her family if she needed help with childcare, a luxury she'd never had while raising Olly in the city.

"Not so much," she said, with a shrug. "Besides, Olly's what's most important and he has thrived living here."

"You're important too, kiddo." Cilla placed her cup back in its saucer. "Kids pick up on their mom's happiness, or lack of, so don't be a martyr, okay?"

Once again, Rose sensed a story behind Cilla's words and wondered if that was the reason Tamsin hadn't been home in years—maybe she blamed her mom for being a martyr to Uncle Vernon?

Before Cilla had visited her at the recovery center, she'd been nine the last time she'd seen her aunt. Cilla had arrived at their place in Brooklyn a year after Uncle Vernon had died, bringing yummy treats for them all, and her dad had thrown Cilla, and her treats, out. He'd ranted like a madman, blaming Cilla for Vernon's death. At the time, Rose had thought if her uncle was half as mean to Cilla as her dad was to her, he deserved it. Before wishing her father would die too.

"Speaking of being happy, my friend Bryce has just moved in here too." Cilla blushed and looked anywhere but at Rose.

Rose knew all about her aunt's flourishing love life but decided to have a little fun.

"Friend?"

Cilla's blush intensified. "Well, he's . . . uh . . . he's more than a friend, really. More of a . . ."

"Boyfriend?" Rose supplied helpfully, trying to suppress a grin and failing.

Cilla nodded, her smile rueful. "I know it's crazy, falling for a guy in his forties at my age, but I can't help it. He's wonderful."

Considering her aunt didn't look a day over fifty with her grey hair cut in a short, trendy style, her lithe body and her funky clothes, Rose wasn't surprised she could attract a younger man.

"You deserve to be happy." Rose smiled. "He seemed wonderful when he came out to the car to help me with some boxes."

Cilla's smile turned positively mushy. "He is pretty wonderful."

"Glad to hear it. But are you sure Olly and I won't be cramping your style?"

"Don't be ridiculous," Cilla said, busying herself with sorting through the cookies to find one she wanted.

But her blush was back and Rose experienced the first pang that maybe she'd done the wrong thing moving in here.

"I mean it, Aunt Cilla. If you think it's getting too crowded in here, let me know and we'll move sooner rather than later."

Rose knew Cilla would never go for that, so she added for good measure, "Moving in here is temporary. When I agreed to come stay in Redemption, I always intended to find my own place."

Cilla frowned, and Rose pre-empted any argument her aunt might have against her moving out. "It'll be good for me. Finding a new place of my own. Re-establishing a routine for Olly." Rose patted her chest. "I need this, Aunt Cilla. A fresh start."

Her aunt's eyes softened with unspoken emotion and Rose knew she'd made the right decision coming here.

"Whatever you want to do, I'll support you one hundred percent," Cilla said, blinking to stave off tears.

"Thanks." Rose managed a wan smile, battling her own emotions and thinking that maybe she should've re-established ties with her extended family and made the move to Redemption a long time ago.

4.

Rose had barely finished her cup of tea when the back door flew open and Olly burst through it, running so fast across the kitchen he slipped and fell against her.

"Mom, you're here!" He wrapped his arms around her neck so tight Rose thought he'd never let go. Which was fine by her.

"Hey, gorgeous boy. I've missed you so much." Her throat clogged with emotion as she hugged him, blinking back tears as she buried her nose in the crook of his neck, inhaling the unique smell, faintly reminiscent of coconut, that was her son.

After what seemed like an eternity but still not long enough for her, Olly eased out of her arms, his eyes wide. "Are we really staying here?"

"Uh-huh." Rose resisted the urge to tug him back into her arms and never let go. "I hear Aunt Cilla's is a great place to live."

"It is, it is, it is." Olly hopped from foot to foot, his excitement contagious: for the first time since she'd arrived in town, Rose felt upbeat and optimistic about her choice. "She's so cool and cooks the best food. And now Doc Madden is here and he's really nice too. He tells me lots of gross stuff that happens when kids don't listen to grownups and get hurt. But it's okay—I'm not that stupid."

"Good to hear, buddy." Jake had entered the kitchen and stood behind Olly, ruffling his hair. "Maybe you should take a breath, though, before you pass out."

Rose laughed at Olly's rueful grin as she stood to give her brother a hug, before resuming her seat.

"Uncle Jake says I talk a lot. But I know he likes it, because he doesn't have a kid of his own." Olly paused and screwed up his nose, as if thinking. "But he has a girlfriend now, Sara, and she's cool too, so maybe they'll have a kid of their own soon."

To her surprise, Jake blanched and glanced away. "Whoa there, Olly. Your mom's only just arrived—let's not bombard her."

Rose met her brother's gaze over Olly's head and knew there was something more going on between Sara and Jake than dating. He had the look of a guy in way over his head. She hoped her loaded glance conveyed the message that they'd talk later.

"Okay." Olly hugged her again. "I've made a surprise for you but it's at Sara's house. She wants to meet you too, so can we go now?"

A tad overwhelmed, Rose looked to Jake for guidance. He gave a brief nod and Rose said, "Okay. Let's go see this surprise."

"Yay." Olly ran toward the door then paused on the threshold. "Aunt Cilla, I'm really hungry. Can you save some of those cookies for me, please?"

Rose blinked. She'd tried to instill manners into Olly for years but it had been hit and miss. The fact he'd said please impressed her enormously. And made her feel a bit of a failure for not succeeding where Cilla and Jake had.

She knew it was crazy, considering how much they'd helped her out these last four months, but she was almost jealous of how comfortable Olly seemed with them. Like having her home again was no big deal for him, when in fact it was all she had been able to think about and work toward during her entire stint at the center.

"Sure, Olly." Cilla winked at her. "Though you won't want to spoil dinner as it's your mom's favorite."

Tears stung Rose's eyes at the thought that this incredible woman had remembered her favorite food from decades earlier and had gone to the trouble to cook it for her. It made her jealousy a moment ago seem even more petty.

"You made roast chicken with tarragon potatoes and pumpkin pie?"

Cilla nodded. "You used to love it so much, I thought you'd like to have it your first night here."

Rose blinked rapidly as the tears threatened to spill over. "Thank you."

"You're welcome." Cilla sounded brusque as she stood and cleared the table, but Rose heard the quiver in her voice and knew her aunt wasn't unaffected.

"Come on, Mom. Sara's waiting," Olly said, leaning against the doorframe. "And my surprise, remember?"

"How could I forget?" Rose stood and gave her brother another quick hug before falling into step with Jake. They walked at a sedate pace behind Olly as he raced ahead, tearing across the yard at a breakneck speed. "Everything okay with you and Sara?"

Jake managed a sheepish grin. "She's asked me to move in, and I've said yes."

Surprised by how swiftly Jake's relationship had moved when none of his previous girlfriends had moved beyond the dating stage, she reached out and squeezed his forearm. "That's great, Jakey. I'm really happy for you."

And she was, determinedly ignoring the tiny flare of resentment and fear: now her brother had a new woman in his life, would he forget about her?

"Thanks. It's a big deal for both of us but we know it's right."

"Good for you."

Jake deserved happiness. He deserved the world on a platter and then some for what he'd done for her. Jake was an incredible brother and she'd never have made it if it hadn't been for him.

Which reinforced her worry of a moment ago: what would she do if she hit the skids again and didn't have Jake around to rely on?

"Sara's had it tough," he said, his tone softer than she'd ever heard. "Her three-year-old daughter Lucy died of pneumonia fifteen months ago—"

"Oh heck, poor Sara." Rose couldn't imagine any pain worse than losing a child and immediately regretted her selfish thoughts. If anything ever happened to Olly, she wouldn't be able to go on. "Has it been hard on her, having Olly around?"

"Initially, yeah, but Olly helped her work through the tough stuff," he said. "Who wouldn't love that boy."

"Damn straight." Rose smiled, only realizing that second how happy she felt. Her heart felt lighter than it had in forever. Being reunited with Olly had done it, but she knew there was more to it. Having Jake and Cilla around, the only real family she'd ever known, made her feel secure in a way she never had before.

She'd definitely made the right decision in coming to Redemption.

"There's something else," he said. "I've bought the local airfield. Planning to open up a charter school, with a small fleet of planes."

Rose halted, the enormity of Jake's declaration sinking in. Considering he hadn't been near an airport in the ten months since he'd quit his job, this was huge.

"That's great news." Rose hugged him. "I'm so proud of you."

"Right back at you." When they disengaged he slugged her on the arm in typical big brother fashion. "We've come a long way, you and I."

"Thank God," she murmured, incredibly impressed by how Jake had dealt with his demons and moved on, including finding love along the way.

"Come on. Sara can't wait to meet you." Jake draped his arm across her shoulder and tugged her forward. "She's a keeper, so don't go all protective on me, okay?"

"Like I would." Rose rolled her eyes. "As I recall, you were the one who almost punched Dyson when you heard I was pregnant."

Jake's mouth compressed in a mutinous line, his expression thunderous. "That guy was no good for you."

"So you've said before," she said, her dry response earning a softening of his expression. "But I wouldn't have Olly if it wasn't for him, so how could anyone regret that?"

"True." He squeezed her shoulders and removed his arm. "He's pretty amazing."

"I'm glad you've bonded," she said, confident enough to voice her fear now. "I was worried he'd be too much for you."

"He was. How did you think I ended up at Cilla's after day one?"

They laughed as the little man in question waved frantically from the open front door as they approached.

Rose caught sight of a slim blonde behind Olly, her smile tentative. She wore a pale blue sundress covered in tiny sunflowers and taupe sandals, making Rose feel like a grub in her denim shorts, tank top and flip-flops.

"I'm so pleased to finally meet you," the woman said, holding out her hand. "I'm Sara."

"Nice to meet you too." Rose shook her hand, surprised by the firmness of Sara's grip. "Both Jake and Olly are rather smitten with you."

"The Mathieson men are fabulous." Sara blushed as she glanced at Jake, and that one look allayed some of the doubts Rose had harbored. Sara looked like she genuinely loved Jake, but while Rose couldn't be happier for her brother, she couldn't dismiss an insistent niggle that this relationship had progressed too fast.

"But I'm not a man yet: I'm just a boy," Olly said, staring at Sara in confusion.

"You're still fabulous," Sara said, tweaking Olly's nose, her affection obvious, eliciting another stab of irrational jealousy deep within Rose.

What the hell was wrong with her? She should be pleased Olly had been so well looked after, rather than resenting the fact her son appeared more at ease with these people than he had with her during the months before she'd left.

Then again, considering her dependency on alcohol to unwind and her erratic behavior because of it, she couldn't blame her son for growing increasingly wary back then.

"I agree, you're fabulous," Rose said, forcing herself to share a conspiratorial smile with the woman she'd just met. "So where's this surprise, young man?"

Olly beamed as he brought a small piece of wood out from behind his back. "Sara helped me with this because she's a grownup and burns wood, but I drew the picture."

Unsure about Sara's status as a pyromaniac, Rose took the wood from Olly's outstretched hands and gasped in surprise.

One of their favorite weekend activities over the last few years had been riding the carousel in Central Park and Olly always drew it for her. But this time, his drawing was etched into the wood.

"I'm a pyrographer," Sara said. "I burn sketches into wood and leather."

"And she's brilliant," Jake said, leaving Rose's side to cross to Sara's and slide an arm around her waist. "Want to come see?"

"Absolutely." Ignoring the sudden hollow feeling and lack of warmth that the removal of Jake's arm elicited, Rose squatted down to Olly's level and dragged him in for a cuddle. "Thanks, sweetie. I love it."

"You're welcome." He squeezed her briefly before wriggling away, way too fast, like he couldn't wait to get away from her. "Can we go in now? Sara has strawberry milk and brownies for us."

Rose wanted to warn him to leave room for dinner but she didn't have the heart when she saw how Olly bounded into the house, comfortable to be there.

A lump formed in her throat as she realized how needlessly she'd worried these last few months. Olly had been well taken care of, by Jake, Cilla and Sara. She owed them all, big time. And she needed to clamp down on her jealousy, because these people obviously loved her son as much as she did.

As they walked up the hall toward the kitchen, Rose had to admit Jake was right. Sara was an amazingly talented artist, in a medium she'd never seen before.

When they reached the kitchen, Rose caught a pointed look passing between Jake and Sara, before he grabbed Olly's hand.

"Come on, champ. We can have our milk outside while Sara rustles up the brownies."

"Yay." Olly didn't have to be asked twice and bolted outside, leaving Rose alone with Sara.

Whatever the woman wanted to say, Rose had no idea if she was qualified to hear it, considering they barely knew each other.

To her credit, Sara didn't waste time. "Jake's told you he's moving in here?"

"Yeah, I'm happy for him." Damned if she didn't sound it, though, and she cleared her throat. "For you both," she added quickly, when Sara's face fell.

"I just wanted you to know that I love your brother very much. We've both been through a tough time and opening up to the possibility of a relationship has been a huge step." She took a deep breath and continued. "Jake's told me a bit about your past and how close you two are, and I wanted to say that I'd never come between you.

And I don't want you to feel like I'm taking him away from you."
She patted her chest. "We'll both be here for you. And Olly. As long
as you need us, which is hopefully forever."

To her amazement, Sara closed the short distance between them
and enveloped her in a hug. "I'd like us to be friends."

While Sara's impromptu hug made Rose vaguely uncomfortable, she could always do with friends, particularly ones with the
potential to become her future sister-in-law.

But she couldn't help but think Jake and Sara were rushing into
this. Moving in together was a huge step and it sounded like they
were both dealing with troubled pasts.

Then again, who was she to judge? She'd only just faced up to
her past recently and didn't like what she'd seen.

"Thanks. I'd like that too." Rose tolerated the hug for a few
more seconds before easing away.

Sara appeared relieved, like she'd been expecting a rebuff, and
Rose wondered what Jake had told his girlfriend about her.

"Give me a hand to take this outside?" Sara gestured at the
plates piled high with homemade brownies, and Rose wondered if
there was anything this elegant woman wasn't good at.

"Sure."

As Rose followed Sara outside and caught sight of Jake and Olly
tumbling in the grass, mock-wrestling, she wondered how long it
would be before Jake and Sara had a child of their own and the
order of things would be restored: her and Olly alone against the
world.

5.

Rose wanted to spend her first full day in Redemption with Olly, but if she was serious about staying in town and making a go of living here, she needed a job ASAP.

After a hearty breakfast of eggs over easy, bacon and hash browns, Cilla had suggested she try Don's Diner in town first, then work her way through nearby towns.

It was a solid plan, but it hit a snag the moment she told Olly.

"Why do you have to go work when you only just got here?" He folded his arms and glared, his mouth mutinous as he flopped onto his bed.

"Because we need money to live, sweetheart." She sat next to him, her heart sinking when he scooted away. "I won't be gone long."

He rolled his eyes. "That's what you said last time, when you were going away to get better, and you took forever."

An ache bloomed behind Rose's breastbone and spread outward. An ache for the months she'd lost with her precious child. An ache for how far she'd spiraled downward before realizing it. An ache that encapsulated her fervent hopes that they could recover their relationship and move forward.

"Sometimes things take longer than we expect." She chose her words carefully, wanting to convey that she understood his resentment but wouldn't condone too much. "And I know you must've missed me as much as I missed you, but I'm back now and we'll do lots of fun stuff together."

"I did miss you," he said, begrudgingly, a smidgeon of frown easing. "Sara and Uncle Jake do fun stuff with me too."

Rose had lost count of the number of times Olly had sung the praises of Jake and Sara over the last twenty-four hours. It had started to seriously grate on her nerves.

But she swallowed her resentment and continued. "Some of that fun stuff requires money. Aunt Cilla, Uncle Jake and Sara have looked after you so well—don't you think it'd be nice to do stuff for them to repay them?"

"I guess." Olly's earnest gaze brought a lump to her throat. "They've been real nice."

"I know. Aren't you lucky?" She ruffled his hair, buoyed when he didn't shrug her off. "Having all these people to love you and look after you?"

His expression cleared as he nodded and bounced up and down on the bed a little. "Yeah, it's cool. Maybe we can go for a picnic later?"

"Sure. That sounds great." This time, when she reached for him, he let her embrace him for a few seconds before wriggling out of her arms and racing to the door. "Aunt Cilla needs help picking herbs in the garden so I'll see you later."

Olly ran out the door before she could respond, leaving Rose to ponder whether they'd ever get their old relationship back.

She shouldn't stress so much—it had only been a day—but deep down she knew the previously insular relationship she'd had with her son had irrevocably changed.

She should be glad. He had more people to love in his life. But she couldn't shake the hint of bitterness that her son had moved on without her.

After heading to her small room next to Olly's, Rose dressed in the only good outfit she owned, a simple black sheath that ended at her knees and kitten-heeled patent ebony pumps. She rarely wore makeup, didn't have any beyond the basics, but took the time to mascara her lashes, dust a bronzer over her cheeks and slick a cherry gloss on her lips.

Confidence had never been her strong suit, and if an outer mask hid the bundle of nerves inside, she was all for it.

The drive into town took ten minutes, a leisurely meandering through vineyard country that looked like pictures of idyllic country living in a glossy magazine.

Gently sloping hills covered in row upon row of neat vines. Lush, green paddocks where horses grazed. Hilltop mansions with three-hundred-and-sixty-degree views. Farmhouses with barns as big as a city block. Boutique wineries with ornate signs promising year-round tastings. Quaint cottages perched on sprawling acreages.

When she'd been here as a kid, her father would arrive at Cilla's and never move, so she hadn't seen any of the countryside. It looked like a nice place to raise a child, and once again she was struck by her predicament. If she didn't find a job within a week, she'd have to consider moving back to the city.

Reconnecting with her family was great, but no way in hell would she mooch off Cilla's hospitality or take handouts from Jake yet again. He'd come through for her in the past, loaning her money when she was desperate, though they both knew she had no capability of paying back a loan.

Now he had Sara, an airfield and a new life in a new town. The last thing she wanted was for him to feel responsible for her too.

Which meant she had to quell her nerves, put on a brave face and nail a job.

Following Cilla's instructions, she drove through town, turned left at the last intersection and spotted Don's Diner on her right. A sprawling old tavern that had been converted into a bright, cheery diner, it spread across an entire block. Cars lined the curb as far as she could see, which surprised her.

It was just past eleven. Too late for breakfast. Too early for lunch. Yet the place looked packed. Which she took as a good sign. Maybe they could do with an extra cook?

It took her five minutes to find a parking spot, another five to walk back to the diner in those stupid heels, and by the time she'd pushed through the double glass doors and stepped inside, she was hot and flustered. And nervous. Incredibly, hand-shakingly nervous.

She stood inside the door behind a potted cactus, taking slow, deep breaths and absorbing the ambience.

Don's Diner appeared eclectic. The right side of the restaurant looked like something out of the Old Wild West, with wooden floorboards, a long bar lined with mahogany barstools and matching chairs and tables.

The left side of the restaurant channeled a diner from the fifties. Black and white tiled floor, red vinyl-covered booths and a jukebox.

She'd never seen anything like it.

"Can I help you?" A grinning hostess in a flared-skirted orange polka-dotted halter dress, bobby socks and sneakers peered around the cactus.

Startled by that much perkiness in the morning, Rose nodded. "I'm here to see Don."

Cilla had insisted she help Rose by ringing the owner this morning and asking if he could spare her niece five minutes for a quick chat. Considering Rose hadn't let Cilla tell him why, Don had been bemused but he'd agreed. An example of small-town familiarity at its best, one that Rose intended to use to her full advantage in this instance.

"Do you have an appointment?"

"He's expecting me," Rose said, determined to do whatever it took, including vaulting that bar, to speak to the owner.

"Okay, follow me."

Rose had to semi-sprint to keep up with the hostess as they wound through the tables to reach a door marked "Office." The hostess knocked twice, stuck her head around the door and announced, "Someone here to see you. Said you're expecting her."

Rose heard a gruff voice from behind the door. "Must be Cilla's niece. Send her in."

Surprised the hostess didn't ask whether she was in fact Cilla's niece, Rose thanked her, stepped into the office and closed the door.

The smell of stale cigar smoke hung in the air and Rose's nose tingled with the urge to sneeze. The office was tiny, at odds with the large diner, and sported a small desk, a bookcase and a filing cabinet.

A scrawny bald man sat behind the desk, wearing wire-rimmed spectacles and a navy wife-beater, a stack of time cards on his right and a laptop on his left.

He glanced up when she entered, his expression harried, and Rose hoped to God she could convince him to hire her.

"Hi, I'm Rose Mathieson, Cilla's niece."

"Yeah, yeah, come in." He waved her closer impatiently, clasped his hands and rested them on the desk. "What can I do for you?"

Here went nothing.

"I'm a qualified chef. Been cooking in New York City restaurants for the last six years. But I've moved to Redemption to be with family and would love a chance to show you my skills."

Don frowned. "You want a job as a cook here?"

He made it sound like she'd asked to dance naked on the diner's bar.

"That would be great—"

"We're not some fancy city place, Missy. We serve good, honest, country fare here. None of that big-plate, tiny-serve crap you're used to."

Hoping she could pull this off, Rose tried her best hard sell. "Actually, I prefer cooking hearty home-style food. Pies and casseroles and pot roasts. Apple pies and lemon tarts. Simple food that packs a punch."

Don's eyebrows rose higher, if that were possible. "Good to hear. Do you have references?"

Heart sinking, Rose nodded. But how likely was it that Don would hire her if he checked her last place of employment and discovered she'd been fired four months ago?

"I do, but I'd like a trial to show you what I can cook."

Don's beady eyes studied her from behind his spectacles for what seemed like an eternity, before he finally nodded.

"You're in luck. One of my cooks broke a leg last week and we've been short-staffed ever since. I can't promise you a long-term job but if you're willing to fill in for eight to twelve weeks, depending when Stella's back, then you're hired."

Elated, Rose held out her hand. "Thanks for the opportunity. I won't let you down."

Don shook her hand. "Stella worked the morning shift, seven to one. That going to be a problem?"

"No, that's fine."

School would be starting back soon and once she had Olly enrolled, she hoped Cilla would be okay with dropping him off. Or she'd check out the school bus. Anything to get her finances ticking over again.

"Good. Then you can start tomorrow." He returned to his time cards, effectively dismissing her, and Rose resisted the urge to run out the door and whoop.

She didn't believe in luck. She couldn't, not with some of the crap that had happened to her, but Don losing a cook to a broken leg around the time she needed a job seemed like fate was finally in her corner.

Having a regular income would give her and Olly freedom of choice. She couldn't see them living with Cilla indefinitely, no matter how insistent her aunt was that it was fine. Bryce sometimes worked nights at the hospital, and she knew it would be impossible and unfair to ask Olly to tiptoe around while Bryce slept during the days. She wanted Olly to have the childhood she'd never had: able to be exuberant and enthusiastic without fear of making too much noise and earning a rebuke. Or worse.

No, she couldn't see the living arrangements suiting them for long, and a wage would ensure she could start looking around for another place.

As she exited the office and stepped into the Wild West dining area, two things happened at once. The aroma of sizzling burgers and onion rings made her stomach rumble, and she almost ran into someone. Literally.

Her foot caught on a bar stool and she lurched forward, bumping into a man's back. He spun around, his arms reaching out automatically to steady her, his eyes widening in surprise, like he recognized her.

"Hey. You okay?"

"Two left feet," she said, grimacing and pointing at her shoes. "Or the cosmos trying to tell me to stick to sneakers or flip-flops and leave the heels at home."

"You look great." His gaze swept over her, his admiration making her skin tingle, his over-familiarity confusing her. Who was this guy?

"Uh . . . do I know you?"

He clutched his chest like she'd wounded him. "I'm crushed you don't remember me."

Wracking her memory but coming up empty, she shrugged. "I haven't been in town since I was a kid, so . . ."

"So I'm still crushed." His grin transformed his face from cute to handsome and she resisted the urge to fiddle with her hair.

"And I'm still clueless as to who you are."

He chuckled. "Maybe I should take your memory loss as a compliment?" He tapped his chest. "Maybe I've transformed into a six-packed, model-like Adonis from the geeky preacher's kid I used to be?"

Preacher's kid . . . no way. This hot guy was Caden Shoreham? The serious, quiet kid who'd been Cilla's neighbor and the friend she'd ditched once he knew too much about her home life?

"Caden?"

He snapped his fingers. "So I'm pretty memorable after all."

She smiled. "Sorry, it's been a long time, and you look . . ."

"Hot? Sexy? Gorgeous? All of the above?"

Definitely option D, not that Rose would admit it.

She settled for "Different," and he laughed.

"Now there's a resounding endorsement for my ego."

"Take it or leave it," she said, enjoying their banter, wondering when was the last time she'd chatted to a guy like this, let alone allowed the flirtation.

He gestured at her outfit. "Hot date?"

"Yeah, that's me, bowling into town and lining up the studs to have lunch with on my first day." She rolled her eyes. "I just had an interview of sorts." She pointed in the direction of the kitchen. "I'll be cooking here, starting tomorrow."

"That's great." His genuine smile made her wish she hadn't ditched their friendship. "Guess I'll be eating here more than usual then."

"You eat here often?"

He shrugged, endearingly bashful. "Often enough. My repertoire of pasta, omelets and steak gets old fast. Plus, I work in town, so it's easier to pick something up here on the way home than cook for one when I get there."

Rose knew what that was like. She had tried to cook healthy meals for Olly daily but usually grabbed a quick snack for herself at the restaurant. While she loved to cook, making anything beyond soup or stir-fry for one seemed like too much hard work.

"What are you doing now?" Caden glanced at his watch. "I was planning on grabbing some takeout and heading back to work, but I've got an hour if you want to have something to eat?"

Rose knew she should head back. She didn't want to leave Olly for too long, not after their awkward confrontation this morning. Or she could start scouting out vacant apartments or cottages.

But with Caden staring at her, a beguiling mix of hope and interest in his clear blue eyes, she found herself remembering how he'd been a good friend when she'd needed one and nodding instead.

"Sure, I'd love to."

"Great." His beaming smile warmed her better than the heat radiating from the kitchen as he guided her to a nearby table. "What do you feel like?"

A perfectly innocuous question regarding her food choices but she found herself staring at her childhood friend, at his broad shoulders and muscly arms and the dark blond stubble dusting his strong jaw, and all she could think was how she felt like doing him.

She hadn't been with a guy since a quickie with a waiter at work once, too long ago to count. Olly was her priority, the only male in her life. Her routine consisted of work and raising Olly. That was it. No dates. No relationships. No sex.

Yet the longer Caden stared at her, the more preoccupied she became with the last.

Rose felt heat flush her cheeks as her eyes lighted on the first thing on the menu between them, and she blurted, "Nachos."

"With or without jalapeños?" He leaned forward, his expression mischievous. "Do you like it hot?"

Rose swallowed and wished she could pick up the menu and fan herself.

She'd never been any good at flirting and when Caden did it, it made her very aware of her shortcomings in the romance department.

"Changed my mind," she said, clearing her throat. "I'll have a burger with the works and a side of fries."

"Okay, I'll have the nachos and we can share," he said, his smug grin alerting her to the fact that he knew exactly how uncomfortable his flirting made her but was enjoying it regardless. "Extra hot."

Deciding to call his bluff, she said, "So when did the shy, reserved boy become a lady killer?"

He laughed, a rich, deep sound that made her insides clench. "There's something about you that brings out my teasing side."

"You weren't always like that," she said, remembering the many times he'd sat with her in the garden, content to pick grass or watch her make daisy chains, their shared silence comfortable. "You were a pretty serious kid."

His smile faded and he gestured to a waitress. "Being an only kid, I was used to being quiet." He eyeballed her, his switch from playful to serious a tad unnerving. "You have no idea how much I looked forward to your visits."

"But you must've had friends at school?"

She never had, because she could never bring them home. Girls in her class had regular sleepovers and manicure parties at each other's houses but she could never reciprocate, so she presented a deliberately aloof front to keep potential friends at bay.

She'd been labeled everything from snooty bitch to ice princess. She'd pretended not to care but it had hurt. Real bad.

After he placed their order with the waitress, he turned his attention back to her. "Yeah, I had friends, but when I hit my teens, most of the guys didn't want to hang out with the preacher's son for fear their parents would find out what they were up to."

She gestured around the diner. "What's the worst kids could get up to in a place like this? Smoking, drinking, partying?"

His somberness surprised her. "Didn't matter. They didn't include me."

Empathy made her reach for his hand before she knew what she was doing and she laid hers on top of his. "Sounds like we both had lonely, crappy childhoods."

He stared at their hands for an eternity before turning his palm up and holding hers. "I'm guessing you couldn't take friends home because of your dad?"

She nodded, hating the stab of fear that, even all these years later, mentioning her father elicited. "You were the only person back then who guessed how bad it was."

His brow furrowed. "I remember that day. I saw you playing soccer with Jake and you accidentally kicked over your dad's whiskey glass. He went ballistic." He hesitated, glanced away. "I saw him raise his hand to you, then Jake intervened and you ran through the bushes into my yard."

Rose should've felt embarrassed that Caden had been privy to her shoddy childhood, but after what she'd been through since then, it didn't seem so mortifying anymore. "And you found me there, bawling, and offered me your prized worm farm."

His frown cleared. "That's why you didn't want to hang out anymore—because I knew the truth?"

She nodded. "I was a stupid kid who was embarrassed you'd seen a glimpse of my horrible life."

"I'm sorry you had it tough." He squeezed her hand, his gaze so sincere her throat tightened. "But I'm not sorry we were friends, for however long it lasted."

Rose swallowed as her eyes started stinging too. Hell, she had to get their conversation back to lighthearted before she cried all over him.

"Jeez, for a lady killer, you sure know how to make a girl nostalgic." She extricated her hand, glad when he released it. "What are you up to these days?"

Thankfully, he bought her change of subject. "I'm an accountant. Have my own business in town. And I'm running for mayor. Can you believe it?"

"I can." She schooled her face into her best prim and proper impersonation. "You're a highly respected, upstanding citizen. Redemption would be lucky to have you at the helm and the first order of business should be to erect a bronze bust of you in the town square."

The corners of his eyes crinkled adorably when he smiled. "Are you making fun of me?"

She held her finger and thumb an inch apart. "A little."

"Honestly? It seemed like the right thing to do when the opportunity presented itself."

He glanced away, pain clouding his eyes, lost in memories that made her curious. What had happened to make this cheery guy so morose?

He pulled a face. "Plus, I've been railroaded into it."

"Your folks?"

He nodded. "Dad's health hasn't been the best the last few years and for some bizarre reason, it means a lot to them. Plus, the accountancy firm is practically running itself and I'm stagnating a little . . ." He trailed off, as if he'd said too much, his expression thoughtful.

"If you're stagnating, you move away. You don't stick around."

That's what she'd done. Made a big move to hustling, bustling, downtown Redemption. Yeah, she really loved to shake it up. But her situation was different. She had Olly and that's what her move was about. Caden had no ties to this town beyond his parents. If she were him, she'd be outta here.

He ran a hand over his face. "You've figured me out. I'm a pathetic homebody who prefers rattling around his house to clubbing in the city."

"*You* know what clubbing is?" Her mouth made a shocked O and she slapped her hand over it in mock surprise.

"Funny." He grinned. "I bet I could outlast you on the dance floor."

She snorted, enjoying their banter. "Shows how much you know. They don't even call it a dance floor in those places anymore."

Bemused, he chuckled. "Then what do they call it?"

"I have a kid and haven't been out in seven years. You think I know?"

He joined in her laughter and it struck Rose how comfortable she felt in Caden's company. For two people who hadn't seen each other in almost two decades, they connected in a way she'd never experienced.

Her fling with Dyson had been typical teenage stuff, filled with angst and intensity and passion, whereas Caden exuded a calm that attracted her on a deeper level. Not that he wasn't sexy; the way her insides jolted every time he laughed and her skin tingled when he'd held her hand was testament to that. But her attraction to him seemed almost visceral, like she wanted him on an instinctive level that defied logic.

"You have a child?"

She nodded, surprised he hadn't heard all about her situation on the grapevine—and glad he hadn't. Small-town gossip could kill reputations and she'd rather have the opportunity to make a fresh start without people judging her.

"Olly's six. And I'm a single mother," she added as an afterthought, not sure why she felt compelled to divulge it. Or not willing to acknowledge why she did: that she found Caden attractive.

Caden snapped his fingers. "Is Olly the kid who's been staying next door at Cilla's?"

Rose gaped. "You still live in the same house with your *parents?*"

She made it sound like she'd rather have her fingernails ripped off one by one, and he laughed.

"Are you crazy? I bought the place from them when I got back from college."

She swiped at her brow in mock relief. "Phew. For a minute there I thought you were still that dorky kid who wore buttondown shirts to read in the garden."

He winced. "Don't remind me."

They smiled at each other and once again, Rose marveled at how relaxed she felt in his company.

"You know, I'm glad you're back in town and ran into me, literally." He raised his glass of water. "To renewing old friendships."

"To friendship," she said, clinking her glass against his.

As she replaced her glass on the table, he touched the back of her hand. "Who knows, maybe we'll get to go clubbing one of these days?"

Rose's heart did a weird little jive that made her breathless. The thought of dancing with Caden made her palms clammy and her stomach roil. She should say something witty to defuse the moment, but the longer she stared into his too-blue eyes and the longer his touch wreaked a havoc she'd never imagined, the more her mind blanked.

So she blurted the first thing that popped into her head. "I'm a terrible dancer."

He accepted her refusal with good-humored dignity as he held out his hands, palm up, like he had no tricks up his sleeves.

"There's no statute of limitations on the offer, so if you feel like a boogie or whatever, you know where to find me."

Yeah, right next door apparently, which suddenly made Rose's fear of small-town life blossom to full-blown panic. She'd liked living next door to a serious kid she could hang out with. But Caden had grown into a charming, gorgeous guy, and having him next door now might be too close for comfort.

"Uh-huh," she mumbled, knowing she should say something articulate and witty but coming up empty.

"*'Uh-huh?'* You really should work on containing your excitement." He made a dorky gun with his thumb and forefinger, and fired it. "Now stop pumping up my ego because our food's on the way and I don't want your gushing to ruin my appetite."

"Idiot," she muttered, returning his grin as their waitress deposited huge plates in front of them.

Rose had never been so glad to see food in all her life because it gave her a reprieve. If she'd valued her friendship with quiet, caring Caden the kid, she didn't stand a chance when faced with his charming, affable adult counterpart.

6.

Rose's upbeat mood after securing a job and having lunch with Caden faded fast when she got back to her aunt's and walked straight into a shit-storm.

Not that Cilla and Bryce heard her as she came in the back door. They were too busy tearing each other's throats out in the living room.

"You need to give me space," Cilla yelled, sounding so anguished Rose wanted to rush in and comfort her.

In fact, Rose wanted to announce her presence immediately but was forestalled when she locked gazes with her aunt through the doorway and Cilla gave the slightest shake of her head.

Great. She'd been caught eavesdropping.

"You're not making any sense," Bryce said, his voice tight with anger. "Why the hell did you ask me to move in if all you want is for me to leave you alone?"

"It's too much. You're smothering me . . ." Cilla trailed off on a sob and Rose carefully backed toward the door. "I know you have needs, but you always knew I'm older and—"

"Cut the bullshit, Cilla. You were all over me when we first got together but ever since I've moved in, something's changed."

Rose had her hand on the doorknob, ready to escape, when the truth hit her.

Olly and Jake had been living with Cilla when Bryce moved in. Were they cramping her aunt's style? If so, adding her to the mix couldn't be helping and in that moment, Rose knew she had to move out ASAP.

Rose heard her aunt sigh. "I haven't lived with a man for twenty years. You can't expect me to change overnight and be ready to satisfy your every whim whenever you want."

Uh-oh. The conversation was fast veering into icky territory and Rose had to bolt.

"This isn't just about sex and you know it," Bryce said, the chill in his tone making Rose want to rub her arms. "You know how I feel about you, Cilla, and you need to let me into your life beyond the superficial. Otherwise . . ."

The pause went on forever and Rose jumped when she heard the front door slam.

She had just turned the doorknob, ready to flee out the back door before her aunt confronted her, when Cilla marched into the kitchen, pulled out a chair and slumped into it.

"Sorry for walking in on that—"

"Don't worry about it." Cilla waved away her apology. "Do you think I'm an old fool?"

"I-I don't know enough about your situation—"

"I think you heard enough to get the general gist." Cilla pinched the bridge of her nose. "I'm just so tired. Keeping the naturopathy business thriving. Doing everything around the house. Looking after . . ."

Cilla compressed her lips, an embarrassed flush tainting her cheeks, and she didn't have to finish the sentence for Rose to know she was adding to her aunt's burden.

"You won't have to look after Olly any longer." Rose sat next to her aunt and patted her hand. "You've done an amazing job and I appreciate it, but it's time for us to move out."

"Please don't." Cilla's plea burst from her lips so quickly that Rose was startled. "Sorry, but I like having Olly, and now you, here as a buffer."

"Seriously?"

Apparently, the problems between Cilla and Bryce were worse than she'd imagined.

Cilla nodded, plucking at her bottom lip absentmindedly. "I can't imagine being in the house, just him and me."

"It could be pretty great," Rose said, wishing she had half a clue when it came to relationships so she could offer stellar advice rather than her half-assed opinion. "Isn't that the point when you ask a guy to move in with you?"

"You're right, but I'm scared . . ."

"Of?"

Cilla stopped picking at her lip, her gaze stricken. "What if I'm not enough? What if he discovers he's stuck here with an old woman who can't satisfy him the way he deserves?"

This relationship stuff was way beyond her expertise level but Rose knew she had to say something to allay her aunt's genuine fears.

"The worst that can happen is that he leaves, and then you'll be back to being independent. Is that what you want?"

"No." At least Cilla sounded certain. "But this is a lot more complicated than I imagined."

Rose didn't know what it was like to live with a guy—discounting her gorgeous little man—but she knew from experience that she valued her space and couldn't imagine answering to anybody.

"What did you imagine it to be?"

Cilla's brow crinkled in thought. "The two of us maintaining our independence but being good friends. Developing our relationship." She blushed. "In and out of the bedroom. But I expected to take our time, not rush headlong into this at a manic pace."

"So tell him."

Easy for Rose to say. She wasn't the one having to tell a handsome doc to slow things down.

Cilla nodded slowly, her expression still worried. "I know we need to talk, but how do I tell him without sounding like I'm pushing him away?"

Rose held out her hands and shrugged. "He's a doctor, which means he's a smart guy. Ease into it. He'll get the message."

A glimmer of a smile tugged at the corners of Cilla's mouth. "How did you get so wise, Missy?"

"I'm very good at giving advice to others, not so good at taking what I dish out."

"You're doing fine." Cilla reached over and hugged her. "Sorry for dumping all that on you, but I'm glad you were around. You've helped."

"I'm glad."

Now, if only Rose could help herself, something she was still figuring out half an hour later at the kitchen table while Cilla worked her frustrations out in the garden. She needed to move out, no question about it, but how could she afford it when she'd spent her life savings on her stint at the recovery center and had only just scored a new job?

Then there was the babysitting factor, trying to find someone other than her aunt or her brother to look after Olly while she was at work and until school started.

She felt like she'd imposed on them enough. Not that she didn't appreciate the amazing job they'd done with Olly the last four months, because she did, but now that she was here she needed to get her life back on track. And that meant resuming full-time care of her son.

She hated to admit it, but being witness to Cilla and Bryce's meltdown had been the catalyst to something she'd already been mulling over since she'd arrived: a small part of her wanted to move out as a result of the petty, stupid jealousy she couldn't shake no matter how hard she tried.

When she'd been discharged from the center, she'd expected Olly to be all over her, to never leave her side. Instead, her intelligent son had made it more than clear this morning that he'd morphed into an independent, confident six-year-old who had thrived under the attention of Jake and Cilla. And if Rose heard him mention how amazing Sara was one more time, she'd run screaming down Main Street.

She hated feeling jealous, knew it was totally irrational. But it had been her and Olly against the world for so long that she couldn't quite believe he'd changed so much in four months.

But with Jake moving into Sara's, and Bryce appearing increasingly resentful of the intrusion of her and Olly, it was time to move.

Bryce entered the kitchen, threw his car keys into a brass bowl on a side table and collapsed into a chair, muttering under his breath as he rested his head back and closed his eyes, reinforcing the decision she'd made.

He hadn't caught sight of her yet and she sidled toward the kitchen door. She'd almost made it when Olly came running into the room and skidded to a stop.

"Hey, Bryce, did you chop up any bodies today?"

To his credit, Bryce's eyes snapped open and he forced a smile. "Already told you, bud, I'm not a surgeon."

Olly's face fell, so Bryce added, "But I did pull a piece of fence this long out of someone's leg."

He held his arms wide and Rose hoped he was exaggerating.

"Wow." Olly perched on the arm of his chair. "Was there lots of blood?"

"Uh-huh."

"And I bet there was a bruise too. Was it purple or blue?"

Before Bryce could answer, Rose took pity on him and stepped in. "Hey, Ol, why don't we go for a walk?"

Bryce's relief was almost palpable as he mouthed a silent "thanks."

Yeah, she and Olly definitely needed to move out. After the argument he'd had with Cilla, the doc had obviously gone for a drive and the last thing he needed when he came home to make up with his girlfriend was an inquisitive six-year-old peppering him with questions.

"Okay, Mom. I can ask the doc more questions later."

Not if she could help it.

"See you later, Bryce." Olly waved and bounded ahead of her, giving her a moment alone with Bryce.

She shouldn't have to apologize for her child's natural exuberance. She'd felt compelled to utter too many apologies herself as a kid and it had sucked, tiptoeing around her father because he was too tired or too drunk or too damn selfish to appreciate everything she did for him in the hope of gaining some snippet of recognition.

She didn't want that for Olly. But she wanted to let Bryce know she appreciated the effort he'd made with her son.

"I know you've only just moved in with Cilla and the last thing you wanted was a kid underfoot, but we'll be out of here ASAP and you'll have some peace," she said.

"You don't have to do that," he said, weariness etched into the lines bracketing his mouth. "You're Cilla's family and she loves having you here."

"But you don't."

If her bluntness startled him, he didn't show it. Apparently he'd mastered a poker face in med school along with cadaver dissection.

"It's been an adjustment," he said, the corners of his mouth curving into a rueful smile. "I'm a confirmed bachelor who has lived alone for years. So to handle living with a woman who's also used to living alone, plus an energetic kid . . . Let's just say it's been challenging."

"I appreciate you being so tolerant with Olly."

And he had been. From what she'd observed, the moment Bryce entered the house Olly would bombard him with countless questions centered on gore. She would have liked to think her son showed an inclination for medicine, but in fact he shared every young boy's obsession with the macabre.

"He's a good kid." Bryce hesitated, as if he wanted to say more, before continuing. "You've done a great job. It can't be easy being a single mom."

"I do my best."

Sadly, it sometimes wasn't good enough, but she was determined to put her weakness for wallowing in the past behind her and move forward.

"You don't have to leave," he said.

"Thanks, but I think we do." She stood and headed for the door. "I'll let Cilla know after dinner."

This time, Bryce didn't protest and as she headed outside in search of Olly, she hoped her aunt wouldn't put up too much of a fight, even though she had no idea where she and Olly might go.

Glancing around, she saw Olly deep in conversation with a neighbor. And it wasn't Sara for once.

This time, he was chatting with Caden, who appeared engrossed in whatever her son was saying.

Her chest tightened with emotion at the sight of her son so at ease with everyone but her. Okay, so that might be a tad over-dramatic, but that's how she'd felt ever since she'd got here, like Olly lit up around other people but only seemed to tolerate her.

Taking a deep breath, she sauntered over. When Olly caught sight of her, he raced over, grabbed her hand and all but dragged her toward Caden.

"Mom, I just met Caden. He's our other neighbor. Did you know he's lived in that house his whole life?" Olly stared at her in wide-eyed wonder, like he couldn't believe people did that. "I told him we'd moved a lot in the city because some of the apartments were yucky."

"My house is yucky when I don't clean it, which is often," Caden said, with a wink. "I'd rather be playing online games than cleaning."

"Awesome. Which ones?"

"I reckon you would've heard of all of them." Caden shot her an intense look she couldn't fathom. "Maybe one day your mom will bring you over for a visit and we can play?"

"That would be so cool." Olly tugged on her hand so hard she could've sworn her shoulder rocked in its socket. "Can we, Mom?"

"We'll see," she said, hating that Caden had put her on the spot.

"Uh-oh." Olly released her hand and pulled a face at Caden. "When she says that, it usually means no."

Caden chuckled. "Maybe she just needs some time to think about it."

"I guess." Olly scuffed a stone with his toes. "Hope she doesn't take too long to think because I really want to play with you."

Realizing she was enjoying watching her son and Caden inter-act way too much, Rose waved her hands in the air. "Hello. I'm right here, guys."

"We know." To emphasize it, Caden's gaze swept over her, assessing and appreciative.

Predictably, she blushed.

"Mom, Aunt Cilla's waving to me from the back door. I better go see what she wants."

"Sure, sweetie. I'll be in shortly."

"'Bye, Caden." Olly waved. "Don't forget I'll be coming over to play real soon."

"Cheeky." Rose tweaked his ear before Olly ran off, leaving her alone with the man who had the power to unnerve her with a single glance.

"He's a great kid," Caden said, leaning on the fence. "Talks a lot."

"Doesn't shut up."

"Considering how damn shy I was, it's a good thing, being able to express yourself." Caden stared at her, like he was trying to convey a message she had no hope of interpreting. "I think we've both been too recalcitrant for our own good."

Rose had no idea if he meant now or in the past and she didn't want to find out. Delving beyond the superficial with Caden could only lead to one thing: trouble.

"So how's the living situation?"

Wishing he hadn't homed in on the one thing she couldn't stop thinking about, she grimaced. "Not good. Cilla's great, but Bryce works long hours at the hospital and it's hard for him to come home to a loud kid."

Caden frowned. "Has he said something?"

She shook her head. "No, he's too polite for that. But I feel sorry for him. He looks so weary when he gets home, and the second he steps inside Olly starts bombarding him with questions."

"He does ask a lot of questions." For a guy who had no kids, Caden's smile was filled with understanding.

"Hope nothing too intrusive?"

He tapped the side of his nose. "Secret men's business."

She laughed, surprised to hear the soft sound spill from her lips. She didn't laugh a lot as a rule. Sure, Olly made her smile or chuckle on a regular basis, but she hadn't had much to genuinely belly-laugh about in a long time.

Yet in one day, Caden, with his easy-going smile and laid-back humor, had made her laugh several times. He was good to be around. Which meant she needed to stay as far away from him as possible if she were to make a go of this new start.

It would be all too easy to fall for a guy like him, to be swept into a fantasy world she'd never inhabited. But she'd learned the hard way that men weren't dependable. Heck, even Jake had let her down when he'd gone AWOL for six months following the plane crash.

Easier to depend on herself and build a stable life for Olly. Nothing else mattered. Her son had to have the secure childhood she'd never had.

He cleared his throat. "This might come out of left field, but I have a vacant apartment." He jerked a thumb over his shoulder in the direction of the garage. "It's been empty for a long time . . ." He trailed off, unable to meet her eyes, and she wondered why he'd issue an invitation that made him so obviously uncomfortable.

She shook her head. "I couldn't—"

He blinked, and she wondered if she'd imagined the flash of pain a moment ago. "Rent free."

Damned if she wasn't tempted, despite her vow to steer clear of Caden. "Even more reason why I can't accept."

He snorted. "You need a place to stay, I've got an apartment. No strings. It's empty and if you don't live in it, it'll still be empty." He shrugged. "It's got to be better than living underfoot of your aunt and her new boyfriend."

When he put it like that, she'd be an idiot to refuse. Yet something held her back. She didn't know if it was his folded arms, defensive posture or sudden evasiveness, but Caden appeared on edge. Like he regretted issuing the invitation for the apartment and didn't know how to retract it.

"You sure it'd be okay?"

He nodded, but his back remained rigid. "Absolutely."

She'd be a fool to refuse an offer like this. It would solve all her problems and give her time to save some cash before finding a place in town of her own.

But she didn't take charity, especially not from some guy she'd only known briefly in childhood. "I'd still rather pay you something."

He pondered a few moments, before snapping his fingers. "You're a chef. I spend a small fortune on takeout. Why don't you cook me a meal or two per week and we'll call it even?"

"That's not enough—"

"My final offer. Take it or leave it."

She should leave it. She should stick to the plan of keeping Caden at bay so she wasn't tempted to depend on anyone. But there was a difference between being savvy and being stubborn to the point of stupidity, and his generous offer could be the perfect solution. She'd still be within walking distance of Cilla and Jake if she needed babysitting, and not having to pay an exorbitant rent would help her become financially stable faster.

Win–win.

But what did Caden get out of it?

Belatedly, she realized he might be expecting her to share those meals she cooked for him. That this could be a subtle ploy for them to hang out together. If that was the case, better to set clear ground rules now.

"Just so we're clear. I'll cook you three meals a week and have Olly deliver them to you when you get home. Is that enough?"

"I was expecting seven a week and you to personally deliver, but hey, I'm flexible." She had no idea if he was joking or not but at least he didn't seem put out that she'd circumvented any possibility of them seeing each other more often. "Give me half a day to air the place out, dust off the cobwebs and do a general cleanup, and you can move in tomorrow if that suits?"

"Sounds great." She reached out to pat his hand where it rested on the fence before thinking better of the contact and letting her arm fall to her side. "Thanks, Caden. You've really come through for us."

"My pleasure, though I haven't really done anything."

His bashfulness was as appealing as the rest of him.

"You've done more than you could possibly know," she said, meaning it.

His gesture of kindness could fast-track her fresh start in a new town. Getting a job had been her first priority, with finding a home of their own her second. Thanks to this generous guy, she could now focus on the third: getting Olly truly settled.

Yet the longer she stood there, with Caden's blue eyes studying her intently, she couldn't help but ponder what would happen if she added a fourth priority to her list.

One that entailed acknowledging her attraction to Caden and seeing how far they could take it.

7.

Rose had been looking forward to spending some quality one-on-one time with her son later that afternoon and this picnic seemed the perfect opportunity.

She'd chosen a quiet lakeside park she'd spotted on her way back from town this morning, had raided Cilla's cookie jars and snaffled an old blanket. Olly had loved their spontaneous weekend picnics in Central Park so she thought this would be the perfect way to spend a few hours getting reacquainted properly with her darling boy.

But her plans for a leisurely, relaxing time hit a snag about five minutes after Olly had demolished most of the cookies and she broached the subject of them moving out.

"Hey, Ol, you remember how you met Caden earlier?"

Olly nodded, dusting crumbs off his hands. "He said he had loads of video games and stuff so he's cool."

"He has a vacant apartment over his garage, and we need a place of our own, so we're moving in there tomorrow."

Considering the tension between Cilla and Bryce when she'd packed for the picnic, she would've moved in tonight if Caden hadn't asked for some time to ensure the place was clean.

"Don't wanna." Olly jumped to his feet and glared. "I want to stay at Aunt Cilla's. I like it there."

Surprised by his sudden mood shift from mellow to angry, she patted a spot next to her on the blanket. "I do too, sweetie, but Bryce has just moved in and sometimes grownups need some time to themselves."

Olly ignored her offer for him to sit next to her and crossed his arms, a deep frown slashing his brows. "Doesn't Bryce like me?"

Oh boy.

"Of course he does. We all adore you. But wouldn't you like it to be just you and me? Like it used to be?"

She expected him to agree wholeheartedly, to hug her, to snuggle into her as he used to. Instead, his frown deepened and a small part of her heart splintered.

"But what if you go away again?" He pouted. "I'm tired of moving around. We had to leave apartments all the time in the city and I like it at Aunt Cilla's, but now you're making me move again and if you go away I'll have to move back . . ." He ran out of breath, his lower lip trembling a little.

Rose's heart fractured a little more. "Sweetheart, I'm not going anywhere."

This time, she didn't give him the option of refusing her offer to sit. She snagged his hand, gently tugged him down next to her and wrapped her arm around him. "I wasn't feeling well for a long time, so I had to go away for a while. But I'm all better now and I'll never leave you again."

A vow she had every intention of keeping, whatever the cost.

Olly gazed up at her, hope smoothing the worry lines from his forehead. "You promise?"

She made a crossing sign over her chest. "Cross my heart."

He hesitated for a moment before flinging his arms around her neck. "I missed you, Mom. Too much. And I don't want to miss you again."

"Same here, darling boy." Battling tears, Rose hugged him tight. "Same here."

She had no idea how long she snuggled Olly. She didn't care. Because having her son articulate his fears and being able to soothe him was the first real mom thing she'd done since she got back.

She owed Jake, Cilla and Sara for taking such good care of her son, but now that she was back, Rose needed to reassert herself in her son's life. Needed to be his go-to person. Needed to be a mother he could depend on.

When he wriggled out of her arms, she wished she could haul him back and never let go.

"So Caden's apartment is next door to Aunt Cilla's?" Olly hugged his knees to his chest and rested his chin on top. "That means we can still visit any time we like, right?"

"Absolutely," Rose said, rapt to be moving out but grateful she wouldn't be going far.

Making a good impression at a new job usually meant taking the crappy shifts and she'd need help with babysitting. She was lucky, having family so close, a luxury she hadn't had in the city.

He shrugged. "Then I guess it's okay, us moving *again*."

"Glad you approve," she said, tweaking his nose. "How about we celebrate with some of Aunt Cilla's homemade lemonade?"

"Yay."

As Olly scrambled to get the plastic cups out of the wicker basket she'd borrowed from Cilla, Rose hoped that the progress they'd made today would continue to the point that her son trusted her fully again.

Olly was her life, and unlike her father, she'd do anything to protect her child.

Her love was unconditional and she'd make damn sure that Olly never had to feel let down or abandoned again.

⁓

They'd returned to Cilla's and Rose had parked and switched off the engine when Olly unbuckled, scooted forward on the back seat and tapped her on the shoulder.

"Mom, what happens if you die?"

Oh boy. Olly was all about the awkward questions today.

Rose swiveled in her seat to face him. "Hopefully that's not going to happen for a long time, sweetie, when you're old enough to look after yourself—"

"But my dad died when he was too young. You said so." His brow furrowed. "I didn't even get to meet him." His face scrunched up. "And you never talk about him, so I don't know what he was like."

Rose had known this day would come, that curiosity would prompt Olly to ask questions about his father. She just wished that day wasn't today, when she was re-establishing a relationship with her son after being absent too long.

Fixing a smile on her face, she patted the passenger seat beside her. "Why don't you hop in here and I'll tell you about him."

"Yay!" Olly scrambled across the gap between the back seat and the front, staring at her with wide-eyed enthusiasm. "What was he like?"

Dyson Patrice had been bold, brash and devastatingly gorgeous, renowned for his outrageous behavior as much as his exquisite cooking.

Rose had met him three months to the day after he'd landed in New York. She had taken one look at the suave Frenchman and fallen in love. Dyson had taken one look at her and seen yet another woman he had to have.

But she'd stick to the less judgmental facts for Olly. "He was a celebrity chef who moved from Paris to New York. He visited the café where I'd been doing an apprenticeship while I was finishing a night course to be a chef."

"A night course? What's that?"

Rose smiled. "I went to a place in the evenings to study different ways to cook."

"Oh," Olly said, the slight wrinkle in the bridge of his nose alerting her to more questions. "How old was my dad?"

"Twenty-one. He was so good at cooking, he was often on magazine covers and in newspapers."

The society pages, mostly, for his hard partying and love of inappropriate women.

"Wow, he was famous." Olly's eyes widened. "Did you always love my dad?"

Rose nodded, remembering the heady, stomach-dropping-away feeling being with Dyson had elicited. She'd resisted him for three weeks after they'd met but Dyson had been persistent. They'd had a fabulous fling that lasted a few months, an eight-week whirlwind of partying and cooking and devouring each other.

Being pregnant at nineteen hadn't been in her grand plans to improve her life after she'd fled home three years earlier, but Dyson hadn't been fazed. He'd charmed her by painting pretty word pictures of a bouncing baby boy with chubby cheeks because his parents couldn't stop feeding him gourmet food. Rose had known she could never hold the attention of a man like Dyson, and there were many nights he didn't come home. But she was having his baby and he'd promised to look after them. Life had been good. Painful, but good.

Until Dyson had gone away with a supermodel and her stick-insect friends for a weekend in the Hamptons, had overdosed on party drugs and wound up dead.

"Sure, honey, I loved your dad very much," Rose said, grateful when Cilla appeared at the back door and waved them in. "And he would've loved you just as much as I do."

She opened her arms, relieved when Olly snuggled into them.

"Thanks, Mom," he murmured, hugging her tight. "My dad sounds like he was pretty cool."

Swallowing a lump of emotion, Rose said, "He was."

She eased away to look him in the eye. "And I don't want you worrying about being alone, okay? Because even if something happens to me, you've got Uncle Jake who loves you, and Aunt Cilla too, so you'll always be looked after."

She pressed her palm over his heart. "And no matter what happens in the future, I'll always be in here. Loving you."

Olly giggled and swatted away her hand. "You're silly. You can't be in there. My heart's in there and Bryce said the heart pumps blood all over our body and keeps us alive."

Rose laughed. "True. Now, Aunt Cilla is waving us in, which probably means she has a yummy dinner waiting."

"Let's go." Olly tumbled from the car and raced toward the house, leaving Rose to follow, marveling that she'd created this amazing little human being.

Dyson might have hurt her, but she'd be eternally grateful to him for giving her Olly.

8.

Caden inserted the key into the lock and jiggled it a little before the door swung open.

He paused on the threshold, finding it difficult to set foot in the apartment for the first time in a year.

It looked the same, bright and cheerful yet functional, and he half expected Effie to come bouncing barefoot out of the bedroom in her signature tie-dyed dress, long black hair tangled, a wide smile illuminating her face from eye-catching to stunning.

She'd been a whirlwind who'd breezed into his life, turned it upside down and left without saying good-bye.

He still resented her for lying to him, for wasting her life on those goddamn pills.

He took a step inside and blinked, catapulted back in time.

"Hey, Gorgeous," he called out, letting himself into the apartment, eager to spend time with the woman who brightened a room just by being in it. "Want to have dinner at that new winery . . ." He trailed off, glimpsing Effie inside the kitchen, a glass of water in one hand, a handful of pills in the other. "Are you okay?"

"Yeah, just some residual muscular pain from an old bout of chronic fatigue syndrome. It bothers me from time to time." She popped about five pills into her mouth and washed them

down, taking the rest with another gulp of water. "Nothing to worry about."

Doubt assailed Caden as he glanced at the three label-less bottles lying in disarray among her beads, incense sticks and a bunch of flowers. "That's a lot of painkillers you just took."

"Don't be an old fuddy-duddy." She poked out her tongue at him, her eyes mischievous. "When the pain flares, I need to take this stuff to get on top of it. Otherwise it makes me catatonic for a week."

"Just be careful, okay?" He strode toward her, his gaze riveted to the loosely knotted sarong tied at her breasts, thinking how easy it would be to undo it. "I've grown used to having you around."

"You're such a softie," she said, flinging herself into his arms and pressing against him. Writhing against him in that way she knew drove him crazy. "Except where it counts, lucky for me."

"Floozy," he murmured, nuzzling her neck, inhaling her signature patchouli fragrance as she cupped him.

"Tell me you don't want this as much as I do . . ." She squeezed him gently and proceeded to eradicate his doubts with her usual abandoned style of lovemaking, like every time would be their last.

How prophetic. Because a few weeks later, she'd been found dead at some seedy motel on the outskirts of Dixon's Creek, a neighboring town, and he'd discovered the extent of her addiction. He'd found a veritable pharmacy of painkillers in the kitchen cupboard, a lethal cocktail she'd been taking for goodness knew how long.

To this day, he didn't know why she'd been in that motel room, who she'd been with, if she'd overdosed deliberately or if it had been accidental. The coroner hadn't helped in that regard either.

In Caden's darkest hours, he wondered if he'd done something to drive her to it. Then the sun would rise the next day and he'd chastise himself for being a fool.

They'd had an impetuous relationship, filled with angst and passion. Fleeting yet fiery. But not once during their six months together had Effie even hinted at being depressed enough to take her own life.

So he'd deemed it an accident, a tragic, stupid decision to take too many pills by a woman who didn't have a lot but had lived life to the fullest.

His eyes burned and he blinked back the sting of tears. Standing here surveying the apartment wouldn't get it cleaned, and he strode inside, slamming the door on his memories.

But they were everywhere.

As he straightened the living room, he saw Effie sitting cross-legged on the floor, meditating.

As he wiped down the kitchen benchtops, he saw Effie drinking some awful green wheatgrass concoction.

As he aired the bedroom, he saw her sprawled naked on the bed, wanton and welcoming.

Damn it.

Caden needed to get out of here.

After the quickest bathroom clean on record, he took one final glance at the apartment and closed the door.

He was glad Rose had accepted his offer to move in. The place needed new memories, ones that wouldn't haunt him.

As for his inner voice that insisted he could be doing the wrong thing, he ignored it.

Better to move forward and forge a friendship than lament the mistakes of the past.

⌒♁

Caden had worked from home the morning Rose moved in.

He'd offered to help but, independent to a fault, she'd wanted to do it on her own, so he'd let her. That didn't stop him peering out the window when her car pulled up alongside the garage. She unloaded six boxes in total, a flabbergastingly small amount for a child and herself. Maybe she liked to travel light? Or maybe she wasn't planning on sticking around all that long?

His computer dinged, indicating an email from yet another frazzled client. Taxes made some people loco and he'd dealt with them all over the years.

When Rose had asked why he was running for mayor, he hadn't told her the complete truth. Sure, he'd been stagnating to the point of boredom. Effie had made him feel that way, constantly regaling him with tales of exotic travels, making him contemplate leaving town with her on a whim. Despite the fact he'd established his firm and had enough work to last him for a decade, he would've done it, too.

But then Effie had died, taking his dreams of traveling along with her.

That still irked the most, the fact he would've left his life behind and followed a woman he hadn't really known at all. He wasn't a stupid guy prone to impulsive decisions, but for that brief time, he'd lost the plot.

Running for mayor would ensure that didn't happen again.

Pinching the bridge of his nose, he sat behind his desk again, only to have someone stab at the doorbell.

Glad for the distraction from work, he strolled to the door and opened it, wondering if his impromptu visitor was Rose.

No such luck. It was his mother.

"Nice of you to drop by, Mom." He stepped back and invited her in, wondering what had his mother so rattled that she'd forgotten the strict protocol she followed.

Never, ever, drop in on anyone unannounced.

"We need to talk, Caden."

Typical Mom. No greeting. No hug. No pretense of warmth.

"Dad okay?"

Caden's father Jeff had survived a heart attack a few years earlier. Since then, Jeff had had occasional angina attacks that required hospitalization. In his less charitable moods, Caden wondered if it was his father's way of escaping his mom for a mini-vacation.

"Health-wise he's fine, though he's just as upset as I am." Penny Shoreham perched on the edge of a chintz sofa he hadn't had the energy to change since his folks had moved out. "What were you thinking?"

"Obviously something at complete odds with you, Mom, so why don't you enlighten me."

Her gaze darted around the room, as if looking for spies. "How could you?" she hissed. "Holding hands with that girl in the middle of the diner."

Caden burst out laughing. He couldn't help it. If the worst the town grapevine could come up with for scandalous behavior was him holding hands with Rose, then it was a slow news day indeed.

Feigning obtuseness, he crinkled his forehead as if deep in thought. "You mean Rose?"

She harrumphed. "And now I see she's moved into the apartment over the garage." Her hands were clasped so tightly in her lap that her knuckles stood out. "Don't you remember what happened the last time you let a woman move in there—"

"Yeah, and here we go again, with you reiterating yet another 'we told you so.'" He muttered a curse. "What do you want from me, Mom? Do you want me to feel guiltier than I already do because I didn't listen to your lectures regarding Effie's many faults? Guiltier that I rarely visited you because Effie didn't like you? Guiltier that I was willing to throw away a good career for a woman who didn't trust me enough to tell me the entire truth?"

He flung his arms wide. "Go ahead, Mom. Lay it all on me again."

Her mouth puckered with distaste. "How do you know Rose isn't like her—"

"Hold it right there," he said, his tolerance at an all-time low. "Rose is nothing like Effie."

"That's where you're wrong." His mother's lips compressed in a thin, mutinous line. "She's in need of rescuing so there you are, stepping up as always." Her expression softened. "You've been doing this since you were a kid. Nursing injured animals. Rescuing stray dogs." Her gaze turned flinty. "And women . . ."

Caden wouldn't give her the satisfaction of reacting. He'd lived with his mother's lectures growing up, had hated how she made him sound like an idiot for giving a damn about the less fortunate. Ironic: for a preacher's wife, she didn't have a generous bone in her body.

"You haven't seen Rose since she was a child. How do you know she needs rescuing?"

Her nose wrinkled like she'd smelled something terrible. "She's an unmarried single mother—"

"She needs a place to stay, and the apartment is empty. I'm helping out an old friend, that's it."

Caden rarely shouted, and certainly not to his mother, but he couldn't help it: she riled him when she stuck her nose in business that was none of her concern.

"No need to take that tone with me." She stood and glowered at him. "If you won't listen to me, maybe you'll listen to your father—"

"For God's sake, don't involve him in this."

She ignored his intentional blasphemy and tilted her nose in the air. "Who do you think sent me here to make you see sense?" Her shoulders slumped a little. "We're concerned, that's all. People are talking, and while you're running for mayor you need to be exemplary."

He couldn't believe the drivel that was spilling from his mother's lips. Or maybe he could. She was nothing if not predictable.

He folded his arms, knowing she hated the defensive posture. "So let me get this straight. Apparently helping out a friend in need isn't exemplary? Wow, if that's the standards this town judges people by, maybe I shouldn't be mayor."

She blanched, her signature crimson lipstick stark against her pallor. "We're only looking out for your welfare—"

"Thanks, Mom, but I'm a big boy now. I'm more than capable of figuring out what's good for me and what isn't."

"You always were stubborn," she muttered, hitching her designer handbag higher onto her shoulder and heading for the door. "You'll regret this, mark my words."

The only thing Caden regretted that minute was allowing his folks to guilt him into running for mayor. Ever since he'd agreed, his mother had been even more intrusive than usual. It was driving him nuts.

His mother paused at the foot of the veranda steps. "What do you really know about this girl? She comes from nasty stock. You were too young to remember, but her father was always bellowing, drunk to his eyeballs. And now she has a child of her own yet no husband. What kind of a woman—"

"Stop." Caden's fingers curled into fists and he thrust them into his pockets, they were shaking that much from anger. "You need to leave and not come back if all you want to do is spread your vitriol."

His mother's mouth gaped, in definite danger of catching flies.

He glared at her, fury making his body vibrate. He'd been angry on occasion but never like this. He didn't like it but no way in hell would he back down. Not this time.

"She will definitely ruin your chances at being elected mayor, so hopefully your father can talk more sense into you." With a final dismissive *tsk-tsk*, his mother marched to her SUV and took off down the driveway like she had a posse on her tail.

Caden had weathered many of his mom's outlandish declarations over the years. Most of the girls he'd dated hadn't been good enough. And his parents had loathed Effie to the point of pretending she didn't exist.

In their defense, he could understand their concern. She'd hitchhiked her way into town and busked to earn a living. She had owned two dresses, one pair of sandals and little else bar her precious guitar. And yeah, he wasn't so self-delusional that he hadn't recognized that his offer for her to stay at his place stemmed from his long-standing rescue complex.

He liked helping people. It made him feel good. The fact that his boring, staid personality had been attracted to her flamboyant wistfulness had been a bonus.

After she'd died and he'd discovered the extent of her addiction, he wondered how someone with little money obtained a plethora of expensive drugs and rented a motel room. He didn't like the answers that came to mind. It made him feel duped all over again.

His parents had caught him at his weakest with their suggestion that he run for mayor, and he hated them for knowing what he needed more than he knew himself. The election had given him something to focus on when Effie's death turned his world upside down. He'd been reinvigorated, falling in love with Redemption all over again while researching the place for his campaign.

It had the added bonus of keeping him too busy to date.

Since Effie's death, his parents had persistently pushed him in the direction of Tully Holmes, daughter of the richest vineyard owner in Redemption. According to them, Tully had pedigree and the one quality "suited to a man of his standing": money.

Pity Caden felt nothing more than a lukewarm friendship for the wishy-washy blonde who ran his campaign—admittedly with a skill and precision he admired. It would've been a hell of a lot easier if he'd fallen madly in love with his parents' choice of bride years ago and gotten them off his back once and for all.

He tolerated their meddling because of his father's health. But his mom had gone too far today, slandering Rose like that.

He kicked a veranda post in frustration, only realizing he had an audience when he heard a discreet little cough.

"Sorry to intrude." Rose stepped forward and held out a stack of magazines. "These were in the bedroom wardrobe and I thought you might want them."

Appalled that Rose might have heard his mother's parting comments, he reached for the magazines, glad they were mathematics journals and not magazines of a different kind. That would've been mortifying. As if he wasn't embarrassed enough.

"Thanks." He took them from her, unsure how to broach the subject of his mom's visit.

"Are you sure you want us here?" She shifted her weight from one foot to another in an action so reminiscent of her childhood that he blinked.

She'd always appeared unsure of herself. Edgy. Nervous. Likely to bolt at any second. Traits courtesy of her nasty father, who'd probably made her jittery and ready to flee to avoid his wrath.

"Of course. I wouldn't have offered otherwise."

A faint pink stained her cheeks. "Look, I heard what your mom said just before she left and I don't want to cause trouble for you—"

"You're not." He held up his hand. "If I listened to every single thing my mother said, I'd be a preacher married to Tully Holmes, squelching grapes with my feet between sermons."

To his relief, Rose smiled, the tension bracketing her mouth easing. "Who's Tully Holmes?"

"Only daughter of the richest vineyard owners in the county. Very *appropriate* choice of bride, apparently."

"So why aren't you married to her?" Her eyes twinkled with mischief. "Because I remember you were a regular stud-muffin with those perfectly ironed jeans and collared shirts your mom used to make you wear."

He grimaced. "Don't remind me. No wonder I didn't have many friends. As if being the preacher's son wasn't bad enough."

She paused, suddenly serious. "You ever think that's why we bonded back then? Because we were two misfits who didn't have anyone else?"

"Probably."

He didn't like seeing the sadness in her eyes, hated even more the thought that his mother had put it there.

So he aimed for levity. "I'm still a misfit. So does that mean you want to *bond* with me now?"

He wiggled his eyebrows suggestively, pleased when she laughed as he'd hoped.

"Have you settled in?"

She nodded. "We needed this, a space of our own, so thanks."

"Don't thank me yet." He mock-frowned. "Because if those meals you cook me are no good, you'll be tossed out on your sweet patootie faster than you can blink."

Her lips curved into a coy smile, the kind of smile he wished he could capture in a snapshot and bring out whenever he needed cheering up.

"You think my patootie's sweet?" She wiggled it in a classic tease as he clamped down on the urge to vault over the railing and grab it with both hands.

"The sweetest," he said, with a wink.

He liked it when they did this, when he stopped second-guessing his decision to let her use the apartment and Rose forgot she was a single mother with responsibilities and allowed herself to flirt a little.

For a woman her age, she was far too serious. Which made him wonder exactly how tough had it been for her since they'd last seen each other. He knew there must be a wealth of information she wasn't telling him, just as he hadn't told her about Effie or anything else deep and meaningful.

"I'd better go. Olly's set up the Monopoly board and that little tycoon waits for no one."

"Sounds fun," he said, hoping she wouldn't ask him over to join in. He wasn't ready to set foot in the apartment again, especially not with an inquisitive kid who'd probably pick up on his freak-out vibes.

She hesitated, and he could almost see her having an argument with herself over whether to invite him or not.

He stifled a sigh of relief the second she squared her shoulders.

"See you round," she said, heading toward the garage, leaving him conflicted, wishing for things he had no right to wish for.

9.

"Mom, why don't you invite Caden over for dinner rather than taking him those meals?" Olly lay on Cilla's sofa, his dinosaur book forgotten as he looked at Rose for an answer she had no hope of giving.

It wasn't as if she hadn't asked herself the same question for the last two weeks, but having Caden eat with her and Olly would be too much, too soon. Bad enough her son adored Caden and that she'd had to rely on her landlord to take Olly to school a few days last week when Cilla or Jake couldn't do it.

Caden had been only too happy to help. It made sense, with him heading into town for work anyway, but with her shift starting at seven, it was those ninety minutes that Olly had to spend with Caden before school that had her worried.

Caden was all Olly had talked about. The cool online games Caden had, the old model train set that took up the entire floor in one of his spare rooms, the stack of comics he'd saved since he was a kid.

Cilla and Jake had teased her about it. How fast she'd moved into Caden's vacant apartment. How she was paying him with meals. How Olly adored him.

Little did they know, it made her all the more determined to keep Caden at bay.

Using him as a babysitter was okay, but no way could she risk letting him into her life further, not when it would impact Olly. Her son treated Caden as a friend and she didn't want to blur that line.

It would be so easy to foster her friendship with Caden. But his mother's words echoed in her head every time she thought about it and no way would she be responsible for him losing out on being mayor.

Everything Penny Shoreham had said was true. What did Caden really know about her? If he knew about her past, would he still be so friendly? Determined to be a better parent than her father, she'd do anything for her child. But the fact remained: what if she was more like her dad than she realized?

She'd already had a near brush with alcoholism, and had sought help before it was too late. But what if it was a weakness within her? She hadn't touched alcohol since she'd been in Redemption, but that didn't mean she mightn't relapse.

Wouldn't Penny Shoreham have a field day with that, if she knew her son's tenant and friend had been in a recovery center?

"Mom, I asked you a question." Olly huffed in exasperation. "You daydream more than me."

Rose smiled and ruffled her son's hair. "Caden's a busy man, honey. It's easier if I cook him the meals and drop them off. Besides, he sees you every morning. He may want some quiet time in the evenings."

Olly scowled. "Caden's my friend. He said it's cool we get to hang out."

"It is, but everyone needs their space."

Olly made a cute little scoffing sound through pursed lips. "Caden's already got plenty of space. He lives in that big house all by himself."

Needing to get off the topic of the man of the moment, Rose slumped in relief when Cilla and Jake strolled into the living room.

"Hey, big guy, how are you?" Jake sat next to Olly and tickled his feet. "Haven't seen you around much."

"I'm busy because I started at a new school." Olly scrambled up and gave his uncle a hug, a simple gesture that brought a lump to Rose's throat. One of the best things to come out of her stint at the recovery center was the relationship that had developed between Olly and Jake. "School's dumb but it's sometimes fun. Mom has to go to work real early so Caden looks after me. He's the best. Then he drops me off."

Jake grinned and Cilla hid a smile behind her hand. If Olly left the room, Rose was in so much trouble.

As if reading her mind, Cilla said, "Olly, Bryce has a new puzzle spread out on the sunroom table and he's really struggling. Think you can help him?"

Olly leapt to his feet. "Yeah, I'm the best at puzzles," he said, and zoomed out of the room, leaving Rose to face the inevitable questions.

"That's one cute kid," Jake said, an odd, wistful expression on his face. "Hope mine's as . . ."

Cilla sank into the chair next to her, shock widening her eyes. "What did you just say?"

Rose assumed Jake had been talking in a "one day" scenario, but as Cilla asked the question, her aunt's nose twitched like a bloodhound's on the scent of a trail.

Jake swiped a hand over his face. It did little to dislodge the rueful goofy grin.

"That's why I asked you both to be here." His grin broadened. "Sara's pregnant."

Rose knew her first reaction should've been joy, but she couldn't help but feel this was too much too soon. Sara and Jake had been dating for a few months and he'd only just moved in. If anyone understood the unexpectedness of an unplanned pregnancy, she did, but what if Sara had done this deliberately, to trap Jake?

An awful, cynical thought, especially when she barely knew the woman, but Jake had been her protector for so long, she couldn't help but want to do the same for him.

Injecting enthusiasm into her tone, she said, "I'm thrilled for you both. Congratulations."

"Thanks, Sis." Jake leaned across and hugged her, making Rose feel like a monster for her doubts a moment ago.

She glimpsed Cilla over his shoulder. Her aunt appeared ashen and tears glittered in her eyes. At least one of them was caught up in the fairy tale. When they eased apart, Cilla managed to pull herself together.

"That's wonderful news," Cilla said, her voice husky. "Is Sara okay about it all?"

Ah . . . So that's what her aunt's funk was about. She was worried for Sara, who'd lost her daughter sixteen months ago.

With all her concern focused on Jake and what this meant for him, she hadn't considered that this baby might be too soon for Sara, hot on the heels of her devastating loss. Rose had never envisaged motherhood in her own future, yet when she'd discovered she was expecting Olly, she'd vacillated between shock, fear and wonder. She'd hazard a guess Sara was feeling the same way, multiplied tenfold because of her loss.

Jake nodded, apprehension darkening his eyes. "She says she's fine but I know she must be terrified." He paused and a slight frown appeared between his brows. "We didn't plan it. And she's come a long way from wanting to avoid contact with all kids five months ago to this. But we've talked about it and she said she'll let me know if she's on the verge of freaking out."

Cilla nodded. "She's a strong woman. Maybe this is the best thing that could've happened? Giving her a second chance at motherhood without overthinking it?"

"Yeah," Jake said, standing. "Anyway, it's early days and she hasn't had an obstetric appointment yet. So we're keeping it quiet, but I wanted to tell you two."

Rose stood and hugged him again. "If there's anything you need, let me know."

Jake squeezed her tight before releasing her and glancing at Cilla. "There's something else."

"Don't tell me it's twins." Cilla clutched her chest and fell back against the cushions. "I'm too old for all this."

"That's not what Bryce says." Rose smirked and blew her aunt a kiss. Cilla waggled a finger at her.

Jake's grin had returned. "We're getting married, and I need your help in pulling together a small garden wedding pronto."

This time Cilla let out a whoop and flung herself at Jake, who laughed at their aunt's enthusiastic congratulations. Rose waited, hoping her inner doubts didn't show on her face. The suspicion of a moment ago, that Sara might've gotten pregnant deliberately to trap Jake, solidified.

Her brother was a stand-up guy. Of course he'd offer marriage if there was a child involved.

Rose didn't want to interfere in Jake's life, but a small part of her couldn't help but think she needed to get to know Sara a whole lot better. Before Jake made a potential mistake that could have long-reaching consequences.

When Jake eyed her with speculation, she joined in the hug and offered her congratulations. If he sensed her doubt, he didn't say anything as he shrugged out of their hug and headed for the door. "I'm taking Sara into town now so I'll see you later."

"Whatever you need, I'm on it," Cilla said, tapping her bottom lip. "I'll meet with you and Sara tonight if you like, get some preliminary ideas down?"

"Thanks. Sounds great." Jake paused in the doorway. "It's nice, that out of adversity comes the good stuff."

His pointed glance focused on Rose. "If you hadn't gone into rehab, I never would've come here, met Sara, fallen in love and considering getting married and being a father."

Thoughtful, Cilla nodded. "And Sara wouldn't have come to live here unless she'd lost her daughter, marriage and gran."

"Meant to be," Rose murmured, not believing it for a second.

She didn't believe in fate. If she did, she would've railed against it a long time ago for the hardships she'd endured.

When Jake left, Cilla collapsed back into the chair, fatigue accentuating the lines around her eyes. "You okay?"

Uh-oh. She should've known her astute aunt would pick up on her recalcitrance toward the happy couple.

"Yeah . . ." She paused, wondering how much to say, before blurting, "You don't think it's too soon? The baby and a wedding?"

Some of Cilla's elation faded and Rose felt like a heel. "It is fast. Maybe too fast. But once you spend time with them, you'll see they're incredibly good for each other."

"Guess you're right," Rose said, feeling guilty for not taking time to get to know her future sister-in-law. "Though I can't help but worry Jake's jumping into this too quickly."

Cilla studied her, thoughtful. "Your brother's a good guy. He'll do the right thing, and not just for Sara. He's been through too much to take a risk on something that isn't real."

Not sharing her aunt's philosophical take on Jake's relationship, Rose changed the subject. "How are things with you?"

"I'm exhausted beyond belief but otherwise all good."

The tightness pinching Cilla's mouth debunked that.

"You shouldn't take on this wedding planning if you're too tired."

"It's what I do best—keep busy." Cilla massaged her temples for a moment, like she had a headache, and Rose knew the problems in her aunt's personal life hadn't been resolved.

"Must be easier with Jake, Olly and me out of the house."

"It's certainly quieter," Cilla said, an unexpected sadness down-turning her mouth. "But I miss you all."

"Bet Bryce doesn't," Rose said, her dry response garnering a raised eyebrow. "Poor guy moves in with his girlfriend and has to contend with all her extended family."

"Bryce wants me to be happy."

"Then why don't you look it?"

Cilla started, as if surprised by her bluntness.

"I told you, I'm tired—"

"It's more than that." Rose patted her chest. "Trust me, I'm an expect at hiding how I'm feeling. I've made it an art form over the years and I can tell something's bugging you." Rose hesitated, before plowing on. "I know we haven't been close over the years and that's my fault mostly. I adored you when I was a kid and I should've come looking for you after Dad died. But I was a typical selfish teenager, too wrapped up in my own problems to care about anyone else. Though I'm here now. You've done so much for me and I want you to know that if you ever want to talk, I'm here."

"Thanks, love. That's sweet." Cilla blew out a long breath. "I haven't spoken to him yet, since you overhead that argument. And I'm still finding it damn tough living with someone after being on my own for so long."

"Know what you mean. Think I'd find it impossible to live with a guy now."

"You already do," Cilla said, the corners of her mouth uplifting a little.

"You know what I mean," Rose said. "Being in a relationship is hard enough. Living with someone? It's tough."

Cilla nodded, slowly. "I know you and Jake had it rough with Ray. Vernon was just as bad. I had a horrible marriage and when he died, I flourished. My independence was like this amazing gift I could unwrap every single day. I didn't need a man in my life and I certainly didn't expect to find love at my age."

"So you do love him?"

To her horror, tears filled Cilla's eyes. "I don't know. It all happened so fast and I allowed myself to be swept off my feet for the first time in my life."

"Heady and exciting."

"Yes." Cilla dabbed at the undersides of her eyes. "When I finally gave in and accepted we could be a couple, I asked Bryce to move in because I thought it'd be short term, 'til the end of his locum stint. Now that he's accepted a year-long contract at the hospital, I'm wondering if I did the right thing."

"You don't like having him here?"

"It's not that . . ." Cilla wrinkled her nose. "Bryce works long hours. When he gets home he's tired but he wants to spend time together. If I'm busy doing other things, he complains, so it's not quite as idyllic as I imagined."

"Relationships never are," Rose said. Not that she was an expert. Far from it. Her one and only involvement with a man had ended with her alone and pregnant. "At the risk of repeating myself, you have to tell him how you feel."

Some of the shadows clouding Cilla's eyes cleared. "That's one thing we're good at. Talking."

"Bet it's not the only thing." Rose winked, chuckling when her aunt started fiddling with the throw rug draped over the armchair, totally flustered.

"Anyway, I've got more important things to worry about now, like organizing this wedding." Cilla clasped her hands together. "I'm so happy for Jake and Sara. They're a lovely couple."

After what her aunt had just divulged, Rose felt compelled to add, "Won't wedding planning make you busier and add to the tension between you and Bryce?"

There was a glint of steeliness in her aunt's gaze, as if she knew exactly what she was doing. "Probably. But you know what? I'm too old to fuss over a relationship. Either it works or it doesn't, simple as that."

Rose didn't think anything about relationships was simple and she gave it one last try.

"I think you both need to work at it, because if one person wants it more than the other, it's doomed."

Cilla darted a quick glance at the door and Rose hoped Bryce hadn't materialized behind her.

"I do want this to work. But I can't banish all my doubts at once. He's eighteen years younger than me, gorgeous and a doctor." Cilla pointed at the slightly sagging skin underneath her chin. "And I wonder on a daily basis what a hot guy like him could want with a woman my age."

This made more sense: Cilla being insecure and inflicting those doubts on the relationship rather than some vague notion of busy lives causing problems.

"You're a beautiful woman and any guy at any age can see that," Rose said. "Don't sabotage a great relationship because you're scared you're not good enough. Or because old self-esteem issues are hard to shake."

Cilla worried her bottom lip before nodding. "When did you get so wise, young lady?"

If only Rose could use that so-called wisdom when it came to herself.

"It's a gift," she said, with a wry smile. "I'd better go check on Olly and make sure he's not driving Bryce batty with his usual twenty questions."

"Bryce loves it."

"Except after a long shift." Rose stood. "He's a good guy, Auntie. Don't screw it up."

"I could say the same to you." Cilla tilted her head, studying her. "Caden's quite a man."

"Just not the man for me." Rose protested too quickly, garnering Cilla's interest because of it.

"Why not?" Cilla started ticking points off on her fingers. "He's single. Good-looking. Kind. Hard worker. Owns his house. Stable." Cilla smiled. "And if Olly's loud laughter as he gets in Caden's car every morning is any indication, he's excellent with your son."

"Well, when you put it like that, what am I waiting for?"

Cilla ignored her drollness. "What *are* you waiting for? No man shows that much interest in someone else's child unless they're keen on the mother."

"We were childhood friends for a while. As you said, he's kind. He offered me a place to stay. That's it."

Her lie sounded hollow even to her own ears.

"Are you planning on sticking around?"

Rose shrugged, wishing she could answer that question herself. "Not sure. It seems like the best option for Olly right now but I can't see myself cooking at the diner for the rest of my life."

Cilla's eyebrows rose. "There are plenty of fine dining establishments on the wealthy wineries in the region. Plus all the high-end restaurants in nearby towns."

"Good to know," Rose said, edging toward the door, increasingly uncomfortable with this conversation. Not because of the employment opportunities mentioned by Cilla, but because of the way her heart leapt at the thought of putting down roots in one town for life. A town that wasn't big enough for her and Caden.

Sooner or later, she'd get tired of maintaining her barriers and allow Caden into her life. And if that were to happen . . . No, she couldn't let him get that close, not without telling him everything.

"Just keep your options open, okay?"

"Sure," Rose said, and fled.

She didn't need any encouragement or prompting to let Caden into her life. If she were completely honest with herself, he'd already insinuated his way in a little, and it terrified her.

10.

re you sure about this?" Rose hovered at Caden's front door,
watching Olly mull over a five-hundred-piece puzzle.

"I wouldn't have offered if I wasn't," Caden said, giving her
a gentle shove. "Go to work. We'll be fine."

"But you're doing so much already by taking him to school in
the mornings—"

"He's a great kid so it's not a hardship. Trust me."

She did trust him and that was becoming a major problem.
Because when Don had called an hour ago, begging her to fill in
for a sick coworker on a Saturday afternoon, she'd known she could
depend on Caden, who had been pottering in the garden.

Cilla and Bryce were having lunch at a winery—and some
much deserved one-on-one time she would never encroach on—
and Jake had taken Sara to the city to check out obstetricians.

She'd asked Don to give her five minutes to arrange babysitting, approached Caden, and here they were. Relying on him
yet again.

"I shouldn't be more than four hours. Someone else is filling in
for the evening shift."

"Take your time." He tapped his watch. "Shouldn't you have
left five minutes ago?"

"Slave driver," she muttered, wishing her traitorous body would settle down when Caden took her by the upper arms and gently propelled her out the door. "'Bye, Olly. Be good."

He didn't look up from the puzzle, his lips compressed into a thin, unimpressed line.

"Olly, I said good-bye." Rose kept her tone well modulated, fervently hoping her son wouldn't cause a scene in front of Caden.

He'd been less than impressed when she'd told him she'd have to work on a Saturday, had been on the verge of a major sulk before he'd learned Caden would be minding him. He'd visibly brightened but now it looked like his bad mood had returned.

Caden shot her an understanding glance. "Hey, Olly, your mom's helping out a friend who's sick at work. Isn't that a nice thing to do?"

To Rose's surprise, Olly looked up, his expression contrite. "My mom's always nice."

"And you are too, kid, so don't you think it's polite to say 'bye to her before she heads off to work really hard on a weekend?"

Olly nodded, gnawing on his bottom lip, solemn. "'Bye, Mom. I'm always good, so don't worry."

"'Bye, sweetie." She blew him a kiss, heartened when he caught it and pressed it to his cheek.

Eternally grateful to Caden for calming a potentially fraught situation, she murmured, "I can't thank you enough for everything—"

"You don't need to. It's what friends do."

Friends she could do. But as he touched her hand, a fleeting caress, she knew she was in danger of yearning for more.

She'd never let any friend get this close before, let alone a guy.

Caden could be so much more, and the faster she recognized that, the easier it would be to reset the boundaries between them.

Though damned if she wanted to.

"See you later." She all but tumbled down the steps and sprinted to her car, Caden's knowing chuckles echoing behind her.

❧

"Puzzles are boring." Olly frowned as he turned the piece between his fingertips over and over, his tongue poking out between his lips as he concentrated.

"They're hard, that's for sure," Caden said, thinking puzzles were a cinch compared with babysitting.

Spending Saturday afternoon with Olly hadn't been on his agenda, not when he'd been ferrying the kid to school daily. Olly challenged him and teased him and even annoyed him with his endless questions. But he was a good kid and Caden liked to help Rose, who appeared to be having a tough time of it.

"Hard stuff is boring." Olly sighed and threw the piece back in the pile.

"It can also be rewarding when you get it right." Caden pointed to a piece. "Remember what I told you? Do the corner pieces first, then follow along the sides and it should be easier."

Olly brightened as he picked up the piece Caden had pointed to. "Oh yeah, I forgot. Thanks, Caden." Olly pushed the piece into place and clapped. "You're really clever."

"Just persistent," Caden said, and wasn't that the truth.

Rose continued to hold him at bay. He should be glad, because the last thing he needed right now was to enter into anything beyond friendship with a woman staying in his apartment.

He might hate his mom's interference but she was right. His old rescue complex had flared to life in a big way when Rose had needed a place to stay, and damned if he wasn't still rescuing her, helping out with Olly whenever he could.

Not that it was a chore by any means. He liked hanging out with the kid. But confusing the urge to help with more potent feelings couldn't end well for him.

It sure as hell hadn't in the past.

In the meantime, he and Rose were doing some weird push and pull dance that might end badly for him, but he wasn't ready to give up just yet. She was too sweet. Too enticing. He wanted to get to know her better, but she wasn't inclined to divulge much beyond superficial chitchat. It should be a good thing. Instead, it was driving him nuts.

"Mom tells me it's important to always try my best."

Caden stifled a smile at Olly's earnestness.

"Sounds like good advice."

"She gives me advice all the time." Olly rolled his eyes. "Stuff like eat all my vegetables so I can grow big and strong. Brush my teeth every night. Pack away all my toys."

"She's smart, your mom."

Olly nodded. "And she's much happier now we're living here."

Caden stilled. They were entering dangerous territory. He would like nothing more than to gently pry information out of Olly but he couldn't do it. Interrogating a child wasn't right.

"We used to live in the city. Mom used to work a lot." Olly wrinkled his nose. "A neighbor who smelled like stinky cabbage used to look after me." Olly grinned and sniffed the air. "I like you much better. You don't smell bad."

"Thanks." Caden returned his smile. "I like vegetables but I'm not real fond of cabbage."

"Lucky for me," Olly said, and they laughed.

This kid really was the best.

"Mom got sad a lot in the city. She'd cry sometimes. It made me sad too." His mouth turned down and Caden hoped Olly wouldn't cry.

He could cope with a lot of things, but tears from this cute kid wasn't one of them.

He knew he was taking advantage of the situation, letting Olly talk without changing the subject, but technically he wasn't prying.

Semantics, and he knew what his preacher dad would say about that. He'd heard that particular lecture a thousand times, same as the rest. His father had been big on preaching at home as much as from a pulpit. Caden had listened intently as a kid, adhering to whatever his guru dad said. He'd wised up as he got older, blaming his dad's job for keeping him friendless. College had been a godsend, yet here he still was, living in Redemption, running for mayor, because he knew it would make his parents happy.

Olly tugged on his sleeve. "Hey, are you listening?"

Embarrassed to be caught ruminating, he nodded. "Absolutely, buddy."

"You know, Mom got sick and had to go away to a place like a hospital and she asked Uncle Jake to take care of me, and that's when I came here and stayed with Aunt Cilla." Olly took a breath and continued. "Though she's really Uncle Jake's aunt, but I need to call her my aunt out of respect."

Rose had been sick? Hell.

"Your mom's better now, right?"

"Yeah. Aunt Cilla took me to visit her at the place and she was better and then she came home." Olly's forehead crinkled, like he was trying to remember facts. "The place was like a hotel, not a hospital. Really fancy. But it smelled funny, like that cleaning stuff Mom uses in the bathroom. And it had locked doors you needed a card to get through."

Caden's mind raced. His curiosity regarding Rose's past raised a host of other questions it would be tough to get answers to. Unless they spent time together. Quality time that didn't involve babysitting or dropping off meals to his door.

He knew just how they could.

One of the local backers for his campaign was throwing a fundraiser, a black-tie ball next week. He'd dithered over asking Rose to partner him. Had chickened out several times now. Time to man up and ask her out.

As a first date it would suck, but once the evening's formalities were done, he could get to know her better in the hope she'd learn to trust him.

Because Caden liked Rose. And having her back in town was making him feel things he hadn't in a long time.

Mainly anticipation for the future.

But if there was more behind her stay at this hotel/hospital, which sounded suspiciously like a rehab place, he needed to know before their relationship progressed. He might like Rose, but he knew it would take a monumental effort on his behalf to get involved with another woman who had an addiction.

He wasn't sure if he had it in him.

Feeling increasingly bad for letting Olly divulge so much private information without stopping him, Caden stood and patted his stomach.

"I'm starving. Ready for a popcorn and milk snack?"

"You bet." Olly didn't have to be asked twice and jumped to his feet.

As Olly ran to the kitchen, Caden brought up the rear, trying to assimilate what he'd learned and match it to the girl he could fall for given half a chance.

Damned if his mother wasn't right.

What did he really know about Rose Mathieson?

One thing for certain, he intended to find out more.

11.

Rose loved being a chef. Loved whipping up meals from basic ingredients. Loved the sizzle of onions and garlic sautéing in a pan, the aromas of spices blending and coalescing into tantalizing brilliance, the textures of mixing flour with water, legumes with stock, pasta with sauces. The compliments from satisfied diners didn't go astray either.

What she didn't love were the aching feet, and as she ducked out behind the diner for a break, she sat on a bench and rotated her ankles, vowing that with her first paycheck she'd buy shoes with better shock absorption in the soles.

The noisy clack of high heels against the nearby parking lot asphalt made her wince. If her feet ached in ballet flats, she couldn't imagine wearing the towering stilettos that many women wore for fashion.

"Did you try the new chef's meatloaf? Rather average, I thought."

Rose stiffened. She couldn't see who her harsh critic was—and didn't want to—but for a moment she felt like leaping up from the bench and defending her exquisitely moist meatloaf covered in her signature tomato relish.

"You should've had the salmon salad as usual, Tully. Better to stick with the tried and trusted."

Tully?

Rose's ears pricked up. Tully was an unusual name, and the only other time she'd heard it mentioned was when Caden had said his folks would love to see him married to her. It had to be the same woman and curiosity kept her seated when she could've headed inside to avoid overhearing anything else.

"I hope that applies to me too where Caden is concerned." Tully snickered. "I heard a rumor he was holding hands with that woman in the diner."

The other woman snorted. "Don't worry, dear. She's a nobody. Some trashy single mother who abandoned her own son for months while she swanned around goodness knows where. Imagine, dumping that boy on Priscilla Prescott without a second thought."

Red spots danced in the periphery of Rose's vision as indignation gave way to anger. How dare these women talk about her like that?

"But Caden's let them move into his apartment, apparently . . ." Tully sounded unsure, like she couldn't fathom him doing such a thing.

"Just my son's old rescue complex flaring to life. You know him, Tully. He sees anyone that needs help, he's the first to offer. It means nothing. Rose is nothing."

My son?

Hell, the vicious woman slandering her was Penny Shoreham, Caden's mom.

Rose should've known. She'd already warned Caden off her. And the old biddy had never liked her, even as a child, but from what she'd just heard, Penny had taken character assassination to another level.

Rose is nothing.

She'd spent a lifetime feeling unworthy. Never good enough no matter how hard she worked or how hard she tried to please. Her father had been a master at battering her self-esteem, but after the recovery center, she'd been doing better at focusing on her positives.

Logically, Rose knew she should dismiss Penny's bitchy character assassination as the rantings of an overprotective mother trying to match-make her son. But as the women's voices faded as they crossed the parking lot, Rose knuckled her eyes to prevent the tears burning her eyes from falling.

Tears of anger and frustration that once again, despite trying hard to fit in, do her best and have a normal life, she was being judged and found lacking.

Redemption had been good for her in so many ways but at that moment, all she could think was she'd never belong.

And it hurt, all the way down to her bruised soul.

೧౨

One glance at Rose's closed expression and Caden knew something was wrong. Seriously wrong. She could barely look at him.

"Thanks for looking after Olly." She shuffled her feet on his top step, unable to meet his eyes as she looked anywhere but at him.

"My pleasure." Before he could second-guess his actions, he reached out and snagged her hand. "What's wrong?"

"Nothing." Her voice quivered and she cleared her throat. "I'm tired from the extra shift, that's all."

It wasn't all, because she hadn't yanked her hand out of his. Which meant either she hadn't noticed or she needed the contact. Either way, he wasn't letting her go without finding out what had her so rattled.

"Rose, you look like you ran over someone's cat on the way home." He squeezed her hand and gently tugged on it. "Why don't you come in and have a coffee while Olly finishes up his painting?"

She was startled. "You have paints?"

He nodded. "I bought them this week because Olly likes drawing in the mornings before school."

To his horror, her eyes filled with tears. "You're amazing, you know that?"

"We like hanging out," he said, resisting the urge to haul her into his arms and offer what comfort he could. "But if the thought of me buying a few paints has you in tears, there's definitely something wrong that you're not telling me."

Rose's lips compressed, like she didn't want to talk, but then he saw a determined glint in her eyes. Like she'd come to a decision.

"I was on a break at work, eavesdropped when I shouldn't have, and heard some women say nasty stuff about me." She blinked rapidly, as if staving off tears, and Caden instinctively stepped a little closer. "Stupid gossip that means nothing but it still affected me, you know?"

Caden cursed under his breath before reaching up to cup her cheek. "Don't let it get to you. Idle women who thrive on the small-town mentality." He reined in the urge to brush his thumb across her bottom lip. "You're so much better than them."

She stared at him with a mix of hope and fear, like she wanted to believe him but thought what he said was too good to be true.

So he set about proving to her exactly how special she was and that he wanted the whole damn town to know.

"Will you accompany me to a ball next week? It's a fund-raiser for my campaign, probably boring as hell, but I need to make an appearance, shake hands, slap a few backs and do the odd foxtrot or two."

She shook her head, dislodging his hand, her gaze instantly wary. "You can't be serious—"

"I've been building up the courage to ask you all week." He hoped his bashful smile would convince her. "Please? It'll be so much easier to tolerate the pompous crap with you there."

"Why are you doing this?" Her eyes narrowed, pinning him with blatant speculation. "Because if it's to prove a point to those gossips, it's not worth it."

"You're worth it," he said, wondering what it would take to get her to believe it. "Please, Rose. I really want you there."

He sensed her capitulation a moment before she nodded. "Okay, but I'll have to see if Cilla or Jake can mind Olly for the night."

"Sure thing." He couldn't hide his elation as he picked her up and swung her around. "We're off to the ball, Cinderella."

She laughed, the first genuine belly laugh he'd heard since she'd arrived in town.

"Put me down, Prince Charming." She smacked lightly at his shoulders and he lowered her, slow and steady, the friction between their bodies making him wish he didn't have to let go.

The attraction between them was undeniable but it was her inherent vulnerability that made him want to slay dragons for her. Rose was sweet yet sassy, fragile yet independent, intriguing contrasts that made him want to delve deeper. To get to know the real woman beneath the brave front she presented to the world.

She rested her palms on his chest and he wondered if she could feel the way his heart pounded for her. "But you'd better speak to Bryce before we go to the ball."

Puzzled, he asked, "Why?"

"Because you'll need a medic and a paramedic on standby when half the town sees me walk in with you."

Her smirk reminded him of the zingers she used to drop as a kid, brief one-liners about her family that made him laugh.

"Leave them to me," he said, meaning it.

He wouldn't let anything stand in the way of his getting to know Rose better, especially not a bunch of nosy busybodies who'd obviously hurt the woman he cared about.

12.

Rose usually grabbed a quick bite to eat in the kitchen for her lunch. But she'd seen the flyers all over town advertising Caden's rally at the town square a block from Don's Diner on Monday at midday, so she made herself a sandwich to go and headed out for lunch.

She could've made excuses for her lunchtime foray—trying to fit into a new town, keeping abreast of local politics, staying up to date with the conversations of the diner's patrons—when in reality, she simply wanted to check out Caden at work.

He'd been such a shy kid, she couldn't imagine him standing on a stage in front of a crowd, trying to convince them to vote for him. Then again, he'd turned into a bit of a charmer, so maybe he had the chutzpah to wow the locals too.

When she reached the town square, with its perfectly manicured lawn framed by sandstone pavers and a gazebo large enough to house a school, she found a good vantage point on a bench beneath a towering oak. Far enough away from the gazebo's stage where all the action seemed to be happening but close enough to hear Caden. Who at that moment was deep in conversation with a well-dressed blonde wearing stilettos that made Rose wince.

The blonde held a clipboard, and while she constantly referred to it by tapping on the documents with a fuchsia fingernail, her attention was fixed solely on Caden. In fact, the woman stared at him in open adoration. Rose couldn't blame her, but as she took in the woman's fitted white sheath dress, her red-soled designer shoes with the staggering heels, her sleek blow-dried hair and immaculate makeup, Rose couldn't help but feel inadequate.

She didn't have the time—or money—to care about fashion or hairstyles. She dressed okay on a tight budget. But staring at the woman, she couldn't help but wish she looked that good.

The woman lowered her clipboard, gave Caden a dazzling smile and touched his arm, a friendly, lingering touch that made Rose's gut churn. It was ridiculous to be jealous when she and Caden were nothing more than friends, so she blamed the hollow feeling in her stomach on hunger and proceeded to stuff the tuna-on-rye into her mouth.

As Caden strode to the microphone with long, easy strides, her chewing slowed. He looked incredible, wearing a charcoal suit, pale blue shirt and burgundy tie. His shoulders were squared yet his posture relaxed, his expression convivial, the epitome of a guy confident in his own skin.

She envied him that.

A small crowd had gathered in front of the stage and he bestowed a welcoming grin on them.

"Thanks to you all for taking time out of your busy day to come here." He pressed a hand to his chest. "I appreciate it."

There was a smattering of polite applause, and Rose leaned forward a little, riveted by the aura of power he exuded.

When the applause died down, he continued. "Because I know we all lead hectic lives, I'll keep this brief. The election isn't for another three months but I'd like to introduce some of the key people working behind the scenes to help me become your mayor." He paused and gestured at the small group of five, four men and the blonde, standing on the fringes. "These generous folk are volunteering their time for the benefit of Redemption—"

"And you," some wise soul shouted from the crowd, and laughter rippled toward the stage, where Caden grinned.

"Yes, and for the benefit of me. So without further ado, let me introduce these big-hearted folk." He waved them forward. "Brent Ziegler, Frank Lott, Dave Gibb, Iain Frommer—and the lovely rose among the thorns is Tully Holmes."

Rose froze. Applause rang out, peppered with a few cheers, while Rose stared at the blonde once again plastered to Caden's side.

It figured that the woman Penny Shoreham wanted her son to marry would look like *that*. Like she'd just stepped off the pages of a glossy magazine, groomed to perfection with a blinding white smile that must've cost a small fortune.

Okay, so Rose was being bitchy, but she couldn't help it. This woman had been happy to slander her without knowing a thing about her. Rose was justified in wishing one of those ridiculous heels would snap so she'd fall flat on her face, right?

But as she watched Tully, totally at ease beside Caden and looking for all the world like a partner rather than a volunteer, Rose couldn't help but wonder why the hell Caden had invited her to the ball and not this woman who clearly complemented him better?

Tully Holmes seemed much more Caden's style. A perfect foil for him in every way. Even discounting her wealth, Rose didn't blame Penny Shoreham for pushing Tully and Caden together. In every way, they appeared a perfect fit.

Caden held up his hands to silence the applause. "I'm extremely lucky to have a team like this." He turned to face them. "Brent, Frank, Dave, Iain and Tully, you're the best support team a guy could ask for. I hope I make you, and the rest of this fine town, proud."

The four men waved to the crowd but Tully went one better. She leaned in and kissed Caden on the cheek. His sheepish grin and shrug made the crowd go wild, as they wolf-whistled and cheered. Rose wanted to vomit.

She shoved the remains of her sandwich back into the paper bag and lobbed it into the nearby trash. She'd seen enough. She stood and took a swig from her water bottle. Time to head back to work and figure out how the hell she could renege on her acceptance to accompany Caden to the ball.

"Now that my old *friend* Tully has embarrassed me in front of all of you, I'd like to outline some of my plans for the town if I'm elected."

Rose wondered if she'd imagined Caden's emphasis on "friend." Maybe a figment of her wishful imagination?

"For a long time, many of you have wanted longer shopping hours on the weekends. A local gym without having to drive to Dixon's Creek. An expanded entertainment complex for our local teens." Murmurs of agreement swept through the crowd. "These are all issues I'll be analyzing with a view to addressing viable solutions. But the main issue facing our community at the moment is a lack of childcare."

To Rose's surprise and embarrassment, Caden stared straight at her. "An old friend of mine recently moved back to town. She's a hard-working mother with a supportive network, but it made me wonder. What about the single parents and working families that don't have access to childcare? How difficult must it be for them?"

Emotion clogged Rose's throat as Caden tore his gaze from hers and refocused on the crowd. "So if you vote for me, I'll ensure Redemption has the best childcare facility for our local families."

The crowd cheered and clapped while Caden sought Rose again, and this time, she smiled.

This incredible man looked beyond the superficial and recognized the needs of his community. It made her like him all the more.

Out of the corner of her eye, Rose glimpsed Tully folding her arms and turning away, like the thought of Caden and Rose smiling at each other was too much to bear.

In that moment, Rose decided to make a stand.

She'd had a gutful of feeling worthless. Her entire life she'd made herself invisible to avoid the wrath of her father, her employers. If there was one thing she'd learned at the recovery center, it was to stop using avoidance techniques and start taking control.

Heck, that's why she'd moved to Redemption: to take back some of the control she'd lost over the last six months, courtesy of her increasing dependence on alcohol to relax before she'd checked in to the center.

Citing some excuse to Caden to get out of accompanying him to the ball would be so easy. But she'd be running scared yet again, intimidated by a woman she didn't even know.

Caden was a stand-up guy. He wouldn't have asked her to the ball if he was dating anyone else, especially not in this small town.

So for once, Rose wouldn't back down.

She'd attend the ball on Caden's arm with pride.

And Tully Holmes, Penny Shoreham and any other bitchy women in this town who deigned to look down on her could go powder their snooty noses while taking a long walk off a short pier.

13.

Rose didn't believe in clichés. But after witnessing Caden's campaign speech on Monday and making up her mind to attend the ball, it had been a peaceful week, and she wondered if the last five days had been the calm before the storm.

She hadn't had a chance to talk to Caden since his speech because he'd received a call-out from an accounting firm in Dixon's Creek, some major software malfunction that threatened their client records, ensuring he'd been away all week.

It had meant juggling her shifts so she could take Olly to school, but she'd coped, despite Don's disgruntled mumblings about single mothers. It made her realize how much she'd come to depend on Caden, how big a deal it was, his helping out by taking Olly to school.

She owed him. And she'd pay him back by being the model date at the ball. Not that it was a date, per se. She couldn't label it that, not without freaking out more than she already was. But she'd found the best damn dress she could afford on her limited budget and had enlisted Sara's help to get ready.

It had been her subtle way to suss out her future sister-in-law, to see how they interacted doing girly stuff. Though Rose had wimped out and invited Cilla too, needing her aunt as a buffer until she felt more comfortable around Sara. For no matter how hard she tried, she couldn't shake the feeling that Jake's relationship with Sara was racing too fast into the future, with marriage and a baby on the way before they'd really got to know each other.

Hopefully tonight she'd get more of a handle on Sara. But first, she needed to get a handle on her nerves.

She stood in front of the full-length mirror in Sara's room, wearing a vintage floor-length gown she'd picked up for a bargain at a secondhand shop, wishing she'd never agreed to go with Caden in the first place.

"That's some dress," Cilla said, strolling into the room and placing a champagne flute filled with soda on the dresser. "You're stunning."

"I agree," Sara said, following behind Cilla, sipping at her peppermint tea. "Designers these days try to emulate that kind of elegance and usually fail."

"I like it." Rose shrugged, the understatement sounding hollow.

She didn't just like the deep pink, shot silk, strapless gown. She loved it. She'd never owned anything so extravagant and couldn't believe she'd found it on a rack at the back of a musty old store, with a price tag that had made her look twice, it was that low.

Caden might have labeled her Cinderella jokingly but she was starting to believe it.

"Caden's eyes are going to fall out of his head." Cilla raised her glass. "Here's to you, my dear, making a statement and then some."

"Can't wait to hear all about it." Sara placed her tea on the dresser and resumed fussing with Rose's hair, which she'd teased into some weird half-up, half-down style that made Rose's cheekbones pop. "Bet some of those uppity types in town won't recognize you."

Rose blushed, almost the same color as the dress. She'd been so nervous earlier she'd made the mistake of blabbing about Penny Shoreham. Not everything, but enough that Sara and Cilla knew tonight would be a slap in the face to Caden's overprotective mother.

"As long as you have a good time with Caden, that's all that matters," Cilla said. "If I listened to every bit of nasty gossip about me and Bryce, we wouldn't be together."

"Oh, so that means I shouldn't be calling my aunt a cougar behind her back?" Rose deadpanned, earning a guffaw from Sara and a mock frown from Cilla.

"Seriously, sweetie, you deserve some happiness and Caden's a lovely man." Cilla patted her shoulder. "Don't let other people ruin that for you."

"Hear, hear." Sara raised her teacup, took a sip and grimaced. "Now excuse me while I go to the bathroom so I don't puke all over that gorgeous dress."

Rose remembered the first trimester well. Too well. The constant vomiting had been a real downer. "Morning sickness still troubling you?"

"Try morning, afternoon and evening," Sara said, instinctively covering her belly with her hand. "I'd forgotten how bad it could be."

Rose hesitated. She wanted to ask if this pregnancy was different to Sara's first, but didn't want to dredge up painful memories.

As if reading her mind, Sara said, "I took a lot of sick days when I was expecting Lucy."

A hint of sadness clouded Sara's eyes, as it usually did if she mentioned her daughter. "But as we all know, it's worth it."

Cilla shook her head. "So long ago I can hardly remember, but I do recall Tamsin making me puke alongside her as a baby." She grimaced. "She had bad reflux problems and I couldn't stand the sight of vomit, so we'd be going in unison."

"Gross," Rose said. "With Olly, once the first trimester passed, I was fine."

Sara crossed her fingers. "Here's hoping."

When Sara made a dash for the bathroom, Cilla perched on the side of the bed. "I know this is none of my business, and you're a grown woman who's coped admirably through the tough times, but there'll be plenty of alcohol on offer tonight." She worried her bottom lip. "Is that going to be a problem for you?"

Touched by her aunt's concern, Rose shook her head. "Alcohol doesn't terrify me as much as the thought of turning out like Dad because of it."

She carefully hiked up her skirt a little and sat beside her. "I checked into the recovery center more to get my head on straight than to fight alcohol addiction. Sure, I'd turned to the bottle to cheer myself up more frequently, but I was never dependent to the point of alcoholism."

Cilla's doubt was almost palpable, and Rose remembered that she too had lived with an alcoholic who denied it.

"Unlike Uncle Vernon and Dad, I love my child and I'd never do anything to put Olly in jeopardy. That night I lost my job, the day before I checked in, I drank a lot. First time I'd ever drunk that much. I was feeling crappy. At my lowest, really. But what drove me to seek help was forgetting to pick up Olly from school."

She realized she was toying with a seam of the dress and stilled her fingers. "The moment my issues affected my child, I sought help. Which is more than Dad or Uncle Vernon ever did."

"You're a brave girl and a great mom." Cilla slipped an arm around her waist and squeezed. "And it's really good to hear you've faced your demons and beaten them."

"Thanks."

But Rose didn't feel brave. In fact, she felt downright sick at the thought of walking into that ballroom on Caden's arm in less than an hour.

Sara emerged from the bathroom, pale and wobbly. "Sorry about that. Bet you're glad I did your hair and makeup first, huh?"

Rose smiled. "Thanks for your help. You've done an amazing job, making me look halfway decent for once."

"You're always gorgeous," Cilla said, fiercely protective, and Rose leaned her head on her aunt's shoulder, savoring the closeness they'd re-established after two decades apart.

"If you think that, maybe the cougar needs to have another eye check?"

Rose sniggered as her aunt gently shoved her away and Sara looked on with fondness.

At times like this, Rose wished she'd made the move to Redemption sooner. And as she glanced at her watch and realized Caden would be picking her up from the apartment in less than ten minutes, she knew it was more than finding family and friendship that drew her to this town.

Kind, upstanding Prince Charming had turned out to be a real draw too.

"I'd better go." She stood and smoothed out her dress. "Thanks again."

Sara hesitated, as if wanting to say more, before rushing on. "Hey, you've got such a great eye for fashion—if you don't mind, could you help me pick out a wedding dress?"

"Me?" Rose made it sound like she'd rather run barefoot down scorching Main Street in the middle of summer, and Sara's face fell.

Rose cleared her throat. "I mean, sure, I'm happy to, but this?" She gestured at her dress. "A lucky find. You've seen the shorts, Ts and flip-flops I usually favor."

"If you know what suits you, you'll know what suits me." A glint of determination lit Sara's eyes, and Rose wondered if she'd picked up on the coolness Rose had tried hard to hide and this was Sara's way of calling her on it.

"In that case, of course I'll help." Rose forced a smile, hoping it didn't come out rigid.

In a way, this could be the opportunity she'd been looking for, to spend some one-on-one time with Sara and probe a little deeper into her relationship with Jake.

Sara beamed, making Rose feel even guiltier for her churlishness. "I'll call you to tee it up."

"And don't worry about picking Olly up early in the morning," Cilla said, her astute gaze swinging between the two of them, like she could see right through Rose's reservations. "Sleep in. It'll probably be a late night."

Not if she could help it. She hoped Caden wouldn't want to stay too late because she had no idea how long she could keep up the pretense of enjoying herself in a stuffy crowd.

"Thanks," Rose said, unable to resist one final glance at her reflection before she left the room.

She looked like a princess.

She just hoped that after an evening with a bunch of backslapping campaign supporters, her prince didn't turn into a toad.

14.

"Ready?" Caden patted Rose's hand, tucked through his bent elbow.

"As I'll ever be," she said, trying not to grimace.

An outright lie, because she'd never be ready to waltz into a room full of people on the arm of a gorgeous man, knowing they'd take one look at her and find her lacking.

No amount of makeup or hairspray or shot silk could change how she felt inside: like the judgmental crowd would see right down to her soul and find a quivering girl too scared to make a noise for fear of being noticed.

Rose had made flying under the radar an art form as a child. And it was damn hard to shake the habits of a lifetime now as she forced her feet to move. One foot in front of the other. Mincing baby steps that had more to do with her nerves than her trusty gold sandals pinching her feet, the only pair of fancy shoes she'd ever owned and had rarely worn.

"You're not facing the executioner," Caden murmured under his breath, tucking her closer into his side.

"Feels like it," she said, fixing a smile on her face as they stepped through the ornate archway of the town hall and into the main ballroom. "Kill me now. Make it quick and painless."

He grinned. "Why, when torturing people can be so much fun?"

Not that either of them had a chance to torture anyone, because the moment Caden guided her into the ballroom, they were besieged. Townsfolk dressed in their finest satins and tuxes surrounded them, all clamoring for a word with the potential incoming mayor.

Caden took it all in his stride while Rose wanted to cower in a corner. But he wouldn't let her.

"Folks, I'd like you to meet my date, Rose Mathieson," he said, addressing the crowd around them.

Rose managed a sedate, "Hi," before an old man half her height tapped her on the shoulder.

"Any relation to Priscilla Mathieson?" His rheumy eyes peered at her and she nodded. "Cilla's my aunt."

The old man beamed. "Though she goes by her maiden name, Prescott, now. Good for her." He tut-tutted. "Never liked that old bastard she was married to."

Rose chuckled. She couldn't agree more.

A tiny woman on the better side of ninety elbowed the old man. "Move over, Gus, and let me get a look at Caden's beautiful date."

Rose blushed, but as the townsfolk introduced themselves one by one, and complimented her on her dress, hair and shoes, she started to feel it.

"You're a hit," Caden murmured, his hand in the small of her back a comfort as another wave of locals bore down on them. "But go easy on the old guys. Your flirting is likely to give them all heart attacks and our local hospital may not cope."

Rose batted her eyelashes. "Bryce is an excellent doctor. I'm sure he can perform a few heart-starters with those paddle thingies."

Caden laughed, earning an approving smile from a couple of seniors hovering nearby. "I'm sure I saw Gus leering down your bodice and he's ninety-five."

"Obviously nothing wrong with his eyesight then," she responded drily, and gave her strapless dress a tug upward.

"All the ladies are gushing too." He tucked a strand of hair behind her ear. "Not that I blame them. You're stunning."

"Flattery will get you everywhere," she said, her body warming beneath the intensity of his stare.

"I'm counting on it."

Thankfully, Dave—a member of Caden's campaign team—interrupted at that moment, and prevented her from melting on the spot; Caden's stare was that hot, that potent.

Wishing she could fan herself, she fixed a smile on her face as several women she hadn't met gushed over her thirty-dollar dress, and happily made meaningless small talk. Until Tully Holmes joined their group and Rose felt like all the air had been sucked out of the room.

She wore a floor-length shimmering emerald halter dress in the finest silk and must've paid a small fortune for some hairdresser to do the elaborate up-do of intricate braids entwining into a French twist. With flawless makeup and a glowing tan that probably came from a booth or a bottle, she made Rose feel insignificant in her cheap dress and old shoes.

"Hi, I'm Tully, a *very* good friend of Caden's." Tully stuck out her hand and Rose went through the motions of shaking it. Though "shaking" would be overstating it. More like a glancing brush of their fingers, like Tully didn't want to catch cooties.

"And an indispensable member of his campaign," Tully added, with a rigid smile and iciness frosting her pale blue eyes. "He can't live without me."

Rose bit back what she'd like to say, something along the lines of "You're a friend, I'm his date, so back the hell off."

Instead, she schooled her face into impassivity. "Caden's campaign is going well and I'm so glad he has the support of *friends*."

Childish, maybe, but Rose knew she'd scored a direct hit when a faint blush stained Tully's cheeks.

So Rose sank the boot in a little harder. "Actually, there's my date now, so if you'll excuse me?"

Mustering her best regal posture, Rose swanned toward Caden, wondering why she didn't feel the daggers sticking out of her back.

When she drew closer to Caden, he swept her into the protective circle of his arm, holding her close as he outlined his plans to extend shopping hours to a councilman, who hung on his every word.

As Caden spoke, she marveled at his skill in making other people feel good. He had a way about him, a natural charm that drew people to him. She should know. Despite her vow to keep things between them platonic, she couldn't help but fall under his spell a little.

Though she knew what would happen if she allowed their friendship to deepen: the yearning for more would solidify in her chest like a weight pressing down, making her breathless. For that's how she felt around him. Lightheaded and lighthearted, a woman who didn't have to worry about her finances or her child, a woman free of her past.

Through the endless meet and greet, Rose was aware of Penny Shoreham hovering on the outskirts of the ballroom, biding her time like a sleek panther stalking its prey, her black satin gown catching the light as she turned to chat with her cronies, her eyes glittering with malice.

Though that could've been Rose's overactive imagination, considering she couldn't see Penny's expression all that clearly from her position near the door. A position she liked. Easy access for a quick getaway.

"They're serving supper soon, then we can escape," Caden said, his breath fanning her ear, sending a delightful shiver through her.

Her hand flew to her mouth in mock dismay. "So soon?"

He chuckled at her sarcasm. "I've slapped all the backs I need to. Can't stand all this phoniness."

"You're not saying that for my sake? Because we can stay as long as you need to. I'll survive."

"Hold that thought, because my mother is incoming," he muttered, his arm tightening around her waist, like he wanted to protect her.

While Rose appreciated the support, seeing Penny here tonight was less intimidating than she'd expected. For tonight, Rose had her armor on and she was determined to make this night run as smoothly as possible for Caden. He deserved that much.

"You're a hit," Penny said, patting Caden's free arm, and Rose felt him stiffen beside her. "Congratulations, son."

He managed a curt nod. "I think I owe a lot of my popularity tonight to the lovely lady by my side. You remember Rose?"

Penny's dismissive glance flicked over Rose, the corners of her mouth barely registering an upward curve, her version of a smile. "I do. You look lovely, dear."

"Thank you." Rose couldn't have been more demure if she'd tried, when in fact she wanted to kick up her legs in a rousing can-can to shock the primness out of Penny.

"Must mingle," Penny said, effectively turning her back on Rose. "Can't seem to find your father anywhere."

"Maybe he's had the good sense to leave," Caden whispered in her ear, and Rose stifled a giggle, just.

Without a backward glance, Penny floated away on a cloud of black satin. Rose might not like the woman, but she had to give her credit. She pulled off a ball gown with aplomb.

"That was relatively quick and painless." Caden turned her to face him. "You okay?"

"Never better."

In that moment, with Caden staring at her with something she daren't label radiating from his eyes, she believed it.

"Actually, I've changed my mind," he said. "Let's ditch supper and get the hell out of here now."

"Really?"

"Yeah. I'm sick of sharing you with this crowd." His hands gripped her upper arms and drew her closer. "I'd rather have you all to myself."

Rose might not have had much experience with men or relationships, but the gleam in Caden's eyes sent an unspoken message that zinged her in a big way.

She should say no. Taking their relationship to the next level could ruin everything.

But the longer he stared at her, willing her to agree, the more she found her resistance wavering. Until it disappeared on a cloud of what might be.

"Okay."

She'd barely given her agreement when he whisked her around for the fastest farewells on record before bolting for the door.

Laughing at his breakneck pace, she said, "Slow down—I'm in heels."

"I can always carry you," he said, with a grin.

"Idiot," she said, well aware he could carry out his threat and she wouldn't mind a bit. "By the way, you took me to a ball and we didn't even dance."

He paused on the top step of the hall and drew her closer. Close enough she could smell his citrus aftershave. Close enough she could see the green flecks in his blue eyes. Close enough to feel the heat radiating off him.

"Later," he said, his voice low and gravelly, short-circuiting the last of her common sense. "We'll dance later."

Rose could hardly wait.

15.

Caden knew he'd cop criticism for bailing on the ball early.

He didn't give a crap.

All that fake backslapping and schmoozing reminded him of his parents' crowd too much and he hated it. What he hadn't hated was having Rose by his side as he did it.

She'd been magnificent. Courteous and sweet and utterly beguiling. She'd charmed the women as well as the men, and he'd experienced an uncharacteristic stab of jealousy whenever any of the old codgers got too close.

She'd handled herself with aplomb, despite her obvious nerves when he'd picked her up. She'd snatched his breath when he first saw her, standing on the lowest step from the garage apartment, looking like a supermodel. The strapless dress accentuated the creamy skin of her shoulders and cleavage, and he'd had a hard time keeping his gaze on her face. The dress had clung to her body like it had been molded to it, highlighting every dip, every curve.

And her hair . . . the sexy, mussed style made him think of how she'd look lying among rumpled sheets, those tresses spread across his pillow . . .

He'd been a goner then. Hadn't been able to get that image out of his mind. Every second since had dragged until they'd reached this moment. Standing at his front door, her hand in his, their bodies close but not close enough. He could've used many lines, many excuses, to ask her in. Coffee. Nightcap. Whatever.

He settled for the truth. "I don't want this night to end."

"Me either," she said, her acceptance so like her. Simple and direct, without artifice.

Knowing he had to be grinning like a loon, he unlocked the door and led her inside. That's when the doubts hit. He wanted her upstairs and naked, but rushing her felt wrong.

He was reluctant to offer her alcohol, considering she hadn't touched the stuff at the ball. It had made him wonder if that was why she'd gone into rehab.

The thought of her being an alcoholic should've put a dampener on his libido. It didn't. Because tonight wasn't about starting a relationship or envisaging a future or anything heavy.

Tonight, he wanted to spend a few sizzling hours with a woman who made his pulse race.

The first woman since Effie.

It was time to lay the past to rest.

So he settled on the one thing he unequivocally knew she liked. "How about a chocolate fondue?"

She smiled in surprised delight. "You still have that old set?"

"Of course." He didn't tell her it had become his favorite meal after the night they'd shared it in his back garden under the stars.

They'd been so young, so innocent, but every time he tasted chocolate it transported him back to that night. The balminess of a summer evening. The smell of freshly mowed grass. The occasional hoot of an owl.

And Rose's giggles as she'd dipped a marshmallow in chocolate and half of it had ended up on her dress when it had fallen off the stick.

"Sounds perfect," she said, squeezing his hand. "Let me help."

"No way. A princess gets waited on." He led her into the living room. "You sit here and relax."

Caden wanted to do this for her. He'd bet a year's worth of wages that she'd never had anyone look after her, not the way she deserved.

She'd always done it and as he knew too well, it was hard to break the habits of a lifetime. Hers was people-pleasing, his was nurturing wounded beings.

Tonight, he wanted to please her and he was definitely up for a bit of nurturing from her.

He saw how exhausted she was when she came home from work and looking after Olly was a full-time job that would tire the hardiest soul.

Rose was a carer. She cared about other people. Did things for other people. At work and at home.

Time to do something for her, and he hoped this corny gesture would remind her that she wasn't alone. That she wouldn't be alone if she let him in.

"Be back soon," he said. "Feel free to put some music on."

He made the mistake of glancing at her before he left the room, and the urge to kiss her slammed into him with the force of a wrecking ball, causing as much damage. His gut cramped with the ferocity of it.

Fierce, relentless desire, the kind that couldn't be ignored, the kind that demanded to be slaked, pounded through him.

It took every ounce of willpower to make his legs move and walk toward the kitchen, away from her.

How the hell was he going to share fondue, surrounded by her intoxicating aura, and not keep his hands off her?

∽

Rose scrolled through Caden's music collection, wishing the butterflies in her belly would stop slam dancing.

Too late to be nervous now. She'd had her opportunity to flee and hadn't taken it.

That moment on his doorstep, when she'd *known* he was going to ask her in, had been the time she should've invented some polite excuse and bolted.

Doubts had plagued her the entire drive home. She'd tried her best, as usual, to please him. To be polite and refined and courteous. To smile and nod. To defer to him during discussions with others. Had she done him proud? Had he really had a good time with her on his arm? Had she really wowed the room as he'd kept telling her? But the main doubt centered around whether one indulgent night would be worth potentially ruining their friendship.

She'd seen the look in his eye when he'd bailed on the ball early. He wanted her.

And the feeling was entirely mutual.

Every time he'd placed his hand in the small of her back tonight, she'd felt a zing. Whenever his fingertips grazed the bare skin on her arms, her shoulders, her skin had come alight. Tingling with enhanced sensory receptors that seemed to be homed in on him. Only him.

But being surrounded by people at a ball while she indulged in a little lighthearted flirtation was very different to being ensconced in his car heading home, all too aware of his proximity. He smelled divine, like freshly showered male with a hint of designer aftershave and something that had to be pure Caden.

As hard as she tried not to stare at his hands gripping the steering wheel, after a while she'd given up. Imagining them on her. Caressing. Stroking. Pleasuring.

It had been pure unadulterated torture, making her acutely aware of exactly how long it had been since she'd been with a man.

Thankfully Caden hadn't noticed her obsession with his strong hands and had kept up a steady stream of conversation. Had made her laugh. Put her at ease. By the time they'd reached home she hadn't wanted the evening to end.

So when he'd verbalized exactly how she was feeling, she couldn't say no.

For someone who didn't believe in fate, she'd sure taken that as a sign darn quick.

But her acceptance went deeper than that and she knew it. Maybe it was the dress and hair and makeup making her feel like a princess. Maybe it was being by Caden's side, his pride in her obvious. Or maybe it was the simple fact that she liked this incredibly caring man.

Whatever the reason, she wanted to have one fairytale evening with him. The kind of night she could resurrect on cold winter evenings when Olly was in bed and the loneliness crept up on her.

The kind of night made of magical memories.

She might be nervous but she didn't have to be. This was Caden. A boy she'd trusted as a child. A man she trusted now.

Smiling, she chose the music, wondering if he'd remember. Even back then he'd looked out for her, those evenings when she'd fled Cilla's and sought refuge in his back garden because her father and uncle were arguing.

He'd had a portable CD player back then: fancy electronic storage devices for songs hadn't been invented. And he'd play her music, doing weird dance moves until she laughed.

She couldn't believe he had all those CDs on his hi-fi system. Men weren't usually sentimental about old stuff, but considering he'd bought his family home and listened to ancient rock, maybe Caden valued memories.

Her? She'd rather forget. Memories made her maudlin. Thinking of the past resurrected how she'd tolerated her father's shoddy treatment and how her battered self-esteem tainted everything she touched.

No, she couldn't allow the past to ruin tonight. She'd remember only the good times with Caden. The music. The laughs. The fondue.

As the first strains of a Bon Jovi ballad filtered through the room, Caden returned and laid out plates, tiny forks and napkins on the coffee table.

"I thought we'd eat in here. More relaxed." He paused and tilted his head toward a speaker, a slow grin easing across his face. "I remember this."

"Thought you might." She pointed at his stereo. "You've filled that thing with enough old hits to have a revival disco."

He shrugged, adorably bashful. "I love the classic stuff. The techno and rap crap being churned out these days doesn't do it for me."

"Agreed," she said, wondering what Olly would be listening to when he grew up. "Sure you don't need a hand?"

He shook his head. "Everything's ready. Be back in a sec."

Feeling restless without anything to do, Rose moved about the room. While it reflected the Spartan life of a bachelor, with its sleek designer modular furniture, low-slung camel-colored L-shaped suede couch and a massive mounted wide-screen television, it also had a warmth to it. The shaggy ochre rug on the floor. The prints of local vineyards in summer on the walls. The open fireplace. The faded chintz sofa in the corner.

It was a comfortable room. The kind of room she could imagine Caden coming home to and relaxing in. *Home* being the operative word.

Everything about this house screamed home. Which made her wonder anew why some wise woman hadn't snapped him up. Not for Tully's lack of trying, from what she'd seen and heard.

Handsome, kind, intelligent, financially stable men were as rare as parking spots in New York. He would've been dragged to the altar long ago in the city.

Though for all Caden's impressive attributes, she could think of one reason prospective brides in Redemption were staying away.

Having Penny Shoreham as a mother-in-law.

Rose glanced around again. That was interesting. No photos. For a guy who respected his parents and valued their opinions, it seemed odd he didn't keep at least one picture. Then again, she wouldn't want Penny's icy glare to mar this beautiful room either.

The dragon had been the epitome of subdued grace tonight when she'd approached them, but her polite act hadn't fooled Rose for a second. Hard to hide the malice lurking in her scathing glare when Caden had turned away for a moment. Rose had stared her down, not willing to give an inch, her bravado vindicated when Penny stalked off to intimidate someone else.

That woman was evil, and the less Rose had to do with her, the better.

"Hope you're hungry," Caden said, and she turned to find he'd brought in a platter covered in diced bananas, strawberries and marshmallows, and the fondue fountain.

Her mouth watered as she rushed to help. "Is now a good time to tell you that I haven't had chocolate fondue since that time in your backyard?" She took the platter from him and laid it on the table. "And that I'm likely to devour this lot myself?"

"I'd like to see you try." He carefully placed the fountain next to the platter and bumped her with his hip. "As I recall, we had a similar argument all those years ago."

She laughed. "And as I recall, you were a gentleman even back then and allowed me to scoff way too many marshmallows."

"You needed them more than me," he said, alluding to her need for comfort food, courtesy of her horrid father, as he placed a hand in the small of her back and guided her down onto the sofa. "Do you ever think about how long we could've been friends if we'd stayed in touch?"

"Nah, I never think about you," she deadpanned, chuckling at his mock outrage.

"That's okay. I think about our friendship enough for the both of us." He scooted closer on the sofa, his solemnity unnerving her as much as his proximity. "At the risk of ruining your appetite, I can't stop thinking about you."

"Maybe you can take something for that," she said, increasingly uncomfortable about where this conversation was heading.

She didn't want to talk.

She wanted to eat and laugh and flirt.

She wanted to forget the past, not think about the future, and live in the present.

"I don't want to get all serious because that's not what tonight's about, but I want you to know that it's been amazing getting to know you again." He clasped her hand, drew it slowly toward his mouth and brushed a soft kiss across the back of it. "I like having you around, Rose Mathieson."

She floundered for the right response, his touch wreaking as much havoc as his declaration.

Emotions weren't her thing. She'd learned to suppress them from a young age, knowing that too much enthusiasm or too much joy garnered attention she'd rather avoid. Her dad had seen to that.

With Dyson, she'd been a doormat. She could admit it now, with the wisdom of hindsight. She'd been a silly teenager in the throes of first love, willing to do whatever he wanted. Stupid at the time, but she'd never regret having Olly, ever.

So she'd never learned to express herself properly, had never had an adult relationship. And no matter how much she dressed up her interactions with Caden as friendship, she knew they'd moved past that. Way past.

"Too much?" He released her hand and reached for a plate, giving her time to compose herself.

"No. I'm just not good with saying how I feel."

"That's okay." He served her a little bit of everything and added a fondue fork to the plate. "I know you think I'm incredible even if you don't say it."

Happiness welled in her chest that he could tease amidst the seriousness. "That's some ego you've got."

"Matches the considerable size of my other attributes," he said, with a wink, his innuendo making her blush. "Want to do the honors?"

He handed her the plate and she took it, grateful to avoid any further talk of emotions. She picked up a forked metal stick, stabbed a marshmallow and dipped it into the chocolate fountain.

The rich aroma of melted cocoa made her salivate and she popped the marshmallow into her mouth without spilling a drop. Sugary goodness flooded her mouth, tantalizing her taste buds, making her moan a little.

"You've got better at that over the years," he said, pointing to her chest. "No massive spills this time."

"Staining a dress like this would be sacrilege, so I'll try to keep my klutziness under control tonight."

"It is stunning." His gaze dipped to her cleavage briefly before lifting again. "You were the most beautiful woman there tonight."

She wanted to fire back a smart-ass remark, about how most of the women there were pushing sixty. But he looked too sincere, and flippant became dull after a while.

"Thanks. I felt amazing." She stabbed at a strawberry this time and repeated the process, making a low, appreciative sound in her throat that was faintly embarrassing.

Her eyelids drifted shut as she savored the slide of silky, warm chocolate down her throat, and when she opened them, Caden was staring at her with blatant lust.

She could've looked away. Could've stuffed her mouth with fondue to defuse the moment. But she'd waited too long to feel this good with a man and now wasn't the time for coyness.

She placed her plate on the table, wiped her hands on a napkin and blew out the small candle firing the fountain.

Caden's eyes never left hers as she performed each innocuous action, as if he thought breaking eye contact might shatter the spell enveloping them.

He needn't have worried.

Tonight was about them and she intended to make every moment count.

"You didn't eat anything," she said, reaching for a strawberry and dragging it through the molten chocolate. "Let's rectify that."

She cupped her hand under the strawberry to catch any drips and wafted it in front of his mouth. Waited for his lips to part. Slowly glided it in.

Before she could remove her hand, his tongue flicked out to lick her finger and she felt the jolt all the way down to her toes.

He took his time chewing, her gaze riveted to his mouth, where the tiniest speck of chocolate remained.

"You have some chocolate right there," she said, pointing at the corresponding spot on her mouth.

"You put it there. You get it off."

A sexy challenge she couldn't back away from, so she closed the short distance between them and kissed him.

An uncertain kiss at first. An awkward melding of lips that had her second-guessing her decision to risk their friendship for one amazing night.

But then he angled his head slightly and suddenly they fit. The kiss deepened. And in an instant, they combusted.

They ravaged each other, hot, long, open-mouthed kisses that lasted forever. Endless kisses that made her lightheaded. Not from lack of oxygen, but from him. Only him.

Every inch of Rose's body felt alight, like the warm chocolate she'd consumed had infused every muscle, every nerve, and sparked a heat that threatened to burn out of control.

She needed air. She needed to cool down. But she demanded neither as Caden eased her down onto the sofa, his body half-covering hers, giving him room to explore.

And he did. With his mouth and his hands, he discovered every inch of her body and came back for more.

As if in a dream, Rose watched him take off her dress and panties. Watched him drizzle tepid chocolate over her breasts, her stomach. Watched him lick every single drop off.

She lost count of how many times he pleasured her before finally, finally, he was inside her.

She didn't do corny. She was far too pragmatic for that.

But as Caden moved inside her and sent her to the brink and over yet again, Rose felt like she'd come home.

16.

Caden's eyelids cranked open slowly, like they did every morning as the first fingers of dawn stole through the blinds. But today was different. Today he had a smile on his face. Must've been some dream. Then he glanced to the right, saw Rose resplendent in slumber, and it all came flooding back.

Not a dream.

A fantasy, come to life.

In the best frigging night of his life.

The smile expanded into a grin. He couldn't help it. She'd made him feel that good.

How many times had they done it? Six? Seven? Twice on the sofa downstairs, once on the stairs, once on the landing and three times in his bed.

He should've been dead. Instead, he felt so energized he could run a marathon.

Though it wasn't just the sex—phenomenal as it had been.

Rose had let him get close last night. Intimate. She'd trusted him when he knew she trusted few. He hoped it would be the start of something better between them. Something wonderful.

But as her eyes opened and she caught him staring at her, he saw the happiness give way to wariness.

Hell.

"Good morning," he said, draping an arm over her waist.

She mumbled something under her breath and drew the covers higher.

"Not a morning person, huh?"

She grunted. Kicked him in the shin. Mumbled an apology. He removed his arm.

"How does coffee in bed sound?" He hoped she said yes because that way, he'd keep her here longer. For as long as humanly possible, because if her reserved reaction was any indication, he wouldn't be getting a repeat of last night.

Not that he was after more sex, per se. But he wanted more of the intimacy. The whispered words. The casual caresses. The cuddling. He could easily keep her tucked in his bed for hours, just looking at her.

He'd never get enough of her.

That's what he'd missed the most after Effie had died so suddenly. The closeness. The comfortableness that came with finishing each other's sentences, with knowing when to give each other space, the way they fit in bed. Not in a sexual way, but the coziness that came with waking up next to someone you knew intimately.

He hadn't expected to feel that comfortable waking up next to Rose. Pity it was one-sided.

"I need to go." She peeked at him over the top of the sheet. "Olly gets up at the crack of dawn and I don't want him seeing me sneak out of here in my ball dress."

"Fair enough."

He respected her decision to leave ASAP so as not to confuse her child, but it didn't mean he had to like it. In fact, her entire demeanor since she'd opened her eyes screamed "Hands off," and he wondered if she was using Olly as an excuse.

"Do you have time for a quick breakfast?" He pre-empted her refusal with, "I make a mean pancake stack."

"Rain check?"

He couldn't read her expression with half her face covered by the sheet, but the genuineness in her stare surprised him. Maybe she hadn't been using Olly as an excuse to escape after all?

"You mean it?"

"Yeah, I do." She scooted into a half-sitting position, more awake than she had been a few moments ago. "Last night was amazing. Don't ever doubt that. But I'm really not a morning person and my priority is always Olly."

She hesitated, gnawing on her bottom lip, and the memory of what she'd done with those lips sent a jolt of awareness straight to his groin. "Perhaps we could catch up for brunch later, with Olly?"

Caden struggled to hide his delight. Until now, Rose had made it pretty clear that she didn't want to hang out with him when Olly was around. Sure, she was fine using him as a babysitter, but she'd never blurred the line for Olly by confusing the kid with friendlier get-togethers with the three of them.

Having brunch together like a pseudo-family was a big concession on her part. Huge.

"Sounds good."

She didn't buy his nonchalance. How could she, when he couldn't stop a smile spreading across his face?

"It's just brunch," she said, trying to temper his obvious happiness.

"I know." He swung out of bed, picked his boxers up off the floor and put them on. "He's a good kid. You don't want to confuse him. I get it."

"As long as you're not confused too," she murmured, and he swung back to face her. "Last night was memorable but it doesn't mean we're dating or in a relationship or anything like that."

His heart sank but he put his game face on. "So what does it mean when two people who are friends and share a sizzling physical attraction finally get it on and realize how fantastic it could be to keep doing it?"

She arched an eyebrow. "So that's all you want? More sex?"

Checkmate. If he said yes, he'd sound like a callous jerk. If he said no, he'd sound needy and she'd bolt fast without looking back.

"I want to spend time with you." He swiped a hand over his face, buying some thinking time, knowing that what he said next could send her into a tailspin. "I get that Olly is the most important person in your life. And you don't want to complicate things. But he picks up on your moods. He sees more than you realize. And if you're happy, he's happy."

Her eyes narrowed and the corners of her mouth turned down. "What has he said?"

"Just general stuff about your life in the city."

He hesitated. Delving into where she'd spent the months before she'd come to Redemption could be disastrous.

But he had confidence in the fact she hadn't run and, better yet, wanted to have brunch. Last night had brought them closer. And part of developing their relationship involved facing the tough stuff.

"There's more," she said, her voice flat. "Did he talk about the recovery center?"

Relieved she'd brought it up, and had enough confidence in him to be honest, he nodded. "He said you'd been sick and in a place that was more like a hotel than a hospital."

"Great," she muttered, a frown creasing her brow as her shoulders slumped.

"Hey, have I ever judged you?" He captured her hand and held it tight. "You know that's not me. I knew about your dad when we were kids. I listened to you. And I'd never think anything less of you because of it."

He squeezed her hand. "So if you want to talk about why you checked into the center, that's fine. If you don't, I'm fine with that too."

Though he wasn't, and he hated himself for lying. He needed to know why she'd really gone to that center and what he'd potentially be dealing with if this thing between them went beyond phenomenal sex.

She sighed and relaxed back into the pillows. "My dad was an alcoholic. A mean one. Mom died when I was four. Jake was eight. I don't remember her much. But Jake said she was amazing and when she died, Dad was heartbroken."

Caden could predict what came next. "He turned to alcohol for comfort?"

"Yeah. He wasn't so bad at first. But I felt like he blamed us for her death." Her hands plucked at the edge of the sheet, catching a stray thread and fraying it. "I tried to make up for Mom's absence by doing everything I could to please Dad. I cooked. I cleaned. I did the grocery shopping. It was never enough . . ." She trailed off, lost in her sad memories, and he waited.

"When pleasing him didn't work, I learned to be quiet and not draw attention to myself. Because Dad turned mean real fast. The meaner Dad got, the more Jake would take the blame." Her eyes shimmered with unshed tears and she focused on that one thread like it held together the fabric of her life. "He protected me all the time."

The thought of a young Rose having to withdraw to protect herself made him want to thump something. It wasn't fair, making a child live in fear. Thank goodness Jake had been around. "He's a good brother."

She nodded. "And he hasn't stopped protecting me. When I left home early, he supported me financially. He took care of me when Olly's father died and I was a pregnant teen." She drew in a breath, blinked several times to clear her tears. "And he came through for me during those months I spent in rehab."

Damn. So he'd guessed right. She'd been in rehab. Where did that leave them now? Because no way in hell could he go through the agony of losing someone to an addiction again.

The entire sheet was in danger of unraveling if she picked at that thread any more. "Olly is my life but it gets hard sometimes, being a single parent. I worked my ass off, going above and beyond at the restaurant, then I got fired for turning up five minutes late for a shift because I helped out a neighbor. That night I hit the bottle pretty hard and forgot to pick him up from school the next day."

She stopped fiddling and clutched the sheet to her chest. "No way would I let myself become a bad parent like my dad, so I rang Jake, asked him to take care of Olly and checked myself into the recovery center the next day."

Confused, Caden needed clarification. "But a one-night bender doesn't make you an alcoholic."

"I'm not, but I found myself having a glass of wine after work more regularly. It eased the pressure. Made me feel less stressed and I looked forward to it. Then I started buying vodka for special occasions. Which became more frequent. Like when the Nicks won. Or a friend got a promotion. Or my favorite cook won *MasterChef.*" Her guilty gaze darted away. "Almost weekly." She screwed up her nose. "But that night I got fired I finished three-quarters of a bottle and knew I didn't want to do that again."

He tried to hide his relief. It didn't sound like an addiction to him. Then again, what did he know? Growing up in a winery region, he'd been allowed a small glass of red with meals from the time he was sixteen. His parents had trusted him that much.

He'd had the occasional bender in college but he didn't like the headache the next day, so he preferred moderation these days.

As for Effie, he hadn't had a frigging clue how badly she'd needed those pills to function.

"Technically, I'm not an alcoholic, but I think I'd hit a point where I'd used it as a crutch too often. So I needed to get away from everything for a while, seek clarification for a few issues in my past and deal with stuff in a mature way so I could be a better parent."

"Wow," he said. "Whichever place you attended should use you as their spokesperson. You're amazingly insightful."

She almost glowed from his praise. "I have to be. I have a little person depending on me."

"You're a great parent." He rubbed her arm. "Olly's lucky to have a mom as loving as you."

She must've heard a wistful undertone. "Your parents were good to you."

"I guess."

"That's not very convincing."

He wondered how much to tell her, considering they weren't in a relationship. Hell, after her disclosure, he didn't know if she'd told him to deliberately drive him away or to prove what his mother said: that she'd be bad for his reputation.

But this was Rose. His Rose. At least, he'd like her to be.

"Ever seen one of those picture-perfect postcards and known it looked too good to be true? That it must be digitally enhanced?"

Confusion creased her brow. "Yeah."

"That's what I think my parents' marriage is like." He rubbed the back of his neck. It did little to ease the tension. "And I sometimes wonder if my entire childhood was fake."

He made inverted comma signs with his fingers. "Perfect preacher in a perfect small town with a perfect family leading a perfect life."

"That's a lot of perfection," she said.

"The thing is, I think having high expectations must grind you down after a while." He huffed out a breath. "My mom's standards are tough to live with and I often wonder if my dad's ongoing heart problems are stress related."

"Is he okay?"

"Yeah." But he remembered a time when his dad wasn't okay. When his heart attack had left him on the brink of death and facing a quadruple bypass if he didn't retire and relax. No surprise he had taken up golf to get out of the house and away from his mom. On the pretext that the walking would be good for him, of course. "Only reason I came back to this town after college was because Dad had a heart attack."

Rose's eyes widened. "Really?"

He nodded. "I had dreams of being a city boy. Turns out I'm a country boy after all."

She ran her fingertips down his arm in an affectionate gesture, the first time she'd touched him voluntarily since last night. "If this is too personal, you don't have to answer. But why do you stick around? Why don't you follow your dreams?"

He'd asked himself the same question on many occasions. Had always come back to the fact he'd established a good life here. But that answer sounded hollow and weak, like he'd been too lazy or something.

So he settled for another truth. But not all of it. Not yet. It was too soon and she'd been spooked enough when she woke.

"Sometimes you make choices in life that snowball, and before you know it you own a house and a successful business and are running for mayor." He gestured around the room, proud of all he'd achieved but wondering if she thought he sounded stagnant and boring. "I'm a homebody. A nerd. Always have been." He chuckled. "Even you knew that way back when."

"I know you liked to read a lot of books. You'd always have one tucked away in the garden somewhere." Her lips eased into a lopsided smile. "It's how I knew where to find you. Follow the book trail."

He snorted. "I was a dork. But you liked me anyway."

"Still do," she said, leaning forward to brush an all-too-brief kiss on his mouth. "I've never shared much of my past with anyone but you're incredibly easy to talk to."

"Ditto." This time, he hauled her closer, crushing her breasts to his chest, wrapping his arms around her. "I know you have to leave now but I hope you understand how much I like you, Rose Mathieson."

He pressed his mouth to hers to prove it in a sweet, sensual kiss tinged with a hint of desperation.

He didn't want to let her go.

He knew he had to let her go.

And what he wanted most, Rose in his life beyond one night, had just become his number one goal.

17.

Rose shouldn't have agreed to have brunch with Caden.

It had been an impulsive decision, one made out of guilt. Because when Caden had asked her to stay for breakfast and she'd refused, he'd looked like a puppy that had been kicked. A guy like him didn't deserve that. He deserved home-baked apple pies and Thanksgiving dinners and a brood of kids to fill his big house.

She also had no idea why she'd divulged all that personal stuff. While she may have been proud of all she'd accomplished at the recovery center, she didn't need the most together guy she'd ever known to get a glimpse into how dysfunctional she really was.

Not that he seemed to care. Along with being understanding and sweet, he was the most nonjudgmental person she knew. She'd felt comfortable talking to him, despite being naked beneath that sheet, memories of their incredible night bombarding her.

It had rattled her to wake and find him staring at her like she'd hung the moon. She'd never been the object of such open adoration before and it unnerved her. That's why she'd been brusque, latching onto any excuse to escape. Using Olly had been the most obvious but truth was, she didn't want her child to see her do the walk of shame.

She could've come up with a believable excuse for Olly but knew whatever she said would be relayed to the rest of the family verbatim, so she'd chosen to slink home, shower and get changed before picking up Olly.

Who was currently doing half-cartwheels across the apartment's small living room area because she'd told him they were having brunch with Caden.

When she'd issued the invitation for brunch, she'd done it out of gratitude. To thank him for a night she'd never forget. No great surprise that Caden's everyday thoughtfulness extended to the bedroom. What he could do with his tongue and his hands and the rest had blown her mind.

She'd lost count of the orgasms, had given herself over to the bliss of being pleasured by a guy who definitely knew how to wield his talents.

He'd explored every inch of her body in intimate detail. Lingering in her ticklish spots. Making her giggle. Tracing her curves. Long, sweeping caresses down her back that made her arch into him. Made her moan when his foreplay went on. And on. And on.

Sex with Dyson, her first, had been quick and frantic, two young people seeking a fast fix.

Sex with Caden was like being played by a master.

"Mom, why are your cheeks red?"

With great timing as usual, Olly lay sprawled on the floor, looking up at her with interest.

"Probably from the oven," she said, hiding a smile at her fib. "Caden's making pancakes so I thought I'd take over a blueberry bake."

"Yum." Olly scrambled to his feet. "Can we go over now?"

She glanced at her watch and decided she'd put off the inevitable long enough. Caden had said ten thirty. It was now ten forty-five.

"Sure, let me grab the bake and we'll walk over together."

A puzzled dent appeared between Olly's brows. "But you let me run over to his house by myself every morning. Why is today different?"

An insightful question she had no hope of answering. When she'd suggested Olly come along to their brunch, she'd known Caden might take it the wrong way, that Sunday brunch was a family thing to do.

But she'd had a much more selfish reason: she'd needed a buffer between her and Caden after that momentous night and Olly was it.

This way, she smoothed over her initial rejection of Caden's breakfast offer and his obvious hurt, plus got past what could've potentially been an awkward morning-after.

That was another thing. It hadn't been awkward. After she'd moved past her initial funk at waking up next to him, their conversation had flowed. And it had progressed to personal revelations fast.

They had an ease between them, a friendship that had rekindled quickly. Last night shouldn't change the friendship they'd built. But what if it did? What if they became awkward and stilted around each other, despite the straightforwardness of this morning? It made her wonder—what would her life be like without Caden Shoreham in it?

The thought made her throat tighten and she had her answer right there.

Perhaps she'd become too dependent on him. Perhaps having sex had changed her perspective. Whatever her reasoning, she couldn't imagine not seeing him on a daily basis.

Which begged the question: what would happen when she decided to move? To find a more permanent home for her and Olly?

She liked this town, liked having her family close and could see them living here for the next few years. But beyond that? She was a city girl. She'd liked growing up in Brooklyn, despite her shoddy home life. She loved the buzz of Manhattan. She wanted Olly to experience more than running around a big garden and playing with chickens in the schoolyard.

Then again, being confined to the city hadn't been so great for her son. He'd thrived out here, emotionally and physically. He laughed spontaneously now, had finally lost his wariness around her.

That had gutted her most before she'd checked into rehab—that her son assumed he would annoy her if he spoke too loudly or dropped a toy. It reminded her of her own disastrous childhood too much and had been a much needed wake-up call.

He must've grown at least two inches too, filling out into a sturdy frame that made her wish she'd made the move sooner. But she never would've moved to Redemption if Jake hadn't re-bonded with Cilla first.

Which brought her full circle back to her initial dilemma: if she fueled her relationship with Caden and they grew closer, she'd probably break all their hearts when she ultimately left.

Olly adored him; she already knew that. And she'd moved past adoration last night, when Caden had paraded her at the ball like a cherished girlfriend.

"Mom, you're daydreaming again. Come on." Olly tugged on her sleeve. "I'm starving and Caden will be waiting."

She'd been doing a lot of that lately. Daydreaming. And starving. Starving for one incredible guy she couldn't get out of her head.

"Let's go." She crossed the small space from the living room to the kitchenette, placed the cooled bake into a basket and covered it with a dishcloth. "Are you going to have one pancake or two?"

Biting back a smile at his obvious indignation, she watched Olly pull up his T-shirt and point to his stomach. "I'm a big boy now. I can eat four. Maybe five."

Her hand flew to her mouth in mock horror. "Five? No way."

"Just watch me, Mom." He smoothed down his shirt and slipped his hand into her free one in a simple gesture she'd never tire of. "I bet Caden can eat more though. Big people have big appetites."

Didn't she know it. Caden had proved that last night. Many times.

Unable to stifle a goofy grin, she fell into step alongside Olly. Though as he tugged on her hand until her shoulder ached, she mentally amended that to "was dragged along by Olly."

They headed for the back of the house, where Caden had said he ate on the weekends.

As they rounded the corner and she caught sight of the picnic table, she experienced one of those surreal moments that rarely occurred in her life but seemed to be commonplace for others.

A moment of such pure, undiluted happiness that her lungs seized and she gasped for air.

Caden had gone to a lot of trouble. A red and white checked tablecloth covered the table that he'd set with crystal glasses filled with orange juice, his best white china, shiny cutlery and enough jellies and preserves to feed the entire town. Three platters were set at equal intervals: one piled high with croissants, another with crispy bacon and the last with berries.

"Mom, it's a feast!" Olly released her hand and ran toward the table, leaving her in awe of what Caden could do. He cooked, he cleaned, he maintained a gorgeous house, ran his own business, looked after her son and ran for mayor in his spare time.

Inadequacy didn't come close to what she felt at that moment. Made her wonder, even more, why on earth a guy like him could be interested in a girl like her.

The guy in question stepped out onto the back porch at that moment, bearing another platter with a mountainous pancake stack. Overkill, on top of everything else, but her stomach rumbled just the same.

"Welcome, guys. Hope you're hungry," he said, his gaze softening when it locked onto hers.

She could read a myriad of emotions in his: affection, appreciation, excitement and something else. Something she dared not define for fear of reading too much into an already loaded situation.

Rose had never been in love. She seriously doubted she'd know what it felt like. But if the tightening in her chest and the fizz in her veins every time she laid eyes on Caden was any indication, she could well be on her way.

"This looks amazing." She strode to the table and nudged the bacon platter aside to make way for her meager offering. "I brought a blueberry bake but I can see you already have the cooking situation well under control."

"Breakfast is about the only thing I'm good at," he said, pulling out her chair and making her feel like a princess all over again.

Then he leaned in close, his mouth grazing her ear. "Though according to your rave reviews last night, I may be good at other things too."

She elbowed him away, heat flushing her cheeks. Thankfully, Olly was too engrossed in serving himself a very generous helping of everything to notice her blush this time. The last thing she needed, while images of exactly how talented Caden was flashed through her mind, was her intuitive, inquisitive son asking why her cheeks were red again.

"Thanks for bringing this," Caden said, spooning blueberry bake onto his plate. Couldn't fault his manners either, choosing the guest's food over his own. "Smells delicious."

She'd never been any good at taking compliments and would normally have dismissed her dish as being not half as good as any of his. But last night had given her a newfound confidence. She didn't need a fancy ball gown or high-heeled shoes to feel good about herself. With the help of Caden, she'd realized she could be good at things besides cooking and parenting too.

She could be good at a relationship.

"Thanks." She smiled and rested her hand on his thigh beneath the table, savoring the flex of muscle beneath her palm. "I'm blown away by how much trouble you've gone to for us."

"You deserve it," he said, his voice husky as he patted her hand under the table before guiding it a little higher on his thigh.

She shot him a mischievous glance from beneath her lashes, kneaded his thigh for a moment before snatching her hand away.

His groan was barely muffled by a healthy swig of orange juice.

Oblivious to their interlude, Olly sat opposite, his attention totally focused on shoveling the four-deep pancake stack on his plate into his mouth as fast as humanly possible.

"Hey buddy, slow down. You don't want to be sick." Caden gave a subtle jerk of his head toward Olly but Rose didn't have to say anything. She liked that Caden showed concern for her son, that he'd gently rebuked him.

Olly mumbled some kind of negative response and Rose laughed. "When it comes to food, word of warning. Don't come between Olly and a plate. Especially when it's pancakes."

"My dad was a good cook too," Olly mumbled, and Rose froze. Last thing she wanted to do was spoil today with talk of her dead ex. "He was famous."

She felt Caden stiffen beside her. Not that she'd ever made a secret of her past. It's just that since she'd arrived in town, she hadn't discussed Olly's father with Caden. Dyson wasn't relevant to her new life here. Now, courtesy of her chatty son, she'd have to reveal more than she'd like.

When an awkward silence stretched between them, Olly continued. "We were talking about families at school and I told Mrs. Hodkinson to look up my dad on the computer."

151

Rose's appetite vanished and she laid down her knife and fork. Realistically, Olly's teacher wouldn't have disclosed the seedier side of Dyson's life—and death—to a classroom of elementary kids. But Rose hadn't told Olly much beyond the basics of her life with Dyson. A life that she had a feeling Olly was about to lay out before Caden.

She could change the subject, but then it would look like she was hiding something. And she didn't want to have secrets from Caden.

"She said he was a really good chef. Cooked for lots of famous people and celebrities." Olly scrunched up his forehead, thinking. "But he died before I was born. That's sad. But Mom's a really good cook and you are too, Caden."

Olly tilted his head and eyed Caden with renewed speculation. "Maybe you can be my dad now that my real one isn't around anymore?"

The sip of OJ Rose had drunk stuck in her throat and she coughed. And coughed. Desperate to get air into her lungs and to her brain so she could formulate an appropriate response.

Before she could speak, Caden rested his elbows on the table and leaned forward, bringing himself down to Olly's eye level.

"We're good buddies, Olly. And your mom's a good friend too. But it's a really big deal to be someone's dad, especially to an amazing kid like you, and only your mom can make that kind of decision."

Olly nodded, his expression thoughtful, before a light sparked in his eyes and Rose knew to expect an incoming zinger. "Mom, do you like Caden? Don't you think he'd be a good dad?" He pointed toward the garage. "Because we already live here, so we wouldn't have to move. And Caden already takes me to school. Plus you cook for him too. And you were Cinderella last night in that dress, even though he didn't take you in a carriage."

He frowned, as if that would be the only impediment to her and Caden getting together for good. "Plus he's nice and we're friends." He grinned at Caden. "I wouldn't mind having him as my dad."

All a flushed Rose could manage was a mumbled "We'll talk about this later," before Olly said, "Can I be excused? I want to go check the strawberry patch at the back of the garden."

Rose nodded in relief and wiped her clammy palms on a napkin. "Sure."

Olly didn't have to be told twice as he pushed his chair back and took off fast, despite having a belly full of pancakes and fruit.

"You okay?" Caden swiveled to face her, his expression torn between concern and amusement. "As much as I loved his rousing endorsement of my potential as a parent, you were trying not to squirm, right?"

"Uh-huh." She pressed her palms to her burning cheeks. "I usually don't mind him being a chatterbox but that much eloquence over brunch is too much."

He toyed with a blueberry on his plate, nudging it around with his fork. "Does talking about his dad make you uncomfortable?"

She shrugged, but wanted to yell *Hell, yeah*. "How much do you want to know?"

He put his fork down and eyeballed her. "Whatever you're happy sharing."

Rose heard the hint of jealousy in Caden's tone and it surprised her. He had no competition, not when Dyson was dead. Even if Dyson wasn't, she knew there'd be no contest. Caden was a far better man than Dyson had ever been. She couldn't imagine the narcissistic, vain Dyson being a father to Olly, despite his empty promises to support her at the time. If he'd been that concerned for her welfare and that of his unborn child, he never would've gone away that weekend and ingested enough party drugs to fell an elephant.

She might've been heartbroken at the time, in the way a desperate, pregnant teenager would be, but she'd never loved Dyson. Not really. Certainly not with any depth of feeling, and definitely not with anything close to what she was starting to feel for Caden.

"Who was he?"

"Olly's father is Dyson Patrice."

She waited for the light of recognition in Caden's eyes but it never came, so she continued.

"He was the toast of New York from the moment he arrived. Son of a double Michelin-starred chef in Paris. Packed out restaurants. We met at one of them, where I was an apprentice."

She struggled not to wriggle around, embarrassed by revealing so much of her past, especially when it painted her in an immature light. "I was smitten. A nineteen-year-old who didn't know better. Fell for him hard. Got pregnant by accident. He seemed happy enough about it. Said all the right things. But Dyson wasn't a keeper. He played the field. Died of a drug overdose at a party in the Hamptons with a bunch of his new supermodel girlfriends."

Caden blanched, his lips compressed in obvious disapproval, but he didn't speak.

She glanced at the far end of the garden where her son chased a butterfly, more carefree than she'd ever seen him. "Olly knows the basics, because I don't like lying to my child. He asked about his father. I told him. General stuff about how we met and what he did for a job and that he died too young."

"How old?"

"Twenty-one." Rose rolled her shoulders a little to release the tension. "Seems like a lifetime ago."

"Not that long," he said, tempering his terse response with a rueful grimace. "Sorry, I sound like a jealous jerk."

"You've got nothing to be jealous about."

He shifted in his chair, leaning away from her slightly, and she hoped he wasn't withdrawing from her on some instinctive level. "I know, but . . ." He trailed off and looked away, focusing on Olly at the back of the garden.

Curious, she prompted, "But what?"

With a sigh, he turned back to face her. "He's a great kid, yet I can't help but wish you hadn't hooked up with that flakey dude so you wouldn't have had such a tough time." He blew out a breath, searching her face for answers when she had no idea what he was asking. "At the risk of sounding totally over the top, the way we've clicked now, I can't help but wonder what would've happened if we'd kept in touch . . . Who knows—maybe I could've been Olly's dad for real."

Stunned, she let the implication of what he'd said sink in. He thought about deep stuff like that? Imagining Caden as Olly's father made her wish they had maintained a friendship. He'd be a great dad and even Olly thought so.

"Too much?" He leaned back in his chair, establishing even more distance between them.

"Just a lot of what ifs." She gestured between them. "We were different people back then. It never would've worked."

"And now?" he murmured, fixing her with a probing stare she couldn't look away from, putting her on the spot so fast she hadn't seen it coming.

She couldn't talk about their relationship now, not when her head and heart were spinning as a result of how they'd connected last night.

She needed time to figure out how she was feeling, to ensure that sleeping together wouldn't ruin a friendship she'd grown increasingly reliant on. Formulating the words to articulate that would be tough and she didn't want to screw it up.

"If you have to think that hard before answering, I guess you don't have to say anything." He scowled and pushed his chair away from the table. "Were you that hung up over this chef guy that you're still pining for him?" He braced his elbows on his knees, hung his head a little, like he couldn't face what she might reveal. "Is that it? Was he the love of your life?"

His bitterness rankled. She didn't owe him any explanations, not when she'd revealed more of her past to him than she had to anyone else.

But this was Caden and she couldn't fob him off. Not when he'd be helping her out with Olly every day for the foreseeable future until she made a decision on a new place in town and saved enough money to move.

She laid a reassuring hand on his forearm, but removed it when he didn't show the slightest indication he'd noticed. "My feelings for Dyson are in the past and have nothing to do with us now."

His head lifted but his narrowed eyes pinned her with a doubtful look. "Then why can't you give me a straight answer?"

Because she needed time to think. Time to assimilate the changes last night had wrought on their relationship. Time to figure out how far she wanted to take this.

Dyson hadn't been a keeper but Caden sure as hell was, and she couldn't jeopardize a possible future with him by botching it now. Guaranteed, rushing into anything too fast would do that, especially considering his standing in the community.

No way would she screw up his life for a fleeting taste of happiness. Because she could move on and he'd be left to face the fallout.

"I need time—"

"For what?"

Damn, Caden wasn't letting this go.

He straightened and squared his shoulders, like he was prepping for a fight. "Not that I'm suggesting I take Olly up on his offer but we need to figure out what we are, Rose. Because in a town this size, news gets around."

Tired of being pushed, her temper rose. "And what, you're scared it might taint your bid for mayor?"

"That's crap and you know it," he growled, tension making his neck muscles stand taut. "I'd walk away from the campaign in a heartbeat if it meant . . ."

He trailed off, his expression pained, as he stood, looking down on her like he wanted to say more but wasn't exactly sure of how she'd receive it.

Rose could ask what he was going to say. But she didn't want to hear his answer. Was terrified of it.

Because having Caden articulate that his feelings for her ran so deep he'd defy his parents and the town to walk away from an important position like mayor meant one thing.

Permanency.

She couldn't look into his beautiful, guileless eyes and guarantee that she was in the same place relationship-wise.

Not yet.

Maybe not ever.

"Thanks for brunch. It was lovely." She stood, leaned in and placed a peck on his cheek. "Olly and I need to head into town so we'll see you later."

"You can run but you can't hide," he said, sadness down-turning the corners of his mouth.

The amazing mouth that had cherished her in so many wonderful ways last night. The mouth that said all the right things; things that made her wish for so much more than she deserved.

Yeah, she'd run scared as usual. It was what she did best.

In response, she raised her hand in a casual wave, mentally reciting, *Watch me try.*

18.

Caden sat at the laden picnic table for a full thirty minutes after Rose and Olly left.

It took him that long to absorb the implications of their conversation. A long half hour where he mentally replayed every word, every revelation.

She'd told him about Olly's father.

He'd almost told her too much.

Last night had been incredible, the type of night he'd fantasized about ever since she'd returned to Redemption and they'd renewed their friendship. But it only served to make his life harder. Because now he knew he wanted her more than ever.

She wanted to take things slow. He didn't.

So where to from here?

He'd stopped himself from blurting the truth just in time: that he'd walk away from his mayoral campaign if it meant settling down with her in a real relationship. In fact, he'd do just about anything if it meant having Rose in his life permanently. To wake up next to. To have family brunches with. To help raise her kid.

That's how he knew this was serious, when he started envisaging raising Olly. It was a huge undertaking, being a dad to a child who wasn't biologically his, a responsibility he wouldn't take lightly.

He even looked forward to the kid bounding up to his door every morning, a huge grin on his face and ten new questions to bombard him with. For a kid his age, Olly asked a lot of questions. A never-ending stream that exasperated him at times but generally made Caden stare at him in wonder.

Yeah, he could definitely see them being a family. But first, he had to do some investigating to ensure Rose's past wasn't holding her back from a future.

She'd said she wasn't hung up on Olly's father, but it would explain her reticence at moving forward. Hell, it would explain a lot more. Like what put the haunted look in her eyes, even now, when she'd dealt with her demons at rehab.

Feeling like an idiot but willing to do whatever it took to win his woman, he cleared the table in record time before heading to the den and firing up his computer.

He typed DYSON PATRICE, CELEBRITY CHEF into the search engine and waited.

It didn't take long for hundreds of hits to pop up before his eyes. The first two pages featured articles about his infamous death.

Caden clicked on the first link and did a rudimentary scan. He wasn't impressed. The guy sounded like a Class A jerk: partying his way through New York, threesomes with supermodels, copious drugs. But as he scrolled through more pages and more articles, he understood why a young, impressionable Rose would've been attracted to the guy.

He looked like the epitome of a movie star bad boy: slicked-back dark hair, dark eyes, a brooding glower, a slight curl to his upper lip. Dyson had a James Dean edge and Caden knew girls went wild for rebels.

Which was probably why Rose had first hooked up with him: associating with a kindred spirit. She'd told him she'd left home at sixteen, not long after her father's death, and Caden knew it had more to do with rebelling against her past and everything it stood for than anything else.

Then there was the cooking angle. By the number of rave reviews, magazine articles and cover shots of Dyson, he'd been a wunderkind in the kitchen.

A stab of jealousy pierced Caden's musings as he glared at yet another cover shot of Dyson.

This guy had once captured Rose's heart.

He'd fathered a child with her.

Considering she'd been alone and pregnant as a teen, she must've loved him very much to have the child.

How could he compete with that?

But after scrolling through a few more articles, reading the same old same old, he shut down the search engine and pushed away from his desk.

He was an idiot.

Researching a dead man wouldn't get him closer to Rose. Being the kind of man she could depend on, the kind of man who would protect her and provide for her, the kind of man who would love her unconditionally, was the way to get the girl.

As for his mom's misgivings that he was attracted to Rose because she was yet another one of his charity cases to be rescued? Couldn't be further from the truth. Rose didn't need rescuing. She was a strong, independent woman who'd faced her problems head on, who'd had the guts to uproot her life and that of her child to move to a new town. If anything, having her back in his life had rescued *him*.

He'd been dead inside since losing Effie and discovering the harsh truth. Reluctant to let himself care about anything or anyone for fear he'd make a monumental misjudgment again.

With Rose, it was different. He didn't have that fear because he knew everything there was to know. She'd told him. Sure, he couldn't dismiss the niggle of concern about alcohol, but since she'd been here he'd never smelt it on her breath once and he believed her when she said she'd dealt with her problems.

Rose had an inherent honesty that drew him to her. It made him feel safe in taking a chance on her in a way he'd never thought possible after Effie.

They were good friends, but it was time to stop lying to himself and admit he wanted more with Rose.

But she kept shooting him down.

Time to up the ante.

He had to tread carefully. Take his time. Not push. Because he had a feeling Rose would bolt like a skittish filly if he mucked this up.

❧

Rose watched Olly clambering over the wooden play equipment in the park on the outskirts of town, determinedly trying to avoid replaying every word she'd traded with Caden since last night. Not that it worked. Because if mentally blocking his words wasn't a problem, trying to forget the way they'd combusted in bed was.

Every time she allowed her mind to drift for a moment, there he was, front and center in her head, totally naked.

She blamed her erotic daydreaming for not hearing Penny Shoreham approach until it was too late. She would've made a run for it if she had. Because Penny wore the same expression she'd reserved for Rose as a child: disapproving and condescending, with a decided tilt to her nose like she'd smelled something bad.

"Am I disturbing you?" Penny halted a few feet in front of her, like she didn't want to come too close and catch anything.

"I'm spending some quality time with my son," Rose said, rising to her feet, not wanting to be at a height disadvantage with the other woman towering over her.

People like Penny Shoreham enjoyed power trips and Rose would be damned if she took whatever Penny wanted to dish out sitting down.

Whatever Penny wanted to say, she'd come dressed for the occasion. Burgundy designer suit with a calf-length fitted skirt and nipped-waist jacket that hugged her bony figure. Matching patent leather pumps. A handbag that would've cost more than three months' salary.

Her plum-colored lips stood out stark against her powdered face, accentuated by the severity of her blonde hair pulled back in a tight bun. She looked ready for a power lunch. Or a takedown. Rose hazarded a guess she was here for the latter.

Penny jabbed a finger in her direction, lips pursed in disapproval. "You need to stay away from my son." Her frigid tone could've frozen the Hudson. "He's an important man in this town, on a fast track to mayor, and doesn't need to be dragged down by the likes of you."

Rose didn't take crap from anyone as a rule. But she wanted to see how far Penny would go before Rose kicked her ass, metaphorically rather than literally, worse luck.

"The likes of me?" Rose kept her tone sugary sweet, refraining from simpering—just.

"You have no husband, no prospects and cook for a living." Penny's nose wrinkled as her imperious gaze swept over her from head to foot. "Plus you have a child." She shot a fleeting glance in Olly's direction and frowned. "A child that you're using to get to my son, and I won't stand for it."

A strange buzzing sound filled Rose's ears. She knew Penny would stoop low but to imply Rose would use Olly to get a guy . . . Heat flooded her face and her heart pounded with outrage.

But Penny wasn't done, not by a long shot. "Everyone's talking about how you're using Caden as a babysitter. How you've moved into the apartment as a stepping stone to the main house." Penny took a deep breath and drew herself up, her spine rigid. "That's never going to happen, because Caden is ready to take the next step with Tully Holmes. So why don't you leave and head back to where you came from."

The next step? She knew Tully and Caden getting together would be Penny's dream, but why would she imply their relationship had reached the commitment stage, unless . . .

"Caden and Tully are friends." Rose hated how defensive she sounded.

When Penny fairly vibrated with triumph, Rose wished she'd hadn't spoken. "Yes, they've been friends for years. *Good* friends. Tully's invaluable to Caden's campaign. A partner in work and play. Surely even you can see they're perfectly suited in every way?"

All Rose could see was her and Caden together last night and she swallowed the bile that rose at the thought of Caden being with her if he was at all intimately connected to Tully.

Penny's vicious grin grated and Rose waited, knowing silence would rile the old cow more than words.

She didn't have to wait long.

"How much to make you leave?"

That did it.

Rose had copped all of Penny's insults with silent fury but to have the woman imply she'd take a payoff to leave Caden alone . . .

She's spent her childhood avoiding confrontation, had grown up shirking any kind of conflict. She hated it. She'd do the best she could to please her father and when that didn't work, she'd hide under her bed or in the closet to avoid him at his angriest. Later, in her teens, she'd run several blocks to Alicia's Bakehouse, her go-to place where the warmth from the ovens and the yeast-scented air would comfort her.

But with the sun beating down on her, and this woman invading a peaceful weekend activity with Olly to spew her vitriol, a fighting spirit resurfaced in Rose that she had deliberately suppressed.

The thing was, insults would only confirm Penny's low opinion of her. So she needed to be smarter. She needed to torture the woman and she knew just how to do it.

Hit her where it hurt the most. Her precious son.

"Why would I leave when Caden and I are getting *acquainted*?" She made it sound like they were doing a lot more than that, and predictably, Penny flushed crimson. "Caden's a lovely guy and my son adores him, so we're staying." Rose made a grand show of looking at her watch. "If you'll excuse me, I need to get Olly. Because the faster he finishes playing, the sooner I can head home to Caden and whip him up one of my gourmet meals he loves so much."

Penny's jaw dropped as her eyes narrowed. But before she could speak, Rose added, "You know the old saying, the way to a man's heart is through his stomach? Lucky me. Caden loves everything I dish up. And more."

As a parting shot, it wasn't half bad and as she half-ran on shaky legs toward Olly and the play equipment, she hoped to God she wouldn't cry.

That woman didn't deserve her tears.

19.

By the time Rose arrived home, her simmering indignation toward Penny Shoreham had given way to full-blown anger.

She wanted to thump something. Or down a bottle of vodka. But the moment the thought popped into her head, she was instantly ashamed. Drowning her sorrows had never solved her problems. The center had taught her that confronting them head-on would.

So that's exactly what she did.

Leaving Olly with a jigsaw puzzle they'd been doing together in the evenings, she marched across the garden, bounded up the steps and pounded on Caden's front door.

However, as she waited for him, some of her bravado faded. What the hell was she doing, running to Caden to snitch on his mother? But she knew there was more to this confrontation than tattling.

Some of Rose's anger was directed at Caden.

Because she remembered the way he'd reacted after Tully had kissed him on stage at his campaign rally. He'd looked goofy, like he hadn't minded her overt display of affection one bit. Maybe Caden liked Tully but didn't know it yet. Men could be really dumb sometimes.

Before she could change her mind, the door swung open and Caden's expression lit up.

"Hey, come on in—"

"How involved are you with Tully, really?"

Damn, not what she'd wanted to lead with, but now that the question was out there, she was definitely interested in hearing the answer.

Penny might have sown the seeds of doubt, but Rose had seen enough of Tully around Caden to know there could be more than a kernel of truth to her implications.

Rose's heart sank as Caden's gaze darted away, oddly evasive: he'd always looked her in the eyes.

"We're friends," he mumbled. "She's doing amazing things with my campaign."

"And?" Rose hated how shrill she sounded and blew out a breath.

"And what?" His brows drew together in a frown. "Why can't you accept what I say at face value?"

"Maybe because your version and your mother's version are poles apart," she snapped, crossing her arms to prevent herself from shaking some sense into him. "According to her, you're ready to take the *next step*—" she made air quotes with her fingers "—in your relationship."

"That's bullshit," he said, but he hadn't lost the evasiveness. "When did you see her?"

"She confronted me at the park. Warned me to stay away from you." She gritted her teeth. "Offered me money to leave town."

He paled. "What the—"

"I took her down in the politest way possible."

The tightness pinching his mouth eased but the shame in his eyes slew her. Was he ashamed of his mother's appalling behavior or because of some secret he was hiding regarding Tully?

"I might've even implied we were a lot closer than we are, just to rub it in," she said, her defiance finally garnering a response beyond caginess when a spark of anger lit his eyes.

"Good for you." Caden's neck muscles stood rigid, a vein pulsing at his temple. "Goddammit, she's interfered in my life for as long as I can remember, but she's never gone to these lengths." His eyes narrowed, resentment making them glow indigo. "This has to end."

Caden's vehemence soothed her own anger. But she couldn't help but wonder: was he overreacting to his mother's meddling or the fact that his mother might have shattered his plans to woo Tully but have her on the side?

"I'm so sorry you had to go through that." His hands balled into fists, like he wanted to pummel something. "She's a control freak. And overprotective."

Rose shrugged. "She's a mother who loves her son and would do anything to protect him. I can relate to that."

"You're nothing like her," he spat out. "Her obsession with Tully and me getting together is making her crazy."

Rose stared at Caden, willing him to say there was absolutely nothing going on with Tully. That he resented the implication. That they had a working relationship and nothing more.

But Caden seemed more upset by his mother's interference than by her statement that they were almost engaged, and that told Rose more than she wanted to know.

After last night, she'd been foolish enough to harbor dreams of her and Caden possibly entering into a relationship, her first.

Now, she couldn't shake the feeling that once again she'd been used and found lacking.

"I don't think you should say anything." She gnawed on her bottom lip, uncertainty making her fidget with the strap on her handbag. "It's not worth it."

"You're worth it," he said, grabbing her hand and tugging, hard enough that she tumbled against him.

"So you've said before," she muttered. This close, her angst only increased, because this thing between them couldn't be denied and she had no idea if she was ready for it. But when he wrapped his arms around her and hugged tight, she couldn't move. It didn't solve anything but it soothed her splintered heart. A heart he'd wormed his way into without trying.

The subtle citrus fragrance of his aftershave tickled her nose and she yearned to bury her face in the crook of his neck and inhale deeply.

Despite her vow to make a stand and confront this problem head on, the longer he held her, the more she wanted to bawl. She held her breath, her posture semi-rigid, holding back the sobs until the wave of emotion passed.

Only then did she wriggle until he released her. "Listen, I think we should cool it for a while."

His mouth opened in a surprised O and she rushed on. "You've been incredible, helping me out, and with everything else, but your campaign should be your focus right now and I don't want—"

"Stop. Forget what my mother said. Means nothing to me." He captured her chin, forcing her to look at him. "And I would never choose a job over a friendship."

She admired him sticking up for their relationship, even if it made her decision to keep her distance harder. "Being mayor isn't a job. It's a prestigious stepping stone to further opportunities."

"Do you think I care about that?" He cupped her cheek and, instinctively, she leaned into his hand. "If you don't already know this, I'll say it again. You're important to me."

She wanted to say, "You're important to me too."

Instead, she stepped away, so his touch couldn't addle her resolve. "But your campaign's important too. Let's leave it at that."

Before he could respond, she turned and ran for the safety of the apartment, far from charming friends she could easily fall for given half a chance.

༾

Caden could've rung ahead to warn his mother he was coming, but he wanted the element of surprise on his side.

Not that it would matter. She probably expected him anyway. She would've assumed Rose would mention her confrontation at the park and would have a host of lies, platitudes or both ready for him. Then again, maybe she thought all her bluster would scare Rose into silence. Whatever, he knew his mom would have loads of trite responses when he asked the hard questions.

Wouldn't matter. Nothing she could say would sway him from doing exactly what he should've done years ago.

Telling her to butt the hell out.

When he pulled into their street, cars lined both sides. Which meant the Shorehams were hosting one of their legendary Sunday twilight suppers.

In his outrage and hurry to get here, he'd forgotten it was the first Sunday of the month, when his parents asked their closest friends and hangers-on over for dinner and classical music.

His dad had given up preaching long ago but they upheld this tradition like it was sacred. He remembered being shunted to his room as a kid and being told to stay there. Yeah, like he'd listened. He'd sneak out and peek through the banisters, watching as the guests arrived. Usually the richest folks in town, dressed to impress, who would stand around drinking sherry and talking in hushed voices. His mom presided like a queen, drifting through the small crowd, air-kissing cheeks, while his dad spoke in animated yet hushed tones, like he did when he preached on a Sunday morning.

Caden had always thought the gatherings boring, had soon tired of spying and returned to his room to read. But the one thing that stuck in his memory from observing his parents with their friends was how fake it all seemed.

He knew the kids of some of those people. Knew them to be drinking and smoking and vandalizing at a young age. Kids who'd lost their virginity at fourteen. Kids who popped party drugs like they were candy. Kids who spouted hate about their parents.

What would those people in their fancy clothes think about that?

It made him value honesty all the more and taught him a better lesson than his dad's sermons ever could. To not put too much faith in appearances because who knew what lay beneath.

He found a vacant spot, parked his car and stormed along the sidewalk. By the time he'd reached his parents' front door, he'd worked up a sweat, and not from the exercise.

Knowing calmness would irritate his mother more than anger, he took several slow breaths and rolled his neck from side to side, easing the tension from his shoulders, his back.

He could hear the faintest strains of Bach coming from inside. Soft music to enhance the mood. No upbeat pop or rock for their guests. Nothing too overt. Nothing to detract from their peaceful home.

Yeah, if the guests only knew.

Because Caden remembered a time when his parents' perfect facade wasn't so perfect. It had stuck with him, the memory of that awful night when he'd seen his father in tears and his mother screaming like a banshee.

"Where the hell have you been?"

Caden froze as he climbed through his bedroom window, caught in the glare of his father's torch and disapproval. Caden could lie but it wasn't in his nature. Guess he had his preacher dad to thank for that.

"Some of the kids from school were meeting down by the river for s'mores," Caden said, banging his knee on the windowsill as he climbed all the way through, the pain of his leg nothing to the pain of embarrassment at being caught sneaking in. "It was the first time they invited me."

His father glowered. "Why didn't you ask permission?"

"Because you never let me go out after ten," Caden said, an uncharacteristic defiance flaring to life. "I'm a teenager, Dad, not some little kid. And you know I'm responsible."

His father stared at him for a long, silent moment, before shaking his head. "Don't let your mother catch you. She'll flay you alive."

"Flay him for what?"

Caden's heart sank as his mother appeared in the doorway, peering around his father.

"What have you been up to?" She pushed past and strode into the room, hands on hips. "Tell me now, Caden."

Caden eyeballed his dad, beseeching him not to say anything. But his father was nothing if not predictable and he'd never seen him do anything but kowtow to his bullying mom.

"Caden went into town to meet up with some friends," his father said. "But he's home now so—"

"This is all your fault," his mother hissed, whirling fast and jabbing his dad in the chest. "The apple never falls far from the tree."

She stomped off, leaving Caden shocked and his father looking resigned as he followed.

A moment later, Caden heard raised voices from downstairs. Startling, because his parents were always coolly polite to each other. No physical displays of affection. No harsh words. No arguments.

But the shouting escalated and he snuck downstairs, feeling increasingly guilty that he'd been the cause of their arguing. When he reached the den and peeked through the crack of the open door, he almost reeled back in shock.

His parents were crying. Bawling. And the expression on his father's face . . . Sheer, unadulterated agony.

Hell, he'd done this. In trying to prove how cool he was, that he wasn't the prissy, prim, preacher's son kids teased him about, he'd caused his parents to have a meltdown.

He crept back upstairs and closed his bedroom quietly, vowing to be the model son from then on, not causing waves or commotion, toeing the line. He didn't like having his orderly life disrupted, didn't like seeing his parents that upset.

He'd do whatever it took to keep the peace.

He'd done it ever since.

Except Effie. She'd been his one rebellion.

Look how that had turned out.

Tonight, he'd come to make another stand. He'd discovered something—or someone, more precisely—worth causing waves for.

He rang the doorbell and waited. The front of their town house still looked as new as when they'd bought it six years ago. Cream rendered bricks. Black trimmings. Gleaming brass fittings. Thankfully, they'd moved out of the family home when he'd returned from college, almost like they'd been waiting for him to come home to make their escape.

He could've left when his dad had recovered but he'd already started work at the accountancy firm in town by then. His folks had bought the town house and practically gifted him the family house. He'd taken on a mortgage, shelved his dreams of a city life and made Redemption his home. At times he resented having been almost dragged back out of familial obligation, but mostly he liked living here. Liked the laid-back atmosphere, the vineyards, the people.

Except today. Today, his mother was one of those people on his dislike list.

He rang the doorbell again, pressed his finger to hold it longer this time and after a few moments, his mother opened the door.

In that split second between recognition and putting on her game face, he saw a flicker of angst. Like she'd been expecting this confrontation but wasn't looking forward to it. Join the club.

"We need to talk, Mom."

She glanced over her shoulder and made a shushing noise. "Not now, dear. We have guests—"

"This won't take long." He stepped forward, leaving her no option but to open the door wider and let him in.

He brushed past her without the obligatory kiss, too damn mad to be anywhere near her.

She must've sensed it, because she didn't push the issue. "We can talk in the den."

He'd already been heading there, well aware she'd rather die than let her precious guests hear a snippet of disagreement. "Of course. We wouldn't want anyone being privy to your appalling behavior."

She frowned, her lips flattening into a thin line, but true to form she waited until she'd closed the den door before uttering a word.

He braced, well aware what her first modus operandi would be: attack.

"I'm sure that girl has been filling your head with lies, but I want you to know—"

"No, Mother, I want *you* to know." He glowered at her, enjoying the first flicker of uncertainty in her usual confident mask. "You don't go near Rose again. You don't talk to her. And you certainly don't dump your prejudiced garbage on her. Is that clear?"

She gaped like a goldfish, clearly not expecting such a cold delivery.

"Rose is my friend. I like her. And nothing you say or do can stop me from spending time with her."

His mother's jaw snapped shut with an audible click. "This is just like that situation with Effie. We squelched the rumors about her when you entered the campaign. But now people are talking again—"

"Let them talk." He shook his head, sick to death of keeping up appearances. "Do you think I give a shit about what people who mean nothing to me say?"

He'd never sworn in front of his mother. Did it deliberately now to ram home his point.

She blanched, a disapproving frown slashing her brows. "If that's the kind of language you're using now, maybe you can see why you should stay away from—"

"Jesus, haven't you heard a word I just said?"

He knew blasphemy, the ultimate sin in their household growing up, would rattle her more than swearing, and she started wringing her hands.

"I love you, Mom. You and Dad mean the world to me. But if you don't leave me alone to lead my own life, with friends of my choosing . . ." He shrugged, not wanting to issue empty threats he wouldn't follow through on, but oh, so tempted. "Let's just say I won't tolerate your interference any longer."

He jabbed a finger in her direction. "Stay away from Rose."

"Caden, wait—"

He didn't. He walked out of the den and made sure he slammed the front door on his way out.

20.

When Sara had called to tee up a time to go wedding dress shopping, Rose had been on the verge of fobbing her off. Making up some excuse. She hated clothes shopping at the best of times, but going with a woman she barely knew who happened to be marrying her brother way too fast had all the makings of a disaster.

But Sara was upbeat and perky and incredibly insistent, so Rose found herself in a Dixon Creek wedding boutique, being plied with champagne she had to continually refuse and having to give her opinion on countless dresses she didn't have the faintest interest in.

As Sara stepped from behind a gold velvet curtain wearing the tenth dress, an A-line, round neckline, chiffon lace, floor-length gown that draped her body to perfection, Rose finally found herself smiling without having to force it.

"That's the one." Rose stood and walked around the bride-to-be as she stood on a makeshift pedestal. "It's perfect."

"I think so too," Sara said, half turning to get a better look at the back. "I knew the second I put it on, but I wanted your opinion."

"Why?" Rose blurted, wishing she hadn't when Sara's eyes filled with tears. "I mean, we hardly know each other so my opinion can't be that important."

Sara blinked a few times, the sheen of tears replaced by a determination that made Rose want to take a step back.

"Because I love Jake and I don't want there to be any bad blood between us."

"There isn't—"

"Do me the courtesy of not lying," Sara said, a frown marring her brow. "I'm not an idiot. I see the way you look at me, like I'm going to steal your family's silver and do a runner."

Crap. Had Rose's doubts about Sara been that obvious? And if Sara knew, did Jake suspect she had reservations about this wedding too?

"We don't have any silver," Rose said, her levity falling flat when Sara's frown deepened.

"Look, I get it. This has all happened really fast and you don't know me." Sara pressed a hand to her chest. "But you've got to believe me when I say your brother is the best thing to ever happen to me." Her mouth turned down. "I tolerated a crappy marriage for years because of my daughter. So I would never, ever, marry again for the sake of a child. It's not fair on anybody."

As Rose digested that revelation, Sara stepped off the pedestal, almost bringing her toe-to-toe with Rose. "I don't prejudge people. If I did, I wouldn't be here with you now." Her eyes narrowed. "I'd be doing everything in my power to avoid you, because I'd be thinking you're a selfish cow for leaving your son to the care of others for so long."

Rose's jaw dropped as she stared at the demure woman who'd morphed into a bridezilla on steroids.

"So all I'm asking for is a little leniency and a lot of respect." Sara jabbed her finger in Rose's direction. "I haven't prejudged you, so don't you dare judge me for wanting to marry your brother and getting pregnant so fast."

Stunned by Sara's outburst, Rose held up her hands. "Whoa. Take it easy."

Sara thrust up her chin in defiance. "I will if you will."

Filled with admiration for a woman who'd stand up to a future in-law like that, Rose chuckled. "You've got some balls, lady. I think you'll do well in the Mathieson family."

Rose could almost see the tension drain from Sara as her shoulders slumped.

"Does that mean you'll give me the benefit of the doubt and at least try to like me?"

"I'll do one better than that," Rose said, feeling increasingly guilty that Sara had picked up on her doubting vibes. "I'll throw you a fully catered bridal shower to show you how much my brother means to me and how I respect you standing up to me. How's that?"

"Fine," Sara said, with a brisk nod. "It's a deal."

When Sara hesitated, Rose reached out and embraced her. "Welcome to the mad Mathiesons."

Sara sniffled but hugged her tight before easing away. "Thanks. Your approval means a lot."

Rose snorted. "It shouldn't. My opinion isn't worth a damn."

Sara looked like she wanted to chastise her but instead she said, "Thanks for today. It was important to me."

To her surprise, Rose found herself agreeing. "Me too."

Sara headed for the dressing room. When she had stepped behind the curtain, Rose said, "Has Jake picked up on my doubts about you too?"

"Are you kidding? Guys aren't as observant as we are."

"Ain't that the truth."

Because if they were, Caden would've picked up on a whole host of signs she'd been sending out, the main one being, was she ready to move their friendship to the next level?

Damned if she knew.

Rose managed to avoid being interrogated by Cilla and Jake for an entire week after the ball. They'd asked how her night out had been, and she'd answered with the standard "fine."

Jake, in the throes of impending fatherhood and upcoming nuptials, believed her.

Cilla, not so much. And Sara hadn't asked much beyond the superficial during their wedding dress scouting mission, because Rose had been frosty on the way there and trying to make up for her recalcitrance on the trip back to Redemption by being verbose about trivialities.

The women hadn't pushed for answers and Rose knew why. They'd saved their interrogation for today, at the bachelorette party she'd offered to host. A garden tea party in her aunt's backyard, just the three of them. Bryce and Jake had taken Olly to the vineyard where the wedding was being held, on the pretext of checking on final details, when in fact they'd bolted for fear of being roped into helping her set up.

Not that she'd gone all out. Well, not much, anyway. She'd wanted today to be special, a way to thank her aunt and Sara for all they'd done for Olly while she'd been away. And to extend the hand of friendship to Sara and show her there were no hard feelings.

Sara had been gracious during their wedding dress shopping expedition, considering how Rose had treated her. Rose respected honesty and once Sara had laid it all on the line, she'd shelved her reservations and decided to give her future sister-in-law the benefit of the doubt.

She hoped today would show Sara how much she really cared and wanted her and Jake to be happy. So Rose had commandeered Cilla's garden and done the lot herself. Decorating and catering. It looked pretty darn amazing, even if she said so herself.

She'd timed it so the afternoon tea would start late, enabling the fairy lights she'd strung in the trees to be seen. She'd draped sheer cream chiffon between the trees too, looping it from branch to branch, creating a marquee effect. Had strategically placed silver stars throughout the garden, what looked like millions of them, to add to the fairytale quality.

All this before she'd tackled the main table, where she'd set out a high tea fit for a bride. Lemon tartlets, carrot quinoa cupcakes, double fudge chocolate brownies, maple syrup cheesecake, almond and polenta strawberry shortcake, white chocolate-tipped strawberries, coconut truffles, cherry and ricotta strudel, orange poppy-seed flourless cakes, vegetable quiches, mini shepherd's pies and dainty cucumber sandwiches cut with precision. Totally over the top, but she'd really wanted to extend an olive branch to Sara. Besides, when the hungry males returned, she knew they'd make short work of the leftovers.

Rose had spent days baking for this, exhausted after long shifts at the diner but wanting to ensure the bachelorette party/bridal shower was perfect. The few times she'd seen Sara this week, there'd been something bothering her. At first Rose had assumed Sara was still annoyed with the way she'd treated her. But they'd moved past that after their heart-to-heart in the wedding dress shop and were tentatively approaching what could be a solid friendship. If something else was wrong with Sara, Rose didn't have a clue what it was. She couldn't pinpoint the problem exactly, because Sara dismissed her concerns with an airy wave and a blasé smile.

But Rose saw the worry in Sara's eyes and hoped to God the woman her brother adored wasn't getting jittery about the wedding, which was to take place in seven days.

She hoped to broach the subject today if the opportunity arose. If Sara didn't want to talk in front of Cilla, she'd find a way to be alone with her later.

Now that Rose had got her head around the speed of her brother's relationship, this wedding had to happen. The Mathiesons had

had enough bad luck to last them a lifetime. Sara and Jake getting hitched would fly in the face of the past and bring happiness to the entire family.

"Hey, Rose, can we come out now?" Sara stepped onto Cilla's back porch and her mouth fell open. "Oh, my goodness . . ."

Hoping Sara's stunned expression signified pleasure, Rose threw her arms wide. "You like?"

"It's . . . stunning." Sara took tentative steps into the garden, like she was afraid the magic would disappear. "You did all this?"

Bashful, Rose nodded. "I wanted you to have a special bachelorette party."

Sara tore her wide-eyed gaze from the garden. "I thought you said this was a bridal shower?" She waggled her finger. "There'd better not be strippers."

"Damn." Rose snapped her fingers. "I'd better go ring the fireman, cowboy and sheriff I had lined up to get their gear off."

"Don't be so hasty," Cilla said, backing out of the kitchen, her arms laden with a tray of elderflower cordial and wine glasses. "I haven't seen enough naked prime males in my time so strippers are fine by me."

Sara shot Rose a horrified glance and Rose laughed. "Sorry to disappoint, Auntie, but there are no strippers. Just the three of us having a very civilized garden party bridal shower."

"Phew." Sara wiped her brow in relief.

"Party poopers." Cilla smirked and placed the tray on the table.

"Don't you have your hands full with Bryce anyway?" Sara teased. "He looks like enough male for any woman to handle."

Rose wasn't surprised when her aunt's smile faded fast and she busied herself pouring cordial into the glasses.

Sara noticed too, and quirked an eyebrow, well aware she'd blundered into a delicate area. But it wasn't Rose's place to divulge the problems her aunt was having in the relationship department, so she gave a subtle shake of her head, relieved when Sara nodded.

Casting a quick concerned glance at Cilla before sitting, Sara said, "Speaking of males, you haven't told us what happened after the ball."

Rose should've been grateful for Sara asking a diverting question. Instead, she floundered a little, not wanting to reveal too much.

What could she say? That she'd spent the best night of her life with Caden, but hadn't known how to handle it the next day? That she'd grown into a cynic at the ripe old age of twenty-six, learning firsthand that she couldn't depend on any man, not long term, and that letting Caden into her heart would be setting herself up for disappointment yet again?

That the longer she dithered over how to move forward with their relationship, the easier it got to talk herself out of having anything to do with him beyond friendship?

She settled for a very circumspect, "He escorted me home like the true gentleman he is."

"And?" Cilla handed them a glass each. "You forget, my dear, that Olly's not the only one around here who's an early riser."

Rose felt heat flush her cheeks. Damn. Cilla must've seen her leave Caden's house early to sneak home to the apartment.

Sara sniggered. "Did you do the walk of shame, Rose?"

Considering her face probably matched the color of the crimson foil hearts she'd scattered over the tablecloth, Rose eventually nodded.

Sara squealed and clapped her hands. "Tell us everything."

Cilla merely grinned as they all sat around the circular table, ignoring the food, more intent on interrogation than degustation.

"Not much to tell." Rose shrugged and helped herself to a sandwich and a tartlet.

"I always could tell when you were fibbing, even as a little girl," Cilla said, pinning her with the same astute gaze she used to way back when. "So you either tell us the gossip or we keep hounding you until you do."

Resigned to having to give them some snippet of truth so they'd leave her alone, Rose settled into her chair.

"Caden's a great guy. We were childhood friends for a while. Since I've been back, he's helped me out, letting me live in the apartment 'til I find a place to stay, taking Olly to school, that kind of thing."

"So far you haven't told us anything we don't already know," Cilla said, her dry response garnering a giggle from Sara.

"Actually, I don't know their background, so it helps set the scene before she gets to the good stuff." Sara rubbed her hands together. "Which is coming next, I presume."

Rose rolled her eyes. "Fine, but once I'm done spilling my guts, I'm turning the spotlight on both of you."

Two sets of eyes turned wary in an instant and Rose vowed to give a little info to get a lot.

"We had a good time at the ball. Caden is attentive and charming, and we escaped before it ended."

"We're getting to the good bit," Sara said to Cilla in an exaggerated whisper.

Rose smiled. "When we got home, he invited me in for fondue."

"Kinky," Cilla said, and Sara laughed.

"I didn't want to complicate our friendship, because he's been so good to me, but . . ."

How could Rose articulate what Caden meant to her without sounding corny and conflicted?

"But you threw caution to the wind anyway?" Sara supplied helpfully.

"Something like that," Rose finished lamely, trying not squirm beneath Cilla's probing stare.

Her aunt knew there was so much more Rose wasn't revealing, but thankfully she didn't pester.

"So how are things between you two now?" Sara rested her elbows on the table and propped her chin in her hands, a faraway dreamy look in her eyes. "Are you dating?"

Rose hesitated, unsure how to answer. She wished she knew how to label her relationship with Caden, she really did.

"He wanted to. I'm holding out."

"Doesn't sound that way to me," Cilla said, sipping at her cordial. "Caden's a nice boy. Getting physical takes your relationship to the next level, whether you want to admit it or not. But if you're having second thoughts, it's hard sending mixed messages."

Her aunt's bluntness made Sara uncomfortable, if her fiddling fingers were any indication.

"I don't think it's right to enter into a relationship with Caden unless I'm in it for the long haul," Rose said, her tone surprisingly steady when in fact her aunt's blunt admonition made her feel a tad shaky. "I won't do that to Olly."

"Fair enough," Cilla said, but something had set her aunt off and she looked decidedly piqued.

"I don't know Caden well but he seems like a really genuine guy," Sara said. "And Olly talks about him a lot. Raves, in fact."

"He does that to me about you too," Rose said. "At least he's got good taste in people he trusts."

Better than she ever had.

When her mom died, she'd trusted her dad. She'd trusted him to love her and support her. She'd trusted him to look after her and Jake. She'd trusted him to provide her with a good home that she could grow up in feeling safe.

He'd disappointed her on every level. She should've learned then but it had taken Dyson betraying her trust too for her to wake up and realize that she'd never give her trust easily again.

"You don't trust Caden, is that it?" Cilla offered a plate of sandwiches. "You know the rumors about him and Tully Holmes are just that—rumors."

Rose sighed. "Yeah, but she's much more his type than I am. They'd be perfect together. Redemption's golden couple."

Cilla snorted. "Maybe in Tully's eyes, but I've never seen Caden show the slightest interest in taking their relationship beyond friendship."

"Maybe he doesn't know what's good for him?" Rose took a cucumber sandwich and laid it on her plate. "Maybe he can't see what's right in front of him?"

Cilla tsk-tsked. "This has nothing to do with Tully and Caden and everything to do with your fear of taking a chance on him." She laid the sandwiches down. "Don't blame you after what you've been through, but not all men are the same."

"Is that why it took you twenty years to take a chance on a relationship again?" Rose hadn't meant it to sound accusatory but her aunt stared at her like she'd been stabbed in the heart. "That wasn't a jibe, by the way. I'm merely trying to get a handle on the stuff I'm going through."

Cilla's dour expression softened. "Sorry, love, I'm just a tad touchy when it comes to Bryce at the moment."

"You're still having problems?" Rose shouldn't have felt relieved, not if her aunt's relationship was struggling, but it took the focus off her and that had to be a good thing.

Cilla nodded and laid her glass down, increasingly morose. So much for a fun bridal shower. Rose never should've answered their questions about her relationship with Caden.

"The age difference is definitely a problem." Cilla poked at the food on her plate, before pushing it away. "I'm not like you girls, who get caught up in the romance of a new relationship and want to spend every spare second in the bedroom."

Sara's accusatory glare spoke volumes: *Why the hell did you bring this up?* The last thing Rose wanted was to listen to her aunt's problems in the boudoir but this was the third time Cilla had brought this up with her and that meant her aunt had resolved nothing. In fact, since Rose had moved to Redemption she'd never seen her aunt so somber. And she obviously felt comfortable discussing her personal life in front of Sara too, which implied that things were at breaking point between her and Bryce.

When Sara and Rose remained silent, Cilla snorted. "Don't worry, I'm not going to give you a blow-by-blow account."

"Rather unfortunate choice of words," Sara said, with a cheeky smirk, and Rose smothered a chuckle behind her hand when Cilla glowered.

"You girls." Cilla shook her head, but at least her mouth had lost its pinched tightness. "The thing is, I've never had a man adore me like Bryce does. And I enjoy all aspects of our relationship." She wrinkled her nose. "But just not so frequently."

Rose wanted to make a joke to lighten the mood but she saw the genuine confusion in her aunt's eyes and knew she needed to offer some kind of help rather than be a smartass.

She settled for a sedate, "You said you'd talk to him about it?"

"I'm embarrassed." Cilla held up her hand and wavered it side to side. "We haven't lived together that long. I'm thinking once the proverbial honeymoon period wears off, he'll slow down a little."

A glimmer of a smile poked through. "Though I could be dead by then."

That alleviated some of the tension, and they laughed. The kind of belly laughs that bubbled up from deep within, a tension release more than amusement, a laugh that couldn't be stopped. They laughed until they cried, swiping tears from their eyes, and Rose got a stitch that required a lot of rib stretching and rubbing.

"Want to know what I think?" Sara asked when she could speak again, and Cilla nodded, pointing at Rose.

"This one's already given me her strong opinion several times now so I'd like to get your point of view."

Rose blew her aunt a kiss and Sara smiled.

"From what you've told me, you've been upfront with Bryce from the start. He's aware you had reservations about the age difference. And he knows you haven't lived with anyone for two decades."

"And?" Cilla prompted.

"Rose's right. You need to discuss this with him." Sara shrugged, like it was the easiest thing in the world to have a difficult conversation. "Are you afraid he'll leave?"

"I've been on my own too long to worry about being alone again." Cilla's forehead screwed up a little, as if she was pondering. "Perhaps it's because he's been so accommodating in fitting in with my lifestyle that I feel bad, bringing up a topic that's so natural for a guy his age."

Rose hated seeing her aunt unhappy, so she chirped in. "Have you ever considered maybe he's making an extra effort for you, because you haven't been with anyone for so long? That he feels if he doesn't you might not be interested in him anymore?"

When Sara glanced at Rose with respect, Rose patted her chest. "When you spend as much time as I have psychoanalyzing yourself, you get pretty damn good at doing it for others too."

Cilla's eyes widened, her relief palpable. "I never considered that."

Rose shrugged. "It's just a theory but it makes sense. You spent a lot of time pushing him away at the start and now that he's moved in, maybe he's feeling a tad insecure that if he doesn't live up to expectations of a younger guy you'll kick him out?"

Cilla nodded, her expression thoughtful. "Guess we really do need to talk about it."

"You should," Rose said, wishing she could sort out her own problems as easily.

"Though speaking of pushing guys away, isn't that what you're doing to Caden?" Sara smirked and Rose poked her tongue out.

"She's right," Cilla said. "That young man must be crazy about you, to help out with Olly as much as he does. Plus take you to a very public ball when he's running for mayor and knows how much his parents disapprove . . ." Cilla trailed off and winced, like she'd said too much.

"What have you heard?" Rose's heart sank. The last thing she wanted for Caden was for gossip to have spread around town about the two of them, gossip that might damage his campaign.

Cilla blushed. "I don't pay attention to rubbish being bandied about, but Penny Shoreham serves on the hospital board and I run into her occasionally when I pop in there."

Cilla mimicked a mouth opening and closing with her hand. "She can't keep her lips zipped. Always flapping them about and letting venom spill out. I wouldn't worry about anything she says."

"You still haven't told me what she said," Rose said, assuming it would be more of the same that she'd copped at the diner.

"And you won't hear it from me." Cilla made a zipping motion over her mouth. "All I'm trying to point out is if a guy is willing to defy his mother, especially one who's had such a controlling influence all these years, he must be head over heels for you."

Sara leaned forward and patted her hand. "Do you love him, Rose?"

The million-dollar question she had no hope of answering.

Because Rose didn't know what love was.

Not in a romantic sense anyway. She loved Olly with every fiber of her being. And she loved Jake and Cilla. But she'd never given her heart to anyone before.

Caden made her pulse trip and her body sing. He made her laugh. He made her feel comfortable and safe. He made her feel cherished. He made her feel like the most wonderful woman in the world.

But was that love?

Damned if she knew.

"I don't know," she said, answering as honestly as she could. "I've never been in love before."

"You'll know when it's right." Sara pointed to her heart. "You'll feel it in here. A persistent feeling you can't shake."

"That's called heartburn and you can take a pill for it," Cilla said, her dry humor making them laugh again. "Now, are we going to share this magnificent feast Rose has prepared?"

"Actually, I've got something I wanted to ask you both," Sara said, her smile fading fast. "I need some reassurance I'm not being completely paranoid."

A sliver of foreboding strummed Rose's spine. Surely Jake wasn't having second thoughts about this marriage—or the baby—that Sara had picked up on? Now that Rose had quelled her concerns about their rushed relationship, she'd acknowledged that Sara had been through a devilishly hard time too and deserved happiness.

"What's going on?" Rose asked, bracing for the worst—a lifetime habit she couldn't shake—hoping she wouldn't have to drag Jake to the altar by his ear.

"I'm worried," Sara said, her hand resting protectively over her belly, and that foreboding Rose sensed blossomed into panic.

Sara's first child had died. She didn't deserve to lose a second.

Cilla blanched and stuffed a tartlet into her mouth, probably to prevent herself from saying anything, leaving Rose to tread carefully.

"Is everything okay?"

Sara's lower lip wobbled. "I've been spotting. Which is completely normal according to my obstetrician. But I didn't have it with Lucy. And I've read so much stuff on the internet that suggests this could be bad—"

"Stop." Rose held up her hand. "Never self-diagnose on the internet. Trust me, I know." She made loopy circles at her temple. "According to the wise faceless doctors of the web, I'm a certified nutcase."

Sara nodded, but she hadn't lost her stricken expression. "I know you're right, but I want this baby so much." She hesitated, the raw unadulterated pain in her eyes making Rose want to hug her. "Losing Lucy nearly killed me. I couldn't go through something like that again."

Rose bit back her first response, which was *Everything's going to be okay*. Because it wasn't her place to give empty guarantees. Not when women miscarried every day. But she had to say something before Cilla's signature bluntness potentially made the situation worse.

"When I was pregnant with Olly, I listened to my doctor like he was God," Rose said. "I was nineteen, clueless and petrified, and had to put my faith in someone who'd delivered countless babies before."

Rose clasped Sara's hand and held it tight, hoping to infuse her with whatever meager confidence she could. "So listen to your obstetrician. Call her if you're having doubts. And try to stay calm, okay?"

"Thanks," Sara said, squeezing her hand. "I know you're one hundred percent right, and it's stuff I've already told myself, but when Jake's asleep and I'm online at night, I can't help but worry."

"Rose is right. The internet is not your friend," Cilla said, her tone soft. "The number of people who come to me asking for this remedy or that after seeing it on the internet is staggering." She shook her head. "There's a lot of misinformation out there, some of it potentially dangerous."

A faraway look clouded Cilla's eyes. "I had spotting when I was expecting Tamsin." Color suffused her cheeks. "I blamed it on Vernon and prayed like hell that he wouldn't ruin the only good thing to come out of our marriage." She pointed at the sky. "Guess the big guy upstairs listened because my baby girl was fine and I carried to full term."

Rose released Sara's hand as she leaned forward. "And your obstetrician wasn't worried either?"

Cilla shook her head a tad too quickly and Rose hoped Sara hadn't picked up on it. "No. Said it was perfectly normal."

"Same as mine," Sara said, looking brighter. "She said to contact her immediately if it got worse or anything else didn't seem right, but apart from the dwindling morning sickness, I'm fine."

"And you will be," Cilla said, pressing her hands to her chest. "I feel it in here."

Rose didn't want to remind her aunt that she'd labeled that heartburn not too long ago, but Sara must've been thinking the same thing because they exchanged an amused glance.

"Now that we've quizzed Rose on her relationship, solved Cilla's concerns in the bedroom and you've both reassured me, let's eat," Sara said, sounding much calmer. "I can't thank you enough for doing this, Rose. The garden decorations and all this food look amazing."

"My pleasure." Rose picked up a fruit platter and handed it to Sara.

There was a flurry of plate filling. Chatting had obviously worked up their appetites.

"How are the wedding plans coming along?" Rose asked out of politeness more than curiosity. She had to be missing the bridal gene because wedding stuff didn't interest her. She hadn't asked Cilla, Sara or Jake anything about the wedding, content to arrive on the day and present them with the wedding cake they'd asked her to make.

"Running like clockwork," Cilla said, dabbing the corners of her mouth with a napkin. "Have to say, when Jake and Sara first chose Winsome Winery as the venue, I was dubious, but James, the owner, has made everything run so smoothly I'm impressed."

Sara nibbled at a cucumber and dill sandwich. "Why were you dubious? James seems lovely."

Cilla screwed up her nose. "I find him a bit full on, with all that overt charm all the time."

Rose sniggered. "Maybe he's got the hots for you?"

"Me and half the women in this town." Cilla rolled her eyes. "But he's been great with the wedding plans. Very accommodating."

Sara nodded. "Nothing seems to faze him. Whenever we make amendments, he just rolls with it."

"So what are you actually doing on the day?" Rose asked, because Sara glowed when she spoke about the wedding. After how worried she'd looked earlier, being distracted could only be a good thing.

"Late afternoon ceremony under a gazebo on the winery's main lawns. Officiated by a minister. Traditional vows. Then an informal party with a band and dance floor." Sara snapped her fingers. "And a buffet, so none of that formal sit-down three-course stuff."

"Sounds great," Rose said, fervently hoping this wedding went off without a hitch. Her brother deserved happiness, and after what Sara had been through, so did she.

Sara glanced at Cilla, her smile soft. "I can't thank you enough for all you've done to help us organize the wedding on such short notice."

"My pleasure." Cilla blushed and reached for a lemon tartlet. "You deserve to be happy."

"We all do," Sara said, her astute gaze switching to Rose.

While Rose wholeheartedly agreed, she couldn't help but think that whole happily-ever-after scenario wasn't for her.

21.

Rose walked Sara home, sensing the other woman needed the company. Since her revelation about her pregnancy fears, Sara looked pale and haunted and Rose sent a silent prayer heavenward that everything would be okay. With Jake absent, she knew reassuring Sara further would fall on her, and she wasn't looking forward to it. Because while Rose had shelved her concerns about the speed of this marriage, now that she'd discovered there could be a problem with the baby, she couldn't help but wonder whether Sara had bailed on her first marriage after her child had died. Would that happen to Jake too?

When they reached the front door, Sara unlocked it and beckoned Rose in. "Want to come in for a drink?"

Rose wanted to say no. The last thing she needed was Sara to pick up on her doubts, not when they'd come such a long way in bridging the gap between them.

But she took one look at Sara's wide eyes filled with fear and found herself nodding. "Sure. I'd love a cup of peppermint tea."

Sara's shoulders sagged in relief as they entered the house and traveled down the long hallway to the kitchen. Rose had been here a few times now but the artwork adorning the walls never failed to capture her attention.

Sara had an incredible talent and Rose envied her ability to work from home and still earn a living. She'd had grand ideas at one time of running her own catering or cupcake business, but that required capital and a large kitchen, two things she'd never had. So she'd ignored her dreams and focused on making a solid living to provide for Olly. Earnings she'd blown at the recovery center. A necessity at the time, but it didn't stop her from feeling inadequate and guilty because she hadn't been strong enough to manage her issues on her own.

"What's wrong?" Sara was propped at the sink, filling the kettle. "You look really sad."

"Just thinking how lucky you are to have such a wonderful talent and be able to work from home." Rose settled for a half-truth. Sara didn't need to know about her envy.

"You've got a great talent too." Sara patted her stomach. "That feast you whipped up was incredible. Ever thought of running your own restaurant?"

Annoyed that Sara had articulated her dream like it was the easiest thing in the world to do, Rose perched on the edge of the kitchen table. "Of course, but I'd need to win the lottery for that to happen."

Sara winced. "Sorry, that was tactless of me."

Rose waved away her apology. "Don't worry about it. I made peace with my lack of funds a long time ago. I do the best I can for my kid. That's all I can do."

Sara's expression crumpled a little. "I know what that's like, so I never should've blabbed like that."

"Truly, it's fine." Not liking seeing Sara so distressed, Rose pointed to the kettle. "How's that cuppa coming along?"

"Almost ready." Sara busied herself spooning peppermint tea into a teapot and readying the cups, but Rose saw how her hands shook and felt even worse for being so touchy.

She needed to change the subject. Maybe if she could get Sara talking about her fears, it would alleviate them. "You sure you're okay, with the baby and everything?"

The teaspoon slipped from Sara's fingers and clattered onto the bench, her other hand instantly covering her abdomen, as if touch alone would protect her unborn child.

"I'm terrified," Sara murmured, "and not just about the baby."

Rose's heart sank as she fervently hoped her innermost fears wouldn't come to fruition: that without a baby, Sara wouldn't be interested in marrying Jake.

"If you want to talk, it won't go any further." Rose almost said "I promise," but held back at the last second. She couldn't promise not to tell Jake if Sara articulated her greatest fear, not when it would affect her brother's future.

When Sara turned to face her, more color had leeched from her cheeks, if that were possible, and Rose crossed the kitchen to lead her to a chair.

"Here, you sit. I'll finish making the tea."

Sara didn't protest and slumped onto the chair like her legs had given way.

Hell.

Rose bustled about, pouring water into the teapot, putting it on a tray along with cups, before heading back to the table.

She had no idea what to say. She'd never had a close girlfriend, or anyone to confide in beyond Jake, for that matter, and she'd been unable to tell her brother half the things that had happened in her crappy life.

But Sara looked on the verge of fainting and Rose had to step up.

"So what besides the baby has you this worried?"

She settled for the blunt approach, hoping she could offer some advice to calm the other woman down.

When Sara's reluctant gaze met hers, Rose had to school her expression into one of blandness so as not to show alarm at seeing the absolute panic in Sara's eyes.

"I'm scared that if I lose the baby, Jake won't want to marry me," Sara whispered, blinking rapidly. "And I'm not sure if I can go through with the wedding, wondering what might happen to our marriage if I do miscarry . . ."

Sara shook her head, tears spilling down her cheeks, but Rose waited, sensing Sara had to get everything off her chest before she could start to feel better.

"When Lucy died, my marriage fell apart . . ." Sara glanced away, focusing on the clock over Rose's shoulder, her mouth contorted as she struggled to hold back sobs.

"And you fear that may happen with Jake?"

Sara nodded and bit down on her bottom lip. "I'd been married to Greg for seven years and we still fell apart after Lucy died. I've known Jake five months, so how could our marriage withstand a miscarriage so early?"

Hearing Sara echo her own fears about this relationship made it easier for Rose to offer sound advice.

"Because Jake isn't your ex," Rose said, reaching out to place a hand on Sara's. "I don't know the first thing about your first marriage but I do know my brother. He stands by those he loves, no matter how hard the going gets. Our childhood was testament to that, and he's stood by me ever since, despite me making some pretty crappy decisions."

Some of the color returned to Sara's cheeks, so Rose continued. "I hope your baby's going to be okay, I really do, but don't let it define your relationship with Jake."

"But what if he's only marrying me because of the baby?"

"He wouldn't do that." Rose squeezed Sara's hand and leaned forward. "He's like me. He's avoided long-term relationships like the plague for fear of letting anyone get too close, because of our pasts. But Jake let you in, *before* the pregnancy. He bought the airfield, facing his greatest fear since the accident. He uprooted his life and moved here to be with you. He agreed to move in with you. Surely that's proof enough of his love, without a baby on the scene?"

Some of the tension eased as Sara's face smoothed. "I guess you're right."

"No guessing involved." Rose tapped her hand and removed hers. "Jake's the best man I know. He won't let you down." Her voice took on a hardened edge. "And I'm expecting the same from you. Don't disappoint my brother, okay?"

A flash of fire in Sara's unflinching gaze signaled she'd weathered the crisis and come out the other side.

"I love him. He's my everything. I'd never do anything to deliberately hurt him."

Rose refrained from pointing out that, moments ago, Sara had been voicing doubts about turning up to her own wedding next week and that that would definitely have hurt her brother.

"Good. Now that's settled, ready for some tea?"

Sara nodded. "Thanks for talking me down off the ledge."

"I'm used to it." Rose shrugged. "Though it's usually inside my own head."

Sara smiled and poured the tea. "You're doing great."

Maybe, but if only solving her own problems were as easy as sorting others'.

❦

Jake arrived home fifteen minutes later and appeared surprised to see Rose in the kitchen with Sara. Which meant maybe she hadn't hidden her reservations regarding Sara and the speed of their relationship all that well.

"Hey, gorgeous." He kissed Sara on the lips before waving at Rose. "Hey, Sis, good to see you here."

Rose poked out her tongue. "Where's Olly?"

"With Bryce at Cilla's." Jake grinned. "When we got back, Cilla mentioned the stack of leftovers and Olly didn't have to be asked twice."

"That's my boy." Rose rolled her eyes. "If he eats this much now, what's he going to be like as a teenager?"

Jake struck a strongman pose. "As big and tough as his uncle."

"Who's a giant pushover," Rose said drily, and Sara chuckled.

"I'll leave you two to it, while I go lie down." Sara stood and stretched, trying to hide a fleeting grimace, but Rose spotted it.

As if sensing her concern, Jake's gaze flew to Sara. "Everything okay?"

Sara nodded. "Fine. But I've got a bellyful of your sister's exquisite cuisine and I'm a tad tired."

Sara turned to Rose. "Thanks for today. It was brilliant."

"You're welcome." Rose smiled, thankful that the effort she'd gone to with the bridal shower had made an impression on her future sister-in-law.

"See you later." Sara mustered a small wave before heading for the stairs, leaving Rose alone with Jake.

And grateful for the one-on-one time with her brother: if she didn't voice her concerns regarding this wedding, she'd burst.

"I feel like I walked in on something," Jake said, pulling up a seat at the table. "What's up?"

Rose mentally rehearsed how to make this easier, but came up empty. Blunt as always, she settled for blurting the truth.

"Have you considered what would happen to your wedding plans, or your marriage, if Sara loses the baby?"

Jake started and stared at her with wide-eyed surprise. "What the hell brought that on?"

"I'm worried, Jakey." Rose shrugged. "Don't get me wrong, I like Sara; she's great. And I've never seen you so happy. But she's been through this before—expecting a baby, marriage, the works—and it didn't work out." She paused and looked at her brother, really looked at him, beseeching him to understand. "What's to say it will this time?"

A frown line appeared between Jake's brows as he leaned forward, fixing her with a no-nonsense glare. "There are no guarantees in any relationship. You of all people know that. So the best I can do is follow my heart and take a risk on the woman I love and hope to God it all turns out okay."

His fervor should've reassured her, but Rose knew she wouldn't be where she was today if it wasn't for her amazing brother and she had to make sure he was one hundred percent sure about Sara and this wedding.

"You sure you've thought this through—"

"Enough." He held up his hand and stood, his glower formidable. "I love Sara. I'm going to marry her. And whatever happens with our unborn child, I'll still love her. So we'll deal with whatever comes our way, together."

"Wow, you're all grown up." Rose didn't push any more. She'd expressed her concerns; Jake had answered them. At some point, she had to let go of her reservations and trust that her smart brother knew what he was doing.

"You're only just realizing this now?" His frown cleared and he grinned. "You're a pain in the ass, Sis, but I love you for caring about me enough to bring up all that stuff."

"What else are sisters for?"

They hugged and she felt better about his speedy wedding. Just because she'd never been in love didn't mean it didn't happen like a lightning bolt for others.

The way her luck ran, lightning would strike her dead before she ever found a lifelong, enduring love.

When they eased apart, Jake said, "Does Cilla mention Tamsin to you?"

Rose shook her head. "Never."

"I've done something that I hope won't backfire." He swiped a hand over his face. It did little to erase the sheepishness. "I've invited Tamsin to the wedding."

"Seriously?" Rose slugged him on the arm. "You big oaf. You know their relationship is strained to the point of being nonexistent. Why would you do that?"

"Because Cilla deserves to be happy and I think despite Bryce being around, she's still obsessing over screwing things up with Tamsin."

Rose nodded, thoughtful. "Guess you're right." She grinned. "I take it you haven't told Cilla?"

He snorted. "Are you nuts? Tamsin didn't confirm whether she was definitely coming or not, and I don't want to get Cilla's hopes up."

Rose knocked on his head. "Good to hear you do have half a brain cell in there."

"Back off, Squirt." He poked her in the ribs and she laughed.

"Seriously, Jake, that's a good thing you did. Let's hope, for Cilla's sake, that Tamsin comes home."

If anyone deserved happiness, her aunt did. And maybe, with a lot of luck, she might get her own taste of happiness too. Yeah, and she'd be the next woman walking up the aisle. Never. Going. To. Happen.

"Why don't you invite Caden?"

Rose started and stared at Jake like he'd suggested she bring a rock star date. "What?"

"You know you want to." Jake's smirk made his eyes twinkle with mischief. "Come on, Sis. He's a good guy. Give him a chance."

"Butt out." She poked him in the chest. "Besides, I already have a date. Olly."

Jake snorted. "You're a sad case. You know that, right?"

"Just because you're in *luuuv* doesn't mean you can poke your nose into my romantic life." She stuck out her tongue.

"*Romantic* life?" He snapped his fingers. "See, I knew there was something going on between you and Caden." He slung his arm over her shoulders. "Seriously, Sis, ask him."

"You're a pain in the ass," she muttered, shrugging off his arm but tempering it with a smile.

Because the moment Jake had suggested she invite Caden, she couldn't dismiss the idea. It niggled and prodded and poked until all she could think about was him accompanying her.

Damn.

She didn't want to send Caden mixed messages. She'd wanted to cool things down between them. Inviting him to a small family wedding suggested otherwise.

But she'd love to have him there. He'd been so good to Olly. Good to her. It would be a nice gesture, a small way to thank him.

Which left her more confused than ever.

22.

After brunch with Rose last Sunday, Caden's week had gone downhill fast.

Since she'd told him she wanted to cool down their relationship so he could focus on his campaign, all he could think about was how much he'd rather heat it up. But whenever he'd tried to flirt or tell the odd corny joke, she'd shut him down. She'd been polite in the mornings when she'd dropped Olly off. Made small talk.

He'd played along, trying to give her time and space, but doing nothing to allude to how badly he wanted her.

God, did he want her.

Their night together had solidified what he'd suspected. They were good together. In and out of the bedroom.

And he had no intention of letting her go.

But if one night together had sent her bolting, no way in hell could he even hint at anything permanent. Instead, he'd bide his time, hoping she'd come around. Figuratively, not literally, which meant seeing her walk up the driveway and hesitate at the bottom step of his veranda was a huge step forward.

When she turned away, he opened the front door so fast it banged against the wall and made her jump and spin around.

So much for playing it cool. "Hey, I've just made a massive pot of stew. You hungry?"

She shook her head, her gaze darting all over the place. "I've just come from Sara's bridal shower and I ate there."

When she didn't move, shifting her feet on the spot like she didn't know whether to stay or flee, he asked, "Do you want to come in anyway?"

He tried to sound casual, like he didn't care if she accepted his invitation. But something in her eyes made him want to drag her in, sit her down and ply her with chocolate.

She looked . . . fragile. Like she needed a hug. He couldn't imagine Sara or Cilla hurting her, yet she had a wounded air, like they'd done just that.

She shot a wistful glance over his shoulder before taking a small step back. "I'm really tired after setting up the bridal shower—"

"All the more reason to relax and let me make you my world-famous hot cocoa." He held his hands a foot apart. "With marshmallows this big."

To his relief, a glimmer of a smile hovered on her glossed lips. Lips he remembered in exquisite, intimate detail. "Now I'll have to come in and show you up for using ridiculous exaggeration to lure a woman inside."

"Not just any woman," he said, with a wink. "Come on, it's getting chilly out here."

She followed him inside and slipped off her shoes at the door. A simple gesture for comfort, but he found himself staring at her feet and remembering how they looked entwined with his.

She'd painted her toenails blue this week, when they'd been ruby that night, to match her dress. And the fact he recalled such inconsequential trivia meant he had it bad. Real bad. Like he didn't already know.

"Take a seat and I'll bring it in." He pointed to the living room, saw her dart an anxious glance toward it and wondered if she feared he'd seduce her again.

Not that the thought hadn't crossed his mind. Hell, he was a red-blooded male in the presence of the woman who made his hormones sit up and howl.

But her shuttered expression and nervous fiddling with her handbag said it all. Rose wouldn't be up for a repeat of their last time on the sofa. Not now. Maybe not ever, if her standoffish posture was any indication.

He jerked a thumb over his shoulder. "Or you can come through to the kitchen if you'd like?"

"Sure," she said, her relief audible.

So much for his confidence that she'd enjoyed their night together as much as he had. She'd just kicked him right where it hurt the most: his ego.

They entered the kitchen and she made a beeline for the island bench, perching on a bar stool and slinging her bag underneath. "You have no idea how much I need a chocolate fix right now."

"That's why I offered," he said, switching off the stove and moving the pot of stew to a back burner. "You looked like you could do with a little TLC."

Her eyes widened in surprise, their glint speculative. "How do you do that? Know exactly what I want?"

"I could BS you about how compatible we are, how I'm tuned in where you're concerned, how I can read you like a book, or any other cliché you'd care to dish out."

"That's a lot of BS," she said, with a wry smile.

He chuckled as he spooned cocoa into milk in a saucepan and set it to simmer. "The truth is, I'm a bit of a mood stone."

She snorted. "Sounds like more BS to me."

"Don't you know sensitive guys know what their woman feels?"

"But I'm not your woman," she said, her tone reserved, her gaze pensive.

"I'd like you to be."

He threw it out there in the vain hope that if he said it often enough she might agree.

Instead, her eyes narrowed and her lips pursed in disapproval. "We've already had this discussion and I said we need to cool it." She jabbed a finger at the stove. "So you'd better make sure that delicious-smelling drink is the best hot cocoa ever or I'm outta here."

"Spoilsport," he said, pretending to knuckle tears from his eyes. "Okay, I'll quit bugging you to make an honest man out of me if you'll tell me what's wrong."

The amusement in her eyes faded and her shoulders slumped. "I had grand plans for the bridal shower but it fell flat."

"Why?"

"Sara's having a few minor hiccups with her pregnancy. Nothing serious, but enough to stress her out." She pinched the bridge of her nose. "Actually, that's the understatement of the year. She told me she's having doubts about marrying Jake if she loses the baby."

Hell, no wonder Rose looked so stressed. Considering Sara's first daughter had died and her marriage had fallen apart, she'd be petrified of losing her next child and repeating the pattern. Providing reassurance in a situation like that would be emotionally draining.

"She's okay though, right?"

"Yeah, for now." She pressed her fingers to her temples and rubbed a little. "When Jake came home, I voiced my concerns to him."

Caden propped himself against the bench, wishing the damn slab of marble would disappear so he could haul her into his arms and comfort her. "Didn't go well?"

She wrinkled her nose in that cute way he loved. "It was tense. But I had to say something." She stopped rubbing her temples and rolled her neck to ease the tension instead. "Jake's one of the good guys and I don't want to see him hurt."

Caden busied himself getting the marshmallows and mugs out. "Was it brutal?"

Rose shrugged. "Not really. He pretty much convinced me of his undying love for Sara and that nothing could keep them apart."

"Good for him." Caden turned off the stove and poured steaming cocoa into two mugs. "Maybe your fear for their relationship has more to do with you?"

"What do you mean?"

He searched her eyes, as if unsure of her reaction. "At the risk of you telling me to butt the hell out, sounds like Jake has been your go-to guy since you were kids. Maybe you're scared you'll lose his support now that he'll have a family of his own?"

"That's incredibly insightful of you," she said, her stare speculative as she studied him. "Let me guess. You completed a psychology degree in your spare time at college."

He topped the cocoa with giant marshmallows and slid a mug across the island bench toward Rose. "I don't think you have to worry. Jake's a good guy. He'd never let you down."

"I'll drink to that." She raised her mug and he did the same.

When she tried to take a sip, the marshmallows kept bumping her nose.

He tried to hide a smirk behind his mug but couldn't stop a guffaw slipping out.

Her eyes narrowed as she lowered the mug. "Is this some kind of test?"

"Yeah." He pointed to her face. "If that marshmallow touches your nose one more time, you owe me a kiss."

"In your dreams."

"You have no idea how often you feature in those, sweetheart."

Their lighthearted flirting gave him hope. All he could think was how easy it would be if she agreed to date him. To sit here every evening, swapping banter and stories about their days. To spend steamy nights together . . . He would give anything to wake up next to those big brown eyes every morning.

Eyes that filled with adoration when they'd looked at him during their momentous night together. Eyes that were usually guarded and jaded, yet could be guileless and sincere. Eyes that really *looked* at him like she could see all the way down to his soul.

She picked up the gooey marshmallows and popped them into her mouth, then proceeded to drink the cocoa.

"My kisses that repulsive?"

She tapped her temple, pretending to think. "I don't like being blackmailed into smooching."

"Then call it gentle persuasion."

She laughed, a light, joyous sound that made him wish she did it more often. "You're making this difficult."

"What's difficult?"

She fiddled with the mug handle, spinning the mug around and around on the bench. When it finally came to a stop, she raised her eyes to meet his. "Don't you find it odd I've kept my distance then suddenly showed up here today?"

He did, but he wasn't one to question good fortune. "You can't resist my charms despite all protestations to the contrary. I get it."

She made an adorable half-scoff, half-snort. "And I've rambled on about a bunch of stuff that happened over the last few hours that you're probably not interested in, but that's only because I'm on the verge of chickening out . . ." Her nose crinkled. "I really don't want to send you mixed messages. And I hope you won't misinterpret this . . . Ah, crap."

"You're talking in circles," he said, his curiosity piqued, her obvious discomfiture making him want to hug her. "Take a deep breath and tell me. Whatever it is, I can take it."

She glared at him, a frown furrowing her brow. "Come to the wedding with me," she blurted. "It's next weekend and I know it's short notice but I think you'll enjoy it. Very small. Family and close friends only. Should be fun . . ." She trailed off and pressed her palms to her cheeks. "I'm babbling."

Surprised she'd asked—and elated—he slid his cell out of his pocket and scrolled through his calendar with infinite slowness.

"Hmm . . . I'm booked solid next weekend—"

"Don't worry about it—"

"But for you I'll cancel my date with the cheerleading team." He grinned and ducked as she grabbed an apple from the nearby fruit bowl and threw it.

"Idiot," she said, amusement making her eyes gleam. Which was a hell of a lot better than her somberness when she'd arrived, or her awkwardness of a few moments ago when she'd hedged around the invitation. "But don't go reading too much into this, okay?"

"Like the fact you find me irresistible?" He squared his shoulders in pride. "I'll try not to."

The corners of her mouth curved upward before she chuckled, trying a mock frown and failing.

He loved making her smile. She had a beautiful smile that transformed her face from pretty to gorgeous. A smile that eased the perpetual tension bracketing her mouth. A smile that banished the shadows clouding her eyes.

"Seriously, I'd love to come." He picked up the apple and tossed it back into the bowl. "Thanks for asking."

She blushed, like it was the first time she'd asked a boy out, and it made him want to hug her all the more. "It's semi-formal, so suit and tie is fine."

"Shame. I was hoping to slip into my tux again." He pretended to smooth down imaginary lapels. "Because I got really lucky last time I wore it."

She didn't look away when he eyeballed her, daring her to remember the night of the ball. He expected her to ignore his playful jibe or to change the subject.

Instead, her expression turned wistful, like she was recalling everything that had happened during their sleepless night in vivid detail.

"Thanks for being a good friend," she said, standing and slinging her bag over her shoulder. "I know things between us are complicated, and I don't want to take things further at the moment, but maybe there's a reason for that."

She stepped around the bench and kissed him on the cheek. "We're too important to get it wrong."

He should've hauled her into his arms and kissed her senseless like he wanted to.

He should've convinced her to stay.

He should've said something other than a garbled agreement.

"Thanks for the chat and the hot cocoa." She paused on the threshold of the kitchen, her lips curving in a coy smile. "You were right. It was the best ever."

He let her go, reeling from her admission. It had sounded like she wanted there to be a "him and her" despite her protestations to the contrary. That she didn't want to muck it up because they were too important.

Hell.

Here he'd been, trying to play it cool over the last week, not wanting to push her, needlessly worrying she didn't want the same things as he did. But inviting him to partner her at the wedding was big, and her admitting to not wanting to progress their relationship *at the moment*—huge.

When he heard the front door close he sat on the stool she'd vacated and pondered another thing that had been bugging him since she'd revealed her concerns about Jake.

If Rose felt like she couldn't depend on Jake anymore once he was married, would she leave?

It hadn't occurred to him before now, because he knew Rose was a good mom and Olly came first. That's why she'd moved here in the first place.

But what if she felt like she was encroaching on her brother's marriage, that she'd taken up enough of his attention over the years?

What then?

23.

Buoyed by Rose's visit, Caden decided to ride into town on his old bike rather than drive. He used to do it a lot when he'd first moved back to Redemption, riding the tracks between the vineyards, to clear his head.

Today, he needed to burn off the frustration coursing through him that having Rose so close yet so far elicited. He appreciated her opening up to him and had struggled to hide his elation when she'd thanked him for taking things slow because she didn't want to get this wrong. But he couldn't shake the feeling she was stalling for a different reason.

That she didn't share the depth of feelings he had for her.

While they weren't at the stage to make any grand declarations—far from it—he wished he could get a better read on her feelings. They joked around, they chatted, they'd gotten physical, but he still didn't know what went on in her head.

Every time they talked about anything beyond the superficial, she'd get this look in her eyes. Like a cloud drifting across the sun. A shadow that lurked, ready to obliterate whatever secrets she had to reveal. A specter establishing emotional distance.

It made him think she was hiding something major from him and he hoped to God it wasn't a repeat of the past.

He'd been in this position before. Had ignored the niggle of misgiving that while his relationship with Effie appeared great on the surface, something sinister lurked beneath. At the time, he'd put it down to her whimsical soul, needing to keep a part of herself separate from their relationship. An independent woman like Effie would do that.

He'd half expected to find the apartment empty one morning, because a wanderer like her would move on when the need arose. Never in his worst nightmares had he expected her to vacate it because her secret addiction had killed her.

He knew Rose wasn't like Effie, but he couldn't help but see the similarities too. Rose was independent too. And she had secret demons, demons she'd recently faced at that recovery center. She also had the same air of bravado, like everything was great, yet an underlying hint that something still bothered her.

In turn, it bothered him. While he couldn't seem to breach her defenses, she could see every damn thing pinging around his head when he looked at her. Maybe that was part of the problem. He revealed too much.

Then again, maybe he was spending too much time dissecting every exchange, evaluating her behavior. He'd always been an overthinker. Analyzing everything to the nth degree. A trait that held him in good stead at work but annoyed the crap out of him in his personal life.

He needed to chill when it came to Rose.

Easier said than done.

Pedaling faster, he picked up the pace. As he coasted around a corner, he spied a car parked on the side of the road, a woman hunkered down next to the right rear tire.

She glanced up as he got closer and his heart sank. The last thing he needed while mulling over his relationship with Rose was an encounter with Tully.

The woman gave persistence a whole new meaning.

"Hey, do you mind giving me a hand? I'm hopeless with changing tires." She stood and straightened out a kink in her back. Caden tried to avert his gaze from the way she deliberately pushed out her breasts.

He'd seen her do the same move countless times during the campaign, trying to gain his attention. If she wasn't so damn good at rallying his team, he would've fired her weeks ago. If he could fire a volunteer.

"Sure. Helping damsels in distress is what I do in my spare time." He pulled over and propped his bike against a fence post, his sarcasm falling flat when she smiled at him like he'd found a cure for cancer.

"I was just on my way back from the city when the car starting swerving to the right."

"You did the right thing in pulling over," he said, biting back his first response, which was to wonder what the hell was she doing out on his back road if she was returning from the city.

"Thought I'd pop in and see you," she added, as if reading his mind. "See if you had any amendments to make to this week's schedule."

"I emailed them through last night." He pointed to the trunk. "If you can pop that, I'll get the jack and the spare out."

"Very organized," she said, folding her arms and flashing him a flirtatious glance from beneath her lashes. "You'll make a great mayor."

"Maybe," he said, keeping his answers noncommittal as he always did with Tully, in case she twisted his words or meaning.

"It's a certainty," she said, stabbing at a button on the remote in her hand and opening the trunk.

"The team's working well," he said, focusing on the campaign so she wouldn't push the flirtation routine as usual. "Regardless of what happens, you should all be proud."

"Thanks." She tilted her head, studying him. "I've had such a great time working alongside you, maybe once the campaign's done, I could work for your accountancy firm?"

"God no," he said, his vehemence garnering a frown she quickly blanked. "What I mean is, my office is at capacity staff-wise so we're good, thanks."

If he thought his blunt refusal would dampen her overt enthusiasm, he was mistaken. "Maybe when the campaign is done, we could spend some time together socially then?"

Hell. The woman was persistent. He grabbed the jack and hoisted the spare out of its holder. "We're friends, Tully. That's all, and I don't want to blur the lines for you."

Tully leaned against the car, pensive rather than annoyed at being rebuffed yet again. "You've never really given us a chance . . ."

Pink flushed her cheeks, like she'd said too much, and she glanced away, staring at some spot in the distance.

"Because I don't see you that way," he said, knowing they would've had to have this conversation at some stage but wishing it wasn't on the side of the road. "Friendship is all I can offer you, Tully."

"Fine," she said, sounding like it was far from it as she brought her attention back to him.

He wished he'd saved this conversation for another time when he glimpsed pain and embarrassment in her eyes.

"Is it because of *her*?" Tully's lips thinned, like she didn't want to discuss Rose. The feeling was entirely mutual.

"This doesn't involve anyone else, Tully." Caden levered the jack and pumped it several times to raise the car. "You know our parents have been trying to push us together for years, but I've made it more than clear we'll never be anything but friends."

An angry blush tinged her cheeks. "Clear as mud," she mumbled, her words frosty. "My folks and yours think we're practically engaged."

Crap. He'd never given off the vibe of a guy showing the remotest interest in her. In fact, he'd been downright blunt at times in rebuffing her overtures, treating her with amused disdain, like he had to tolerate her.

"Meaning?"

She huffed out a breath, like she couldn't believe he was this obtuse. "Friends can be a good platform to build something more. Something lasting."

"You can't be serious." He unscrewed the wheel nuts and maneuvered the tire loose. The faster he finished changing her flat, the better.

"Deadly." She tapped her foot, her pointy-toed shoe kicking up tiny puffs of dirt. "We'd be the golden couple of the district. We both come from respected families. We have similar life goals. We could have a solid future together."

He slid the spare tire on and started re-screwing the nuts as fast as humanly possible. "I'm not cut out for a marriage of convenience."

She snorted. "It wouldn't have to be."

She'd made that abundantly clear. But this had to stop. He needed to end Tully's hopes once and for all, so she wouldn't put them through this excruciating torture again in three months. Or six. Or even a year.

While he wracked his brains for an honest response that would convey his disinterest but not hurt her, she tut-tutted.

"Rose is a lucky lady."

The wheel brace slipped out of Caden's hand.

Her chuckle sounded far from amused. "You certainly don't waste any time. Hasn't she only recently moved to Redemption?"

Annoyed by her presumptuousness, he tightened the last wheel nut and stood. "We were childhood friends."

"She has a child." Tully studied him with disdain. "You must really like her to be willing to take on a kid too."

"Olly's great," he said, hating how defensive he sounded. He didn't owe this woman any explanations and her relentless pursuit was really bugging him.

"We're all done here." He replaced the tools in the trunk and slipped the punctured tire in too. "You'll need to get a new tire in town tomorrow."

"Thanks." She leaned forward, as if about to kiss his cheek, and he stepped back.

"You're welcome."

He waited until she started the engine, steered back onto the road and disappeared with a slight squeal of accelerator.

With a little luck, Tully had finally got the message that they'd never be more than friends.

Leaving him to pursue the woman who'd captured his heart without trying.

24.

Rose fussed around Sara, adjusting her veil and smoothing her skirt, glad the bride had asked her and Cilla to help her get dressed.

It kept her mind off how foolish she'd been in inviting Caden to accompany her to the wedding today. She'd initially done it to thank him for all he'd done for her. Though deep down she knew it was more than that. More to do with how bone-deep weary she was of always being the single one surrounded by couples. A wedding was guaranteed to make her feel lonelier than ever.

So after the bridal shower she'd gathered her courage and asked him. He'd been happy enough to accept. And then that same afternoon she'd seen him changing Tully's flat tire and her buoyant mood had soured fast.

Not that she'd seen anything overtly *couple-like* between them, but Tully's body language had been fairly indicative of a woman comfortable around a man. While Caden tended to her car and they chatted, Tully had repeatedly flicked her shiny blonde hair over her shoulder, pushed her chest out, smiled and stood with her feet pointing fairly and squarely at Caden.

At a distance, the scene had looked like two people relaxed in each other's company and Rose had made herself watch the entire exchange. Not out of some weird masochistic tendency, but to prove to herself what she'd already known.

Tully was the woman for Caden.

Poised, elegant, baggage-free.

Rose's exact opposite in every way.

Caden was her friend. She should be happy for him, should be thrilled he had a woman to match him. Instead, all she'd felt for the last seven days was a gut-wrenching sadness that she'd let herself hope for even one second that they could have a future.

When he'd picked her and Olly up for the wedding today, she'd been coolly polite, determined to present a brave face if it killed her. While he hadn't said anything, Caden had picked up on it, occasionally shooting her a concerned glance when he thought she wasn't looking.

The moment they'd arrived at the winery, she'd left Olly in his care and bolted for the sanctity of the bride's dressing room. Easier to ignore the pain tightening her chest when listening to Cilla gush over Sara's exquisite gown or trying to calm a pale Sara, who was on the verge of fainting when she discovered the tiniest grass stain on her ivory satin shoes.

"I need air." Sara fanned her face, terror tightening her mouth. "God, why did I ever agree to get married?"

"Uh, because you love my brother and he adores you right back?" Rose patted Sara's arm. "You know you want this."

Sara's lower lip trembled a little. "Yeah, I know. I'm being an idiot."

Cilla, fussing around the bottom of Sara's gown, glanced up. "You're in a funk. Entirely normal for a bride on her wedding day."

"But I've already done this before—" Sara bit her lower lip, looking horrified. "Crap, I'm a mess. That came out wrong. What I meant was I wasn't nervous at all the first time, so the fact I'm a basket case now must mean Jake's the one, right?"

"Of course, sweetie." Cilla stood and grabbed Sara's upper arms. "I was numb when I married Vernon. Didn't feel a thing." She snorted. "Which should've spoken volumes. So the fact you're nervous? A good sign."

Rose had never been close to an altar with a guy—and wouldn't be for a long time, if ever—so she kept quiet and opened the door to let some air in the room.

"You're right." Sara took several deep breaths and blew them out slowly. "I'm fine. Just an attack of last-minute nerves." She glanced at herself in the mirror and smiled. "I'm almost good to go."

Relieved a mini-crisis had been averted, Rose started tidying up the makeup paraphernalia, when she felt a stare boring into her back. Glancing over her shoulder, she saw a woman standing in the doorway, her expression guarded.

"Uh . . . Aunt Cilla, I think one of the guests has popped in for a preview of the dress," Rose said, keeping her voice low. "Though she looks rather intense."

Cilla glanced toward the door and froze, the comb in her hand falling and clattering onto the floorboards with a jarring clang.

She looked like she'd seen a ghost, her back rigid.

"Is everything okay, Auntie?" Rose hovered, ready to confront this woman causing her aunt such obvious distress.

But before she could move, Rose heard Cilla whisper, "Tamsin," and it all became clear.

Sara mouthed "daughter?" and Rose nodded, feeling intrusive as she watched the reunion unfold.

Sara must've felt it too, because she whispered, "Should we leave?"

Rose murmured, "You're the bride: we can't leave yet."

Cilla rarely spoke about Tamsin, so she had no idea if her aunt would welcome this impromptu visit or be thrown by it. In case it was the latter, she'd stick around. Cilla had supported her when she needed it most; the least she could do was return the favor.

Cilla took a few steps forward and waited, her uncertainty palpable. Leaving Tamsin to broach the distance between them.

As Tamsin entered the room, Rose wondered how she could've mistaken her cousin for a local. Tamsin wore a tailored designer suit that would've cost more than Rose made in a year. An ebony pinstripe skirt and jacket ensemble with a wide-collared ecru silk shirt beneath. Exquisite black suede pumps and matching handbag. Immaculate makeup. And hair that had been styled into a sleek brunette bob that skimmed her shoulders.

Rose had never known Tamsin well, had seen her only a few times when she'd visited Cilla's as a kid and Tamsin would hide away in her room, music blaring. The last time they'd crossed paths had been at Uncle Vernon's funeral. Back then, the sixteen-year age difference had seemed massive. Now, she felt like she could hold her own. Tamsin might have a career as a high-flying city lawyer, but Rose had a kid she doted on. She knew which she'd rather have.

"Hi, Mom." Tamsin paused when she reached them and only then did Rose glimpse the uncertainty beneath her poised mask.

Tamsin's eyes darted around as she took in their group. And she tugged at the hem of her jacket continually.

"Good to see you, Tam." Cilla moved forward and enveloped her in a hug that looked stilted and awkward rather than like a natural embrace between mother and daughter.

When they disengaged, neither woman had lost her wariness. They eyed each other with open speculation.

"Jake rang me and invited me to the wedding, so I thought I'd take some time off and come." Tamsin eyeballed Cilla, as if daring her to disagree. "Hope you don't mind. I wanted it to be a surprise."

"It's certainly that," Cilla said, sounding like she didn't know whether to scold her daughter for not ringing ahead or throw a party. "You're staying at home?"

"God, no," Tamsin said, her outburst not lost on her mother as Cilla recoiled slightly.

Tamsin winced. "Sorry, Mom, I didn't mean that the way it sounded. I don't want to be in the way with you and Bryce, so I booked accommodation here at the winery."

Cilla's shoulders slumped in relief. "The B&B here is beautiful."

Tamsin nodded, her hair swinging in a shimmering chocolate wave that Rose envied. "Seemed like the best option."

Before Rose could break the awkward silence, Sara held out her hand. "Hi, I'm Sara."

"Pleased to meet you. You look gorgeous." Tamsin shook Sara's hand. "Thanks for inviting me to the wedding."

"Our pleasure."

Rose saw the way Cilla glared at Sara. Apparently her brother and his blushing bride hadn't wanted to spoil the surprise and had kept the news of Tamsin's arrival to themselves.

Considering the emotional distance between mother and daughter, Rose thought they should've warned Cilla. Then again, maybe the happy couple hadn't wanted any tension before the wedding and didn't want to get Cilla's hopes up in case Tamsin pulled out at the last minute.

Interesting that she'd made the effort for family she hardly knew. From what Cilla had told her, Tamsin never took time off work, ever.

When Tamsin's curious gaze swung to her, Rose smiled. "Hey, Cuz. I'm Rose."

She deliberately chose an informal approach, wanted to see if she could rattle the elegant woman.

But Tamsin merely returned her smile. "You were tiny the last time I saw you."

"Eighteen years is a long time," Cilla said, the judgment in her tone cutting.

Looked like Cilla wasn't about to forgive or forget her daughter's absence.

"Would you like to join us?" Sara gestured at the crimson velvet chaise longue nearby. "We're just chatting, waiting for the ceremony to start so I can be fashionably late."

Tamsin took one look at Cilla's closed expression and said, "I don't want to intrude."

"You're not." Rose picked up a champagne flute and thrust it at Tamsin. "Here. You're family."

Tamsin hesitated, glancing at Cilla again, who merely sank into a chair like she couldn't give a damn.

Oh boy. The faster this ceremony got under way, the better. These two needed some serious one-on-one bonding time.

"So how's Jake coping with this speedy wedding?" Tamsin barely sipped at her champagne, which explained her trim figure. "He didn't tell me much beyond how much he adores you."

"He's a sweetheart." Sara smiled. "And the feeling's entirely mutual. As for the quickie wedding, lucky we had Cilla. She's been our rock and has virtually planned the whole thing."

The outer corner of Tamsin's eyebrow quirked, like she doubted the couple's sanity in assigning such a huge task to her mother or her mother's ability to complete said task. "But didn't you want more of a say in your wedding?"

"They trusted me," Cilla said, the glimmer of a frown appearing.

Which is more than you ever did hung unsaid in the air, which was so thick Rose could hardly breathe.

If her mother's jibe registered, Tamsin didn't show it. "The venue's beautiful from what I saw online and the little I saw outside. And the manager seemed lovely from his emails when I booked."

Cilla snorted. "That's James Winsome's MO. Trying to charm every woman he comes into contact with. Don't take it personally."

"Noted." Tamsin seemed to run out of small talk as Rose wondered anew what could keep a mother and daughter apart for almost two decades.

She would have given anything to have her mom around, a woman she could confide in one hundred percent, a woman to accept her faults and all, a woman who could be her best friend as well as her champion.

Tamsin had had that, yet she'd walked away. What had Cilla done that was so terrible?

Whatever their dreaded secret was, Rose hoped they confronted it and moved on.

"How did you manage time off work?" Cilla sat back in her chair and folded her arms, a classic defensive posture, and Rose could almost hear the gloves sliding off. "You're a busy lawyer."

Tamsin's eyes narrowed a little, the snark hitting home. "Actually, it wasn't so difficult. I've taken a month off."

Cilla was visibly startled. "You're staying around that long?"

"I might." Tamsin made it sound like a month in Redemption equaled a daily root canal for thirty days. "I've got a few things I need to sort out."

Hopefully top of that list of things was repairing her relationship with her mother, but given the tense standoff between these two, it would take a lot of compromising on both sides to achieve any kind of thaw.

When Cilla made an odd *hurrumph* sound, Sara jumped into the silence with "What kind of law do you practice? Criminal?"

"Corporate." Tamsin abandoned all pretense of drinking and put her glass down.

"The most lucrative," Cilla added, making Tamsin sound shallow and mercenary with three little words.

Anger pinched Tamsin's mouth and Sara glared at Rose, then made a subtle head jerk in the direction of the door.

Rose couldn't agree more. The faster they escaped, the easier it would be for these two to really slug it out.

"Thanks for keeping me sane, ladies, but I think we should get this show on the road." Sara stood and placed a hand on her belly, the simple reflexive action of mothers around the world.

However, there was nothing simple about Tamsin's reaction. She blanched, her pallor stark against her ebony suit.

Mistaking Tamsin's reaction for prudish shock, Sara chuckled. "I take it Jake didn't share the rest of our news?" Sara glanced down at her belly and glowed with pride. "This wasn't planned but we're ecstatic."

Tamsin visibly swallowed twice before responding. "Congratulations."

She sounded so strained that even Cilla stared at her with concern.

"I'll walk you out," Rose said, sliding an arm around Sara's waist, more to give her a hurry on than for support. "Coming, ladies?"

"Soon," Cilla said, eventually tearing her gaze away from her strange daughter.

"See you outside," Rose said, giving Sara a gentle shove in the direction of the door. "Good seeing you, Tamsin."

"Family calls me Tam," she said, shooting Cilla a quick glance, as if expecting confirmation or affirmation.

But Cilla had already started tidying up the bride's stuff and missed the wistful expression on her daughter's face.

"Let's go," Rose muttered, propelling Sara forward. Thankfully, her sister-in-law-to-be was only too happy to join her in a brisk walk to escape the confrontation waiting to happen.

Rose had valued her time re-bonding with her aunt over the last few months. Cilla was important to her. But there was something beneath Tamsin's polished exterior that called to her on an innate level . . . Rose recognized Tamsin as being on the edge. Like the slightest thing could push her over into an abyss she'd have difficulty recovering from.

Rose could empathize. She'd been there and thankfully come out on the other side.

For Tamsin's sake, she hoped her cousin could do the same.

25.

When Rose had first asked Caden to accompany her to the wedding, he'd seen it as a sign their relationship was progressing.

Now, as he stood in the front row, minding their seats as she went with Olly in search of a toilet before the bride arrived and the ceremony commenced, he wondered why the hell she'd invited him.

She'd been silent the entire car trip to the winery. Content to let Olly bombard them with questions, his usual exuberance magnified tenfold at the thought of seeing two of his favorite people, Jake and Sara, get married. The few times Caden had tried to engage her in conversation, she'd answered in monosyllables, her mind obviously elsewhere.

He'd put it down to the concerns she'd already expressed regarding this marriage, but deep down Caden wondered if there was more.

Had her demons resurrected their ugly heads again and she didn't want him to know? Or was her withdrawal a simple way of telling him she'd come to a decision and really didn't want anything beyond friendship between them?

Whatever was bugging her, he hoped to get to the bottom of it after the ceremony. He was done trying to read women's minds. It hadn't worked last time and look how that had turned out.

"Thanks for coming." The groom, obviously tiring of being the only one at the makeshift altar, stepped forward and held out his hand. "My sister looks happy for the first time in ages and I think I have you to thank for that."

"We're friends." Caden shook Jake's hand, not in the mood to be interrogated on his intentions toward Rose. "She needs a hand and I'm happy to help."

Jake's eyes narrowed slightly, his gaze speculative. "Rose hasn't dated since Olly was born, so the fact you're here at a private family wedding suggests you're more than friends."

Damn the guy for being so perceptive. Rose hadn't dated at all? That surprised him. A young, beautiful woman living in the city would've had guys bashing down her door. Which made him wonder why she'd shut herself off from men. Had her bastard ex done more of a number on her than he'd first thought?

As Jake continued to study him, Caden knew he'd have to give the guy some semblance of the truth. "I care about your sister."

"Good to know." Jake slugged him on the arm. "But in case you haven't figured it out, I've always looked out for her. I'm over-protective." He winked. "Which means if you hurt her, I'll have to kill you."

"Noted." Caden forced a tight smile, glad Rose had a brother like Jake to look out for her, considering how crappy her father had been. "For what it's worth, I'll do whatever it takes to make her happy."

Surprise flitted across Jake's face. "You two are that serious?"

"I'd like to be." Caden held up his hand and wavered it. "Your sister, not so much."

"She's been through a rough time." Jake slid a finger between his bow tie and collar, loosening it a bit. "Not that I'm trying to warn you off or anything, because you seem like a stand-up guy from all accounts, but Rose may need more time than you're willing to give to sort through her issues."

Caden wanted to ask "What issues?" but he didn't want to hear what was truly bothering Rose from Jake. He wanted to hear it from her, for her to show how much she trusted him.

Because the way he felt right at that moment sucked, big time. Like Rose was using him, happy to have him involved in fragments of her life without showing him the whole picture.

His mom's meddling came to mind: what did he really know about Rose Mathieson?

It soured his mood further.

With a brisk nod, Caden said, "Thanks for the advice. I'll keep it in mind."

"Good . . ." Jake trailed off, his attention riveted to something over Caden's shoulder. "Holy hell."

Caden turned and caught sight of the bride, waiting patiently at the end of the red carpet, her smile radiant as she locked gazes with her groom.

"You're a lucky man." Caden slapped Jake on the back and gave him a gentle shove toward his spot under the flower-covered arbor.

Jake didn't answer, too busy trying to shut his gaping mouth, and Caden grinned. The guy was smitten. Not that he could blame him. The few times he'd met Sara she'd seemed like a lovely woman, someone who'd survived the loss of her child and a marriage breakdown and come out on top. He admired her ability to take a risk, considering what she'd been through.

He hoped Rose would be willing to do the same.

"Olly, come on. We're going to miss it." Rose slid in beside him, tugging on Olly's hand and barely glancing at Caden.

"Sara looks like a princess," Olly said, hopping from one foot to the other. "And Uncle Jake is her prince."

A tight smile played around Rose's ruby-glossed mouth and Caden had no idea if it was because she still harbored doubts about this wedding or she was pissed at him for something.

"Would you like to play princes and princesses one day?" Caden murmured under his breath, bumping her with his hip.

She sent him a scathing glare that left him under no illusion that he was the cause of her funk. If only he knew why.

The sounds of a harp prevented him from asking as Jake straightened and tugged the ends of his jacket, his slightly fearful gaze fixed on his bride as she drifted up the aisle toward him.

To the bride's credit, she never faltered once, her steps sure and steady as she broached the distance between her and the groom, until she was standing alongside Jake, smiling at him.

Caden didn't know a lot about weddings, having been to only a few of his college buddies' when they tied the knot. Grandiose affairs with countless bridesmaids decked out in gaudy satin and sleazy groomsmen debating which of the bridesmaids would end up drunkest and most likely to be up for a quickie in the broom closet.

But this wedding was very different, in a good way. Cilla had done an amazing job pulling it together on short notice, creating an intimate atmosphere in the shadows of the vineyard with the white wooden chairs tied with alabaster satin bows, an arbor covered in gardenias, a string quartet alongside the solo harpist and a minister who beamed at the happy couple like they were his own children.

He liked the lack of artifice, the informality of a garden wedding. It seemed more natural somehow, like two friends pledging their lives to each other without all the fancy trimmings.

As Jake and Sara exchanged vows, he felt Rose stiffening beside him. Hoping to allay her worries, he reached for her hand, intertwining his fingers with hers. He expected her to pull away, and when she didn't, he relaxed.

He squeezed her hand and sensed her looking at him. When he glanced her way, he glimpsed the sheen of tears in her eyes and his throat tightened. She looked so vulnerable, like the slightest breeze would blow her over, and his grip on her hand tightened.

She stared at him like she wanted to say something and as the minister pronounced Jake and Sara husband and wife she leaned toward him. He bent lower, expecting her to whisper in his ear. Instead, her lips grazed his cheek in a fleeting kiss that was so soft he could've imagined it.

When they straightened, he quirked an eyebrow and she gave the barest shake of her head, sorrow darkening her eyes to molasses.

She couldn't be sad about the wedding, which could only mean one thing.

Something was wrong with them.

Drastically wrong.

Caden's gut tightened in dread as he smiled during the longest kissing of the bride in history, during the flinging of the rose petals over the happy couple, during the playing of some haunting song that hinted at love and happily-ever-after. And the sick feeling didn't let up as the small wedding party strolled toward the back of the winery, where a mini dance floor and buffet table had been erected along a shaded veranda.

Rose had deserted him after the couple had waltzed back up the aisle, on the pretext of chasing after Olly to stop him from throwing too many petals.

But Caden knew better. She was avoiding him, and whatever that all-too-brief kiss tinged with sadness had been about, he hoped it hadn't been a good-bye.

❧

Rose's antipathy for weddings kicked in as she watched her brother marry Sara, and felt little beyond warm affection for the happy couple.

She had no grand hopes to get married. In fact, the thought of being tied to one guy for the rest of her life made her edgy.

Then again, as she glanced at Olly cavorting under the floral arch where Jake and Sara had exchanged vows ten minutes ago, she realized she already was.

Though being a mother and being a wife were poles apart. A kid would love her unconditionally no matter how much she screwed up—or had done so in the past. A husband wouldn't be so understanding.

"They look happy." Caden leaned in close to murmur in her ear. "Do you think that's something you'd like to do one day?"

Rose stiffened, hoping he meant in general and not to him. If entering into any kind of relationship with Caden scared her, contemplating a long-term commitment like marriage terrified her.

Caden was a keeper. The kind of guy who'd expect more kids and would dote on them and her. Who'd expect to raise their family in the same house he'd grown up in. Who'd want to hold her hand when they were old and grey. Who'd have high expectations that she'd eventually fall short of.

Because if there was one thing Rose knew, it was that no matter how much you did for another person, no matter how hard you tried to make them happy, they eventually grew tired of you and didn't appreciate anything.

Caden was one of the good guys, she knew that. But she also knew that marriage could deteriorate into a prison to be tolerated. She'd seen it with Cilla and Uncle Vernon. How much her aunt had done for him, striving to provide the perfect meals and keep a perfect house. Doing whatever it took to please him. She'd been verbally abused for her troubles. And the fallout resulted in her aunt shutting herself off emotionally for twenty years.

Not that Caden was anything like her uncle, or her father for that matter, but Rose had no intention of putting herself into a position to find out. Her self-esteem had always been low courtesy of her father. She didn't need to enter a full-blown adult relationship only to have the fact rammed home that regardless of her efforts to make it work, she wasn't good enough.

That's what had hit her during the ceremony, as Jake and Sara exchanged vows: that no matter how hard she tried to fit into Caden's world, she'd never be good enough.

She didn't wear the perfect clothes or style her hair to perfection. She couldn't stand beside him on a stage and act like the mayor's proud partner. And she'd be foolish to put herself in that position, knowing it would stress her out, potentially triggering a relapse where she'd start depending on alcohol again to unwind.

For that's exactly what entering into a relationship with Caden the mayoral candidate would do: stress her out. In a small town like Redemption, she'd always be found lacking. People gossiped. They'd discover her past. They'd judge. And they'd take it out on Caden.

No way in hell would she be responsible for him losing out on a prestigious position.

She could move away to protect Olly, but once the damage of having been involved with her was done, who would protect Caden?

Once the realization hit, a bone-deep sorrow had filled her, flowing through her veins and seeping into her muscles until it had taken every ounce of willpower not to cry.

Caden had picked up on her distress, had provided stoic comfort when she needed it most. But she'd known in that moment that their relationship couldn't go anywhere and she'd have to end it before it had a chance to really begin.

"Too tough to answer?" he asked.

So she forced a laugh. "Being shackled to one person for the rest of my life? Think I'll pass."

He straightened and stepped away, and she immediately missed his closeness. "We all need to settle down some day."

"When I feel like it I'll let you know."

She'd meant it as a flyaway comment, and realized her mistake too late as he visibly flinched.

"I'm a patient man, Rose. You asked to cool things down; I'm doing that." The indigo flecks in his eyes darkened with anger and regret. "But I won't wait around forever."

He stalked away, shoulders rigid with disappointment.

Damn, she was making a mess of this.

Then again, what was new? She had a habit of wrecking everything she laid her hands on.

"You look like someone snatched the bouquet out of your hands." Her cousin Tamsin appeared by her side, as Rose wished everyone would leave her the hell alone so she could have a pity party in peace.

"I'm having a moment." Rose scowled, hoping it would encourage her cousin to leave.

It didn't.

"I have those moments all the time." Tamsin pointed to a wrought-iron bench under a willow nearby, hidden away from other guests. "Let's hide out for a while."

Rose didn't enjoy heart-to-hearts with women in general, especially those she hardly knew, but something in Tam's tone made her think her cousin needed to chat more than she did.

She'd noticed the odd expression on Tam's face every time she glanced at the bride during the ceremony. Like she'd wished it was her getting married.

Considering her age—Rose had done the math and figured Tam had to be early forties—it wasn't surprising. Though the last thing Rose needed right now was a maudlin cousin waxing lyrical about how she wanted the big white dress and veil.

Wanting to go on the offensive to avoid discussing her own problems, Rose said, "Are you seeing anyone in the city?"

"No. You?"

"Would I be holed up here if I was?"

Tamsin nodded in Olly's direction. "You might be if you were doing it for his sake."

"You're perceptive." Rose followed Tam's line of vision and smiled when she saw Olly trying to dance with Jake and Sara. "He has flourished since he's been in Redemption."

"Which is why you're still here."

"What's your excuse?" Rose couldn't help the snark. She wanted to brood and sulk in peace for driving Caden away, perhaps once and for all. Tamsin was interfering with that.

"I came for Jake's wedding—"

"Cut the crap. You haven't been home in almost two decades, so why would you return now for the wedding of a cousin you barely know?"

To her surprise, Tamsin chuckled. "You don't pull any punches."

"I have a low tolerance for bullshit." Rose shrugged. "I've seen too much and done too much to tolerate lies."

"Then why are you living one?"

"Excuse me?" Rose frowned and glared at the cousin who knew jack about her. "You don't know the first damn thing about me—"

"I know that man over there is crazy about you." Tamsin pointed at Caden, deep in conversation with Bryce. "He can't look at you without lighting up. It's sickening." Her tone softened. "But kinda sweet too. I wish I had someone that ga-ga over me. So why aren't you with him?"

"It's complicated," Rose said, sincerely wishing it wasn't.

Nothing would make her happier than to embrace a relationship with Caden, to create a real home for Olly and live happily ever after. But she'd given up believing in fairy tales a long time ago.

"Every freaking thing worth fighting for is complicated," Tamsin said, sounding like she'd learned the hard way too. "Is it your dad? Because if he was anything like mine, he would've screwed you up real good."

Startled by Tam's honesty, Rose waited for her to say more.

"He kept me away from my home, even after his death eighteen years ago." Tam's expression softened as she stared at Cilla, tossing back champagne with abandon. "I blamed Mom for so much, when I was the one with the problem. Thanks to *him*. So don't let it stop you from going after what you want."

Impressed by Tam's insightfulness but increasingly uncomfortable being analyzed, she turned the spotlight on her.

"What do you want?"

Confusion creased Tam's brow. "What do you mean?"

"You barely know Jake and me, so showing up for his wedding is out of character."

Tam eyed her with respect. "I've stayed away long enough. It's time I made peace with Mom."

Rose couldn't agree more. "Did you and Cilla talk earlier?"

Tam shook her head. "I chickened out. Bolted out of the room not long after you did, saying I didn't want to hold up the wedding. But I will talk to her."

"Don't leave it too long. Your mom's amazing."

Tam nodded, her expression grave. "I'm staying around for a few weeks in the hope we can sort things out. I've worked at my firm a long time so I've got stacks of leave owing."

"Lawyers take vacations? I thought you were workaholic, driven drones with no souls."

She'd meant it as a joke but Tam's expression crumpled a little.

"Shit, I'm sorry. I didn't mean it—"

"It's okay," Tam said, with a wobbly smile. "You described me to a tee 'til recently."

Curious, Rose said, "What changed?"

Tam took an eternity to answer, and to Rose's horror, her eyes filled with tears.

"God, you must think I'm pathetic," Tam said, dabbing the corners of her eyes with the tips of her little fingers. "I guess being at a wedding reinforces that I want more than a career. I'm supposed to have this amazing life, being the high-flying lawyer in a glamorous city. But I'm forty-freaking-two, single and my job is my life. Plus, I've screwed up everything with Mom over the years . . ."

Tam trailed off on a small sob and Rose slid her arm around her cousin's shoulder, flattered she'd confided so much but helpless to know how to comfort her.

"Sorry." Tam swallowed a sniffle. "I'm such a sad case. Please ignore everything I said."

"Hey, at the risk of sounding trite, everything will be okay." Rose squeezed her shoulders, feeling helpless to comfort the cousin she barely knew. "And you're here now, so you can fix things with your mom."

"Who made you so wise?" Tam leaned into her a little. "Do you realize I'm sixteen years older than you?"

"Who gives a flying fig? We're cousins; that's all that matters."

"And hopefully we can become friends," Tam added, sounding optimistic. "I'm glad I came back to town."

"Me too," Rose said, removing her arm when Tam straightened. "Guess having fathers who were bastards bonds us like nothing else."

"True." Tam pointed at Caden. "So what are you going to do about him?"

"Damned if I know." Rose watched Bryce head toward Cilla, leaving Caden alone. But not for long. Within five seconds Olly had bowled up to him, tugging on his jacket to say something.

Caden knelt, his expression softening at whatever Olly had murmured in his ear. Then the two men in her life looked at each other like co-conspirators and high-fived.

Seeing them that close hit Rose hard and she absentmindedly rubbed her chest. Caden would be a great dad. But she didn't want to enter into a relationship for the sake of her son, no matter how wonderful Caden could be as a father.

"Want to know what I think?" Tam elbowed her. "Because I'm going to tell you regardless."

"Go ahead."

Even though she didn't know Tam well, Rose liked her cousin's bluntness.

"If you've got a good thing going with Mr. Handsome over there, don't muck it up." Tam blew out a long breath. "Or you'll end up like me. Alone in your forties and wishing you hadn't been so damn picky along the way."

"You're not doing so badly," Rose said. "You've got a great career and an interesting life in one of the best cities in the world."

"And I'd give it all up in a heartbeat to have a guy like that look at me the way he looks at you," Tam murmured, her voice husky. "Anyway, I've got a bottle of champagne with my name on it over at the bar so I'll see you later."

"Sure." Rose stood alongside Tam, touching her cousin's arm before she walked away. "Hey, if you ever want to drop around, I make the best brownies in town."

Tam's eyes lit up, making Rose wonder how many female friends her cousin had. "Thanks. I'd like that."

As Tam headed for the bar, Caden drew Rose's gaze again. He was holding Olly's hand, their arms swinging in unison, as they strolled toward the dessert table.

Rose's chest tightened to the point where she had to sit again.

She could be a part of that if she wanted. Holding hands with Caden. Forever.

He chose that moment to glance over his shoulder and lock gazes with her. Hers conflicted, his flinty.

She willed him to understand how difficult this decision was for her.

Instead, he gave a little shake of his head, like he couldn't believe she was putting them through this, and walked away.

26.

When I grow up, I'm going to marry a girl as pretty as Sara," Olly murmured, snuggling into Caden's arms, his eyelids almost closed. "What about you, Caden?"

"I certainly hope so, buddy." Caden locked eyes with Rose over Olly's head as he gently laid the boy in his bed.

Predictably, she looked away.

Clamping down the disappointment, he slipped off Olly's shoes and pulled the covers over him. "Goodnight, Olly. Sleep tight."

He heard a mumbled, "Don't let the bedbugs bite," as Olly drifted off to sleep.

Caden allowed himself the luxury of watching the boy sleep for a moment. A bundle of energy when awake, Olly looked like an innocent cherub when slumbering.

Caden swallowed the inevitable resentment against Rose when he turned away from Olly and caught her staring at him with those wide eyes filled with wariness.

He could stick around and try to convince her yet again of why they should be together, of how much he'd like to tuck Olly in every night. But he'd tried everything to make her open up and take a chance on her feelings, to no avail. Her flippant response to his question regarding marriage at the wedding earlier had been the proverbial last straw.

Time for some tough love.

That meant walking away from her every time he was inclined to stay and make her believe in them.

Starting now.

He followed her out of Olly's room and closed the door. "Thanks for inviting me to the wedding."

The corners of her lush mouth curved upward. "It was a great day."

It had been, until she'd shot him down in a blazing heap after he'd hinted at a forever after. So as part of his grand last-ditch plan to treat her a little mean and hopefully keep her a lot keen, he nodded in agreement and headed for the door.

"Would you like a coffee?" She fiddled with her watchstrap, her fingers plucking at the clasp. "We need to talk—"

"No thanks." He willed his feet to keep moving despite their instinct to stay. Because he had a strong suspicion he wouldn't like what she had to say. "Early start tomorrow."

"It's Sunday," she said, disappointment lacing her tone.

Welcome to the club. He didn't mean to be petty, but every overture she ignored left a disappointment he was tired of swallowing.

"Can I ask you something?" He paused at the doorway, knowing he should leave but needing to know what was really biting her ass so he wouldn't be up all night pondering. "Why did you invite me to the wedding?"

"Because you're a good friend—"

"If this is how you treat friends, I'd hate to see how you treat your enemies." He sounded bitter and felt like a bastard when she blinked as if he'd struck her.

"I'm sorry if inviting you to the wedding sent the wrong message . . ." She sagged against the wall, like the simple act of standing was too much. "You're an incredible guy and I value our friendship, but that's where it has to end."

Hating how every word slashed at his hopes, he snorted. "Don't you think we've moved past the old 'let's just be friends' routine?"

She blushed. "We're heading in different directions. You're on a fast track to mayor and I don't have a freaking clue if I'll even stick around. Can't you see it's pointless to start something with an inevitable expiration date?" She shook her head. "I can't do that to Olly. I won't."

Damn, she was leaving? Was that the reason she'd totally withdrawn?

"I get it. Olly has to be your priority. But don't you think it's worth taking a risk on having something wonderful, even if only in the short term, rather than not taking a chance at all?"

She worried her bottom lip with her teeth, her gaze darting around the room like she'd rather look anywhere than at him. "I'm not a risk taker. Especially when it involves my son."

He couldn't argue with that. In fact, he was done trying to convince her they'd be great together. Maybe leaving her alone for a while might work where his persistence hadn't?

"See you later, Rose." He yanked open the door and was five feet away from the garage when she called out.

"I'm sorry."

He didn't break stride as he flung over his shoulder, "So am I, babe. So am I."

Weariness seeped through him as he let himself into the house and slammed the door without looking back.

He couldn't do this anymore.

Couldn't keep putting himself out there with Rose, only to have her jiggle his strings like a goddamn puppeteer.

Something had to give, and he had a sinking feeling it was him.

He slipped off his jacket, tugged off his tie and flung them both on the sofa. His usual Saturday night ritual of watching sitcom reruns didn't appeal so he headed for the den. Maybe losing himself in boring tax documents would dull the pain.

Because that soul-deep ache that kept gnawing like a persistent tooth abscess wouldn't go away in a hurry, no matter how many ballsy decisions he made to toughen up when it came to Rose.

Walking away from her a few minutes ago had been the hardest thing he'd done in a long time.

He could be holed up in the cozy apartment over the garage right now. Sharing coffee and cake and conversation. Flirting a little. Orchestrating the occasional touch. But they'd done that dance and it hadn't got him anywhere. Much smarter to try a different approach.

He wanted Rose in his life. Permanently.

He wanted to shout it from the top of Redemption's highest hill.

If only the woman in question would agree.

Scowling, he fired up his computer and opened the last file he'd been working on. His eyes glazed a little at the numbers so he checked his inbox out of habit rather than necessity, surprised to find one titled ROSE MATHIESON: PRIVATE.

Hoping some scammer hadn't hacked either of their accounts, he scrolled down to scan the email.

His heart stopped.

Someone had investigated Rose and laid out her most private details.

Like her affair with celebrity chef Dyson Patrice, a notorious playboy who'd died of a drug overdose while partying in the Hamptons.

Her teenage pregnancy citing Dyson as the father.

Her father's untimely death.

And most recently, citing her battle with the bottle as the reason for her stint in rehab.

Hell.

He rubbed his hand over his face, but it didn't scrub away the awful sordidness from seeing Rose's privacy invaded and her secrets laid bare. Whoever had sent this to him thought he didn't know about her past. But he did, so they'd wasted their time.

Then his gaze landed on the last line and he knew this wasn't just about Rose. It was a threat to him too.

THIS INFORMATION WILL BE MADE PUBLIC IN A RELENTLESS SMEAR CAMPAIGN TO RUIN HER REPU-TATION AND BY ASSOCIATION, STOP YOU RUNNING FOR MAYOR. SO DISTANCE YOURSELF FROM ROSE MATHIESON OR FACE THE CONSEQUENCES.

Shit, who would do something like this?

Caden's blood chilled as his mind leapt to the obvious conclusion: his mother. But her dream was to see him elected mayor, so it didn't make sense for her to taint his campaign this way.

Unless she was trying to call his bluff? Expecting him to walk away from Rose for a shot at being mayor?

If so, she was in for a rude shock. While being mayor would enable him to do a lot for this community and shake up his mundane life, he'd give it away in a heartbeat if it meant losing Rose.

A no-brainer decision.

The problem was, if it wasn't his mother behind this, who else would care enough to threaten him?

Tully.

He'd rejected her overtures so many times. Yet she kept persisting in the vain hope they'd end up a couple. And she had a PI friend she'd used to get the dirt on his mayoral competitors, something he'd admonished her for. What if she'd used that PI to get this information on Rose?

After his last snub, when he'd changed her tire, he'd got the impression she finally got it. That they'd never have a chance. Not that his rejections had stopped Tully from pursuing him in the past, though. The woman couldn't take no for an answer.

But his theory that Tully could be behind this had a major flaw: Tully would never ruin his campaign for mayor. It was the one place where they got to spend time together and she wouldn't wreck that.

Which could only mean one thing.

His mother had to be the perpetrator of this travesty.

Outrage warred with disbelief as he re-read the email. He didn't want to believe it. Couldn't believe his mother would do something like this. But sadly, the niggle in his gut couldn't be ignored. He'd seen his mom fight for what she believed in over the years, from petitioning the state for a new church to driving out a minority alternative religion that dared to want to set up house in Redemption.

Nothing stopped Penny Shoreham from getting what she wanted. She'd made it pretty bloody obvious from the outset that Rose wasn't good enough for him.

It had to be her.

Swallowing the bile that rose to his throat, he shut down the computer and started pacing. His first instinct, to drive over to his parents' town house and confront her, had to be tempered. The way he was feeling now, he'd instantly cut off all further contact with her and that would be the end of it. But he had no proof, and their relationship had already been strained lately following the last time he'd done this very thing, when his mother had confronted Rose at the park. It would do irreparable damage if he ranted at her again tonight for something she hadn't done.

It would be better to think this through rationally, and if he still couldn't ignore his gut instinct in the morning he'd confront her then.

For a day that had started off with so much promise, it had turned to shit pretty damn quick.

He'd turned his back on Rose deliberately at the wedding, he'd ostensibly given up on their relationship fifteen minutes ago, and now this.

As he trudged upstairs, he realized he was more pissed at the thought of anyone smearing her reputation than any possible damage to his campaign.

In fact, he'd happily walk away from being mayor to protect Rose.

If his mother was behind this, he'd enjoy ramming that fact down her throat.

27.

Rose didn't give herself time to second-guess her decision. She changed out of her dress, slipped into yoga pants, a hoodie and sneakers, grabbed the baby monitor and locked up.

Olly had sleepwalked on occasion when they'd been living in New York and she'd taken to using the baby monitor in his room to ensure she didn't wake up one morning to find him gone. He'd also had infrequent nightmares since she'd returned from the recovery center and this way she could hear when he needed comforting.

It also came in mighty handy for leaving her son for a few minutes while she confronted the guy who'd stolen her heart without trying.

The desolation on Caden's face when he'd left thirty minutes ago . . . She couldn't stand it. She wouldn't be able to sleep, knowing he thought she was a flighty bitch who kept yanking his chain. Because that's how he had to see her, the way she kept vacillating over their relationship.

They couldn't go on like this. *She* couldn't go on like this. It sure as hell wasn't fair to him.

She had two options.

Tell him the whole truth.

Or end it between them and walk away completely.

As she ran across the garden toward his house, she knew what she had to do. It made her feel physically ill.

Taking the front steps two at a time, she pounded on his door, her bravado fading when it took him an eternity to answer.

When he did, she wished he'd taken longer. Making the decision to move out and end their relationship had been hard. Caden made it harder by appearing at the door shirtless, with a towel knotted at his waist.

She tried not to stare, she really did, but her greedy gaze ate him up. The defined pecs and abs, the muscled chest, the light tan, the smattering of hair that arrowed low on his belly . . .

She made some weird half-strangled sound and masked it with a cough. From the knowing glint in his eyes, he didn't buy it for a second.

"Is everything okay?" He tightened his hold on the towel as her inner vixen wished the damn thing would disintegrate.

"Yeah, Olly's worn out so he'll sleep 'til the morning." She shifted her weight from side to side, increasingly uncertain she was doing the right thing. "I've got the monitor so I can hear him if he needs me, and I was hoping we could talk for a minute?"

For a horrifying second Rose thought he might slam the door in her face, he looked that unwelcoming.

But then he shrugged in resignation and swung the door wider. "Come in. I'll get dressed and be down in a sec."

She bit back her first retort, "Don't get dressed on my account." This wasn't the time for flirting. It was the time to figure out what the hell she would say to make this easier on both of them.

She watched Caden climb the stairs, appreciating the shift of back muscles beneath his smooth skin, admiring his muscular legs. He was such a beautiful man, inside and out. Yet here she was, preparing to break his heart.

That was the problem, though. His perfection. If she were to take a massive risk on a relationship, would he end up finding her lacking somehow?

She liked how he looked at her. Like he could see beneath her ornery surface to the softer woman beneath. He'd quickly become an invaluable friend and accepted her, faults and all. Could she handle having her closest friend in the world turn his back on her when he knew the truth?

She entered the living room and set the monitor down, ensuring the sound was set to maximum. She'd hate for Olly to wake and panic if he found her missing. She'd had night terrors as a kid—no great surprise considering the monster she lived with every day—and Jake would comfort her. He'd cuddle her and tell her fairy tales until she drifted back to sleep. He'd be a great dad.

Just like Caden.

The thought popped into her head, ramming home the momentous decision she had to make.

Closing her eyes, she rubbed her temples, willing the pressure in her head to ease. She didn't get headaches usually but it had been a long day and she had a lot to consider, so no surprise the pain behind her eyes had intensified in the last half hour.

She heard footsteps descending the stairs and her palms grew clammy. Swiping them down the sides of her yoga pants, she stared at the sofa, unsure whether to sit or stand or make a run for it.

When Caden stuck his head around the door, she was still standing like a doofus in the middle of the room.

"Would you like a coffee?"

With her shredded nerves making her jumpy, that was all she needed—a caffeine hit. Then again, she'd be sleepless tonight anyway, regardless of the outcome.

She nodded. "Thanks. That'd be great."

He didn't invite her to follow him into the kitchen like last time, which spoke volumes about how their relationship had deteriorated. But the way she kept pushing him away, what did she expect?

She perched on an armchair, her gaze repeatedly drawn to the sofa where they'd made out, and made love, the night of the ball. It felt like a lifetime ago, the sheer exhilaration of forgetting her responsibilities—and her past—for one incredible night.

"Here you go." He re-entered the living room and placed her mug on the coffee table. "It's hot, so give it a minute to cool."

"Thanks."

With nothing to stop her fingers fiddling, she clasped them tightly in her lap.

"Something on your mind?" He sat in a chair opposite, avoiding the sofa as much as she was. Yeah, his mindset had definitely changed.

He'd also lost the flirtatious twinkle in his eyes. In fact, when he looked at her now, all she could see was sadness.

Great. Just freaking great.

She'd screwed this up big time.

"Yeah, I wanted to talk," she said, searching for the right words and coming up empty.

"Actually, I wanted to talk to you too." He sounded so solemn she couldn't help but think he might end this before she'd had a chance to explain. "Do you have any enemies back in the city? Anyone who'd want to discredit you?"

Whatever Rose had been expecting, that wasn't it.

She shook her head. "I don't have enough friends to make enemies out of them. Olly took up all my time. When I wasn't working, I was with him."

"Jake said you haven't dated anyone."

"No." Rose didn't count a quickie with a waiter in the alley behind the kitchen at the restaurant where she'd worked as a date. More like a tension release. "Why?"

He sighed and placed his untouched coffee on the table between them. "Because someone has had you investigated. Dredged up every detail of your past. And emailed it to me, threatening to go public to embarrass you."

Shocked to her core that someone would go to that much trouble, she scooted to the edge of her chair, wishing she hadn't sat so far away, trying to get a read on his expression. "Why would they send it to you?"

The moment the question popped out of her mouth, she knew the answer.

Blackmail.

Anger sparked in his eyes. "If I don't distance myself from you, they'll go public with the information," he said, disgust twisting his mouth.

"And ultimately ruin your bid for mayor," she added, the enormity of the situation sinking in. "Who would do something like this?"

His gaze shifted away, like he couldn't meet her eyes. "That's why I asked if you had any enemies."

"But I don't have any . . ." She trailed off, the truth detonating and making her head ache more.

Only one person had made it obvious how much she despised her hanging around Caden.

His mother.

He knew it too, because when he finally met her gaze, she saw the resignation in his.

"I'm going to confront her in the morning." He clasped his hands behind his head and leaned back, his expression pained. "I can't believe she'd do something like this."

"Already told you—mothers will do anything to protect their sons."

"But this?" His grimace made her want to hug him. "Surely she knows I wouldn't . . ."

He looked away again, more tortured than she felt. She had to ask, even though the answer terrified her.

Surely he wouldn't give up everything he'd strived for with this campaign for her?

"Wouldn't what?" She held her breath as he eventually dragged his gaze back to hers.

"Wouldn't walk away from you," he said, so softly she had to lean forward to hear.

Those five words solidified Rose's resolve to end this.

She couldn't let him risk everything for a future with her. Not when she was inherently flawed and would ultimately let him down.

Initially, she'd come over here to tell him she was moving out and ending any hopes he might be harboring for a future. But she'd also toyed with telling him the truth and letting him decide whether she was worth the risk. But now?

She couldn't tell him how much she'd fallen for him.

She couldn't tell him anything.

What she could do was make the decision for him easy.

She could walk away.

But in order to do so, she'd have to tell a whopping lie guaranteed to drive him away once and for all.

"Don't stand by me." She stood, willing the hurtful words to tumble from her numb lips. "That's why I wanted to talk to you tonight. Seeing Jake and Sara marry made me see how we couldn't have the same thing."

She dragged in a breath and let it out slowly, the monstrous lie lodging in her throat like a stone. "I'm never going to change my mind, Caden. I don't love you, so it's not worth you protecting me."

He stared at her with heart-wrenching devastation, and her legs turned to jelly.

She'd done that to him. Her. With her stringing him along and her selfishness.

She'd never be able to forgive herself.

Unable to tolerate his shattered stare one moment longer, she forced her feet to move toward the door.

"Is that really what you came here to tell me?" He was by her side in an instant and she regretted not making a run for it. She could keep her voice steady but no way could she hide the pain in her eyes, on her face. "Because I don't believe you."

She reached for the doorknob but he grabbed her arms and spun her around to face him, leaving her staring at the buttons on his polo top. She had to stay focused on those damn buttons, because if she looked up and met his eyes, she'd be lost.

"Look at me," he said, his tone cold and commanding.

"I—I can't." Her voice hitched and she swallowed a sob, a stabbing pain ripping her in half from gut to chest. The devastating pain of loss.

"Why not?" He gave her a gentle shake. "Dammit, Rose, why are you doing this? You know I'm crazy about you and you feel the same way—"

"I can't ruin your life like I've ruined mine," she yelled, pulling out of his grip and finally eyeballing him, her chest heaving with the effort of dragging in air. "Don't you see? I've made crappy decisions my entire life and I live with the consequences every freaking day. I can't add you to the list."

Confusion creased his brow. "Decisions?"

She almost told him then. All of it. But she knew what would happen. He'd comfort her. She'd welcome it. And they'd be back to the start, him wanting to give up his life for her.

So she dredged up the only other excuse she could think of. "Olly's thriving in this town. I don't want my past to taint that. So if you care for him at all, if you care for me, you'll stay away from us and keep that info about my past private."

Remembering the monitor at the last minute, she grabbed it and headed for the door, mentally willing him to let her go.

"Is that what you really want?" He reached out and she sidestepped him, her heart pounding so hard she could hear it in her ears.

"Olly comes first. You've always known that," she said, unable to hold back the tears any longer as the vice-like pain clamping her chest intensified to the point of agony. "If you stay away from us, we all get what we want."

His stoic mask of the last few moments cracked as she opened the door and stepped outside.

This time, he let her go.

28.

Caden let Rose walk away.

He didn't have any other option. If her tears hadn't slugged him enough, hearing her articulate how ruining her reputation would taint Olly too would've done the job.

Not that he hadn't already considered that. Once his outrage at someone invading Rose's privacy had subsided, Olly had been at the forefront of his mind.

The kid deserved better. As did Rose.

She'd battled hard to establish a new life for herself and her son. Working long hours. Seeking help with babysitting. Checking out rental properties.

If he didn't love her so damn much, he'd admire her tenacity regardless.

It was because of that love that he let her walk away. A love that was reciprocated, he was sure of it. Actions spoke louder than words, and the way she'd acted at the ball, that night in his arms, the brunch . . . Something about the wedding today had sent her into a tailspin and her knee-jerk reaction was to push him away.

She couldn't have come here tonight to end it. She'd already done that in the apartment forty minutes ago. Which meant she'd probably had second thoughts. Hell, if he were being really fanciful, maybe she'd come here to tell him the truth about why she kept pushing him away? But the moment she'd learned about the smear campaign, she'd latched onto it as an excuse. He'd expected it. It was why he'd told her.

As a test.

A jerk thing to do, but he'd wanted to see her reaction, to see what she would do.

If she didn't love him, she never would've lied and walked away.

She thought his dream to be elected mayor was all-important. That's why she'd walked away, not because of any sense of self-preservation or for her son.

For him.

He knew it because he'd done a thorough internet search after he'd received the email and most of that information, bar her stint in the recovery center, was readily available. Hell, the kids at Olly's school could discover it with a computer and a few keywords.

Which meant she was more concerned about him being tainted by association with her.

So she'd let him off easy. Saying she didn't love him was her way of ensuring he let her go.

Like hell.

Caden had a clear plan. Confront his parents in the morning and tell them his decision.

A decision that would change the course of his life.

For the better.

๏ฉ

Caden timed his morning visit to perfection. His mother had a strict routine. He should know: he'd lived with it for years. She'd shower, dress, apply makeup, style her hair, and only then come downstairs for her coffee.

She didn't appreciate being disturbed before that morning coffee. He'd learned that the hard way as an eight-year-old, when he'd barreled into her room to get a form signed for school and she'd yelled so loud his ears had rung for ten minutes.

He'd only heard her yell like that one other time, the night she'd had a meltdown and he'd seen his father cry. The night he'd rebelled and caused so much tension in the house he'd sworn never to do it again.

He had a feeling what he had to say today would eclipse the tension of that night. He didn't give a damn. Because if his mother was behind that email . . . He couldn't imagine cutting her out of his life but it would take a long time before he could look her in the face.

He glanced at his watch, knowing she'd be doing her usual Sunday morning prep for church. If she'd sabotaged his relationship with Rose, all the penance in the world wouldn't save her today.

Stabbing at the doorbell, he mentally counted backwards from ten, a calming technique he'd seen online once. It worked. Until his mom opened the door: he took one look at her face and saw the guilt.

"Caden, what brings you by so early on a Sunday?" She pasted a false smile on her face, opened the door wider and beckoned him in. "We're heading off to church shortly if you'd like to come—"

"Church can wait."

He pushed past her without the obligatory kiss. He couldn't feign affection. Not today. Not when he'd seen his mother's furtive look-away and knew the truth before he'd asked the question.

"Where's Dad?" He strode into the formal living room and planted himself in front of the fake fireplace, knowing his mother would choose her favorite armchair by the window, far away from where he stood. Perhaps not far enough, the mood he was in.

An imperious eyebrow rose. Faking it to the end. "What's this about?"

"I want Dad to hear this too, so can you please get him?" He thrust his hands into his pockets and glared, channeling every ounce of his inner rage into that stare, not surprised when his mom scuttled from the room.

Yeah, she knew why he was here, no doubt about it. Though he wondered if she'd perpetuate her sin by lying about it. After having Rose investigated and trying to blackmail him with the info, he wouldn't put anything past her.

His father entered the living room a few moments later, took one look at Caden, and mouthed, "I'm sorry."

Jeff wore the look of a resigned man, the same look he'd seen on his father for years. But Caden wasn't buying into his father's helpless act. If Jeff Shoreham had any balls he would've stood up to his wife before she sent that damn email. He loved his dad, he really did, but he'd lost all respect for him after this stunt.

His mom stood next to his father, her shoulders squared for battle, her lips compressed, her glare defiant.

"You know why I'm here," he said, his gaze shifting between them. "Did you have Rose investigated and send me that threatening email?"

He'd never know if his mom opened her mouth to deny it, because his dad leapt in with, "I told her not to do it, Son, but you know what your mother's like."

"Sadly, I do." Caden shook his head, waiting for the anger to subside. Loathing roiled in his gut and he mentally counted backwards again to stop his abhorrence from bubbling up and spilling out in a torrent of hateful accusations.

His mother had gone too far this time with her interference in his life, but to learn his father was so weak-willed he couldn't stop her really rankled.

His dad's instant confession should've calmed him. It didn't. If anything, seeing his mother so composed and nonchalant, and his father worried yet deferential, made him more furious.

"Do you have any idea how much you disgust me right now?" He couldn't hide his repulsion but it made little impression on his stoic mother.

Her eyes flashed with barely concealed irritation. "You're our only child. We'd do anything to protect you—"

"Yeah, Mom, I know. I was your miracle child, conceived after many years of trying, blah, blah, blah."

He scowled, not caring when she flinched from his raised voice. That was another thing that had annoyed the crap out of him growing up. He would've rather endured loud, honest arguments than the usual tiptoeing that they did around each other to express displeasure.

"Don't you think I've felt the burden of that every day of my frigging life?" He was yelling now and didn't care. "Hell, I gave up my dreams of leaving this place because Dad was sick and I felt obligated to do the right thing and come back."

His father looked away, his cheeks flushing crimson. And yet another truth hit home.

"You weren't so sick, were you, Dad?" Coldness laced every word. "You used your heart attack to get me back home after college, then played it up so I'd stay."

"This place has always been your home," his mom said, a deep frown slashing her brows. "You can achieve so much here—"

"I can't live my life according to what you want!" He bellowed so loud, the china figurines on the mantel wobbled. "I know you want me to marry into the region's richest family and be elected mayor and enhance your *social standing*." He thumped his chest. "But that's not me. And it never will be."

His father stared at him in mute apology, his shoulders slumped, while his mom continued to glare, her stubbornness holding her posture rigid.

"Remember that night you had a meltdown, Mom, and you made Dad cry? I thought I caused that, because I'd snuck out to meet those kids and you caught me. So you know what I did? I became the model son. Did my best to be perfect, just to live up to your *expectations*." He spat the last word. "But you know something? I'm tired of living up to your standards." He blew out a long breath, his rage petering out but the indignation remaining as a reminder that he couldn't trust the two people he should have been able to count on the most. "I'm done."

His mom puffed up in outrage. "What does that mean—"

"That night was never about you, Son." His dad crossed the room to stand in front of him, his expression repentant. "Your mother and I—"

"Don't say another word!" His mother screeched, her face flushing an ugly puce. "Don't you dare."

But his dad continued as if she hadn't spoken. "That perfect facade your mother and I have worked so hard to maintain all these years? Exactly that—a facade." Jeff held his hands out, as if asking for forgiveness. "I had an affair, and to get back at me, your mother had a one-night stand. What you saw that night was her taunting me with it, saying your rebellious behavior was a result of me putting our family in jeopardy because of my bad choices."

Caden's jaw dropped as his gaze flicked between the people who'd raised him, parents he thought he'd known, when he really didn't know them at all.

These upstanding folk, who rammed their morals down everyone else's throats, had been unfaithful. Hypocrites.

That was the moment another unpalatable truth detonated in Caden's brain. "You stayed together because of *me?*"

His mother refused to speak, refused to look at him, so he turned to his father.

Jeff nodded, his jowls wobbling. "Partially, though there was more to it. I loved preaching. We had an orderly life in a town we both loved. So we forgave each other and moved on. Forged a solid partnership."

His father's shoulders lifted in a half-hearted shrug. "There were so many townsfolk divorcing, giving up, and we didn't want to do that. We wanted to be seen as better than that."

Caden could hardly comprehend that these infinitely polite people had stayed in a sham marriage for the sake of appearances. And in doing so, burdened him with their crap.

"You're just as flawed as everyone else, yet you made me believe I had to be perfect," he said, rage making him shake. He dragged in deep breaths to calm down. "Do you have any idea what it's like growing up like that?"

To his horror, tears stung the back of his eyes but he'd be damned if he cried in front of these phoneys. "And you're still bloody interfering."

"I'm sorry, Son." His dad clapped him on the back. Yeah, like that would erase their lies. "For everything."

Caden managed a mute nod in acceptance as he glared at his mother who, even now, couldn't bring herself to apologize.

"Everything I've done has been for you," she said, her tone clipped. "I stayed in a loveless marriage. I built a good home. I raised you right."

Caden sniggered. "Do you have any idea how self-righteous you sound? And you still can't bring yourself to say sorry."

Unrepentant to the end, she tilted her nose in the air. "I'm not sorry for doing whatever it takes to protect you. Rose is an addict, just like Effie—and look how that turned out. You need to end this before it's too late—"

"Enough," he roared, striding toward the door before he swept every one of her precious figurines onto the floor and smashed them to pieces.

Hearing his mom call Rose an addict terrified him as much as the thought of losing her because of what his parents had done.

His mom was wrong. Rose would've told him if alcohol was still a problem. She'd told him she'd handled it at the recovery center.

But what if she was lying to him, just like Effie had?

He wrenched the door open, pausing on the threshold to deliver the news he hoped would shut his mother up once and for all. "I'm withdrawing from the mayor's race. The only reason I ran in the first place was because Effie had died. I was floundering and you guilted me into it with your infamous 'I told you so.'" He paused for dramatic effect before delivering the final blow. "And I'm asking Rose to marry me."

At least, that was the plan. Whether she'd have him after all this, he doubted.

His mother's jaw dropped but his dad nodded his approval. "Good for you, Son."

His mother merely glared at him with icy disdain.

He didn't care. Not anymore.

He'd discovered the two people in this world he'd respected the most had been living a lie, happy to perpetuate the sham so they could control their only child.

It made him sick.

He left without a backward glance, slamming the door on his way out.

29.

Rose was returning from checking out possible job opportunities in Dixon's Creek on Sunday morning and had reached the outskirts of Redemption when her cell rang.

Clamping down on the instant, irrational fear every mom experienced when a phone rang and her child wasn't with her, she pulled over and glanced at the screen.

The number wasn't Cilla's, and she sighed in relief before answering.

"Hello?"

"Is that Rose Mathieson?"

Rose couldn't place the short, clipped tone but the voice sounded vaguely familiar. "Yes. Who's this?"

"Penny Shoreham."

Rose almost dropped the cell in shock. Why the hell would Caden's mom be calling her and how did she get this number?

"Hope you don't mind me calling. I got your number from Don at the diner."

That ratfink. So much for confidential employee information.

"I'm afraid I told him a little white lie, that it was dreadfully important I contact you on the weekend."

Still clueless as to why the nasty woman who had confronted her at the park to warn her off Caden would be calling, Rose kept her tone civil despite wanting to hang up.

"What can I do for you?"

Rose heard the faintest sigh before Penny responded. "I was hoping you could stop by my house for a few minutes today. I have something I'd like to say."

Rose bit back her first retort—"Hell, no."

"If this has anything to do with Caden, don't worry: we're not involved."

Not anymore. The thought brought an instant lump to Rose's throat.

"I'd really like to see you, if you could spare the time," Penny said, her authoritative voice brooking no argument.

So Rose found herself agreeing to meet the last person she wanted to see after the soothing day she'd had.

"Fine. Where and when?"

"How about now, at our place?"

Wow. Whatever Penny had to say must be earth-shattering to demand an instant audience.

Rose knew this had to be a fool's errand. Probably more of Penny's vitriol and another warning to stay away from Caden. Which Rose would promptly pre-empt with the news she was moving out this week and that would be that.

She needed to keep her distance from Caden in order to heal, and living over his garage wasn't conducive to that. So she'd take a lease on a small cottage near the center of town, tighten her budget and hope she maintained a steady stream of shifts at the diner while job-searching in neighboring towns.

As for school drop-offs, she'd sweet-talk Don into letting Olly sit quietly in a booth for an hour every morning, and allowing her to duck out to drop him off.

Besides, after giving Penny her private cell number, he owed her. "Text me the address and I'll be there in fifteen minutes."

"See you then," Penny said, clearing her throat. "Thank you."

Rose stabbed at the disconnect button, thinking Penny shouldn't thank her yet. Rose might have been ambushed last time. This time, she wouldn't be such a pushover.

Her cell pinged a moment later and after plugging the address into the map app, she followed the voice instructions until she reached a trendy town house on an immaculate tree-lined street. She could imagine someone as image conscious as Penny Shoreham living here. What she couldn't imagine was why on earth the pretentious woman had invited her here for a chat.

Squaring her shoulders, Rose marched up the pathway and stabbed at the doorbell, intent on staying the requisite two minutes. Long enough to hear what Penny had to say. Not long enough to get an earful and care about it.

The door opened straight away, like Penny had been hovering on the other side, waiting for her.

The woman looked awful. Dark circles under her eyes no amount of concealer could hide. Tear streaks channeling the foundation on her cheeks. Pale. But it was the expression in her eyes that struck Rose the most: like someone had died.

"Please come in." Penny stepped aside and beckoned her in.

"If it's all the same to you, I'd rather stay here." Rose tapped her watch. "I don't have long."

"Considering how I badgered you at the park, I don't blame you for wanting to remain outside," Penny said, her tone oddly subdued. "But I'd rather the neighbors didn't hear what I have to say, so if you could spare a few minutes?"

Not wanting to appear churlish, Rose entered, immediately struck by the difference between this town house and the Shorehams' old family home.

While Caden had added a distinct masculine edge to his house, this place seemed devoid of . . . everything. Pristine white walls. Polished marble tiles. Minimal pictures and knick-knacks. A complete lack of personality.

"Would you like something to drink? Or a snack perhaps?" Penny wrung her hands, but obviously couldn't resist playing the polite hostess.

"No thanks. I'd rather hear what you have to say so I can leave."

Penny winced. "I deserve that for how I've treated you."

Rose remained silent. Agreeing would be redundant.

"I owe you an apology." Penny clasped her hands together to stop from twisting them, her serene pose at odds with the tension making her neck muscles stand rigid.

"Don't worry about it. The park and diner incidents are in the past."

Penny was startled. "What diner incident?"

Rose refrained from rolling her eyes, just. "I overheard you and Tully talking about me. You said I was worthless."

Penny had the grace to look embarrassed. "I'm sorry for that. And for threatening to expose your past," she said, her gaze glassy with tears. "I did a stupid thing, trying to get Caden to stay away from you. You have to know I would never have allowed that information to go public. It was a spiteful thing to do, a mother's deluded attempt at maintaining control over her son's life."

Rose shrugged, not surprised by Penny's admission and not particularly caring. She'd been through tough times in her lifetime. Whatever this narrow-minded woman could dish out was nothing compared to that.

"It's irrelevant, because we're not together," Rose said. "So if that's all?"

Penny's eyes widened as she swiped at a stray tear trickling down her cheek. "You don't love him?"

Annoyed to be ambushed, and not wanting to discuss her romantic life with this woman or anyone else right now, she said, "That's none of your business."

"But he's going to . . ." Penny bit back the rest of what she was about to say and for a moment, Rose wished she'd continued.

Then again, she didn't want to know what Caden was going to do. It was irrelevant. She'd made up her mind to cut him loose and if there was one thing she'd learned through her experiences, it was to stick by her decisions.

"Whatever happens, promise me you'll keep an open mind and not break his heart." Penny took a step forward and for a horrifying second Rose thought she might embrace her.

Rose had no intention of making promises she couldn't keep, so she backed away and held up her hand, as if to ward Penny off.

"Thanks for apologizing, but I need to go now."

Penny looked stricken, like she hadn't finished what she had to say. "I only did it because I thought you were like the other one and I didn't want him going through the pain again."

The other one?

Rose wanted to bolt, but curiosity kept her feet rooted to the spot.

"My son has a penchant for rescuing wounded things. Always has." Weariness deepened every wrinkle on Penny's face. "When he was young, it was animals. Birds with broken wings, limping dogs, even an injured porcupine once."

A glimmer of a smile tugged at the corners of her pinched mouth. "In college, he was constantly doling out money to his friends. Bailing them out of tight spots. Then when he came home, a few years later . . ." She visibly swallowed. "Effie moved into the apartment."

Rose tried to hide her surprise. Caden had never mentioned a relationship with anyone called Effie, let alone the fact she'd lived in the apartment too.

Not that she had any right to be jealous, but a stab of envy for the faceless Effie had her rubbing a spot beneath her ribs.

Penny continued like Rose's silence meant little. "Effie drifted into town, a pauper. One of those hippie types who float through life on patchouli and not much else." She wrinkled her nose. "I never knew what the attraction was but Caden seemed smitten. He asked her to move in within a week."

Penny's stare took on a mean glint. "She used my son, while feeding her secret addiction to painkillers."

A chill swept over Rose.

"The woman kept it from Caden. He found out when she was discovered dead in a seedy motel nearby, from an overdose."

Rose didn't know whether to be indignant on Caden's behalf for being duped by a woman he'd cared about or outraged that Penny had lumped her into the same tarred bucket.

"When you arrived in town and Caden asked you to move in a few days later . . ." Penny shrugged. "I knew nothing about you and my son didn't either, and it seemed like he hadn't learned from past mistakes."

"I'm not an addict," Rose said, her tone frosty.

"But you were in a recovery center because of problems with alcohol." Penny shook her head. "I'm sorry, dear, but that sounds like an addiction to me."

Rose compressed her lips to prevent herself from telling Penny to eff off. What irked her the most was that Penny was partially right. If Rose had continued to use alcohol as a relaxation method and a way to decompress, she would've been well on her way to alcoholism.

Thankfully, she'd taken steps to avoid that, but she didn't owe this woman any explanations.

"None of this matters," Rose said. "I'm not involved with your son."

Penny's shoulders sagged and she appeared to age a decade before Rose's eyes. "Caden has made it more than clear he wants nothing to do with me. But I know my son. If you're his new pet project to rescue, he'll convince himself he wants you."

Having Penny label her a pet project to be rescued meant it was time to leave. Way past time.

She'd heard enough. Sticking around to hear Penny wax lyrical about her son wasn't conducive to moving on.

Getting home to start packing was.

30.

It didn't surprise Caden that Rose sent him a text message late Sunday night saying she'd take Olly to school in the morning. She'd gone into avoidance mode. She'd asked him to stay away from her and Olly for their own good, but he had no intention of doing that.

When he received the text, he marched across the yard to the garage and pounded on the apartment door. She opened it a crack, enough for him to spy boxes in the tiny living room, some taped, some open but overflowing.

It slugged him in the gut, seeing cold, hard evidence of how far she'd go to avoid him. But it only served to steel his resolve.

"Let me in, Rose. We need to talk."

She didn't budge. "Olly's asleep so now's not a good time."

Her swollen, red eyes indicated now *would* be the perfect time. The woman he loved was hurting and he needed to be there for her.

"If you don't let me in, I'll pound this door 'til Olly wakes up and you wouldn't want that."

A low blow, appealing to her mothering side. Not that he'd go through with it, but he had to speak to her, tonight.

"Whatever you say won't change a thing," she said, grudgingly swinging the door open to let him in. "And for goodness sake, keep your voice down."

Relieved, he pushed past her and waited until she shut the door before reaching for her.

"Stop," she said, shoving him away so fast that he stumbled a little. "Don't come near me."

Uncertainty warred with his resolve for the first time since he'd made up his mind to fight for them.

"What's wrong?"

She barked out a harsh laugh, devoid of amusement. "I don't need to be rescued, Caden. I'm not *Effie*."

Caden felt the blood drain from his face. "What?"

"You heard me." Her frigid tone added to the chill sweeping his body from head to foot. "What I can't figure out is why you didn't tell me about her. Especially when I asked if there'd been other women in your life."

Hating that he'd have to divulge the disaster that had been his relationship with Effie, when he'd rather be focusing on Rose, he shrugged.

"I didn't tell you because it wasn't relevant to us in any way."

His response angered her, as her fingers curled into fists, her arms rigid by her side. "So the fact you make a habit of taking pity on financially strapped women who arrive in town and offering them a place to stay almost immediately isn't relevant?"

"This is bullshit," he said, stalking toward the kitchenette to avoid the tiny voice inside insisting she was right.

"No, it's what you do, apparently. Rescue things. Try to fix them." She drew in a breath and hissed, "I don't need to be rescued by you or anyone. Got it?"

Stunned by how fast his plans to woo her over to his way of thinking had turned to crap, he leaned against the benchtop and tried to gather his thoughts.

That's when he spied the bottles, tucked away behind an upright cookbook. Brandy and whiskey. Both half full.

In that moment, the threat of betrayal catapulted him back in time. Discovering Effie's cupboards stocked to overflowing with medication. Knowing she had nothing to sell to buy the stuff but herself. Having the world as he'd known it ripped out from under him.

He'd asked Rose about the recovery center. She'd played down the alcohol aspect.

But what if he was staring at proof of an alcoholic struggling to hide her addiction?

Indignation made him whirl back to face her, so he could see her reaction. "Why do you have half empty bottles of alcohol hidden away?"

Rose's jaw dropped. "What the hell are you talking about?"

"Over there." He jerked a thumb over his shoulder. "Are you drinking again?"

Rose's mouth snapped closed with an audible click as she glowered at him with disgust. "Get out."

"I'm not leaving 'til I get answers," he said, sick to the stomach at the thought of being duped again.

Worse, that his mother might be right.

"You want *answers*?" She made it sound like he'd asked for an arsenic cocktail. "How about trusting me? How about giving me the benefit of the doubt that after spending four freaking months in rehab, away from my precious son, which is why I went there in the first place, I wouldn't touch the stuff again?"

She jabbed him in the chest, hard. "How about figuring that I'm a cook and making a wedding fruit cake involves using copious amounts of brandy and whiskey? How about *that*?"

She shoved him again before backing away, shaking her head, as he struggled to keep the tears burning the back of his eyes at bay.

"You know what, Caden? I thought you were one of the good guys. And having you in my life lately has been a godsend."

She sniffled a little and swiped at her nose. "I even let myself fall in love, probably for the first time ever. I gave you the benefit of the doubt with Tully, even though every time I've seen you together you appear to be a cozy couple. But I believed in you. I took what you said at face value. And I was willing to walk away from you so you could be mayor and follow your dreams."

Mortified, he reached for her. "Rose, I'm sorry—"

"You need to leave. Now." She pointed at the door. "There's nothing more to say. I need someone in my life I can trust. Someone who sees the best in me. Someone I can depend on to not judge me if the going gets rough." She shook her head and a small sob escaped. "Want to know the irony in all this? I'm not the addict: you are. You're so addicted to helping people to make yourself feel good, you can't see the truth when it's right in front of your face." She patted her chest. "I'm not Effie. I've never hidden anything from you. And if you'd had the guts to tell me about her rather than treat me like some goddamn pet that needed to be saved, who knows—maybe we could've worked this out."

Devastation made him shake. "We still can—"

"No, we can't."

With that, she trudged toward the bedroom and closed the door.

Leaving him bereft and with no frigging clue how to make this right.

31.

Caden had screwed up. In a big way.

He'd lain awake the entire night, replaying the awful scene in the apartment over and over, like some horror film stuck on rerun.

Rose had been right.

About all of it.

So he tried calling her. Predictably, she didn't answer, but that wouldn't deter him. He had to apologize and tell her how he felt.

Her cell rang five times before her perky message kicked in.

"Hi, this is Rose. Can't take your call right now so please leave a message."

He waited for the beep, took a deep breath, readying himself to blurt the things he should've said to her last night.

Then hung up.

What if Rose wouldn't be convinced with words, no matter how honest his declaration was? He'd already tried telling her, and look how that had turned out. Words were useless. He needed to show her how far he was willing to go for them to be together, with a grand gesture even she couldn't ignore.

Waiting until the diner opened half an hour later at six a.m. killed him, but he bided his time, going over his plans in his head until he knew what he intended to do couldn't fail. Not when he'd have an audience. Rose thought being mayor was all-important for him? Well, he'd show her.

When Don picked up the phone on the second ring at a minute past six, Caden outlined his plan, grateful that the diner's owner had a romantic bone or two in his body. Yeah, Caden was done with words. It was time for action.

❦

He stepped into Don's Diner at eleven a.m. The place was packed with local media, townsfolk and the woman of the moment, Rose.

Their gazes locked across the crowd and, predictably, she bolted behind the counter and into the kitchen. He couldn't blame her, not after last night. Hopefully, she'd come out of hiding when he delivered his prepared speech.

It took a while for him to work his way through the crowd, the townsfolk shaking his hand or clapping him on the back. A cynic would consider their friendliness as sucking up to the incoming mayor, but Caden had lived here too long to see it as anything other than small-town camaraderie. Supporting one of their own.

He hoped they were as supportive when he dropped his bombshell. Not that he cared. He didn't give a flying fig what anyone thought of his decision. Only one person's opinion mattered, and he hoped to God she'd come around to his way of thinking.

Don was waiting for him by a small podium he'd set up at Caden's request. "This okay, Caden?"

"Perfect. Thanks." He shook Don's hand and took the cordless microphone he offered. "This shouldn't take long."

Don chuckled. "Take as long as you like. We haven't had a crowd like this since last year's wine growers' festival. And they're mighty hungry."

"As long as you let one of your chefs take a few minutes off."

Don winked and tapped the side of his nose. "Trust me, Rose will be out here to hear your big news."

Don didn't know the half of it. Because once Caden had delivered his announcement, he had something else to say. Something life-changing.

"Thanks."

Taking a deep breath, Caden faced the restless crowd. Some were chatting, some were laughing, some were cramming Rose's signature mini quiches into their mouths. He knew, because she'd made them for him as the first meal in lieu of rent. That seemed like an eternity ago.

After she heard what he had to say, he hoped he had a lifetime of great home cooking ahead of him.

He waited until he spotted Rose being ushered from the kitchen by Don. He had no idea what her boss had said to her, but Rose's mutinous expression and crossed arms indicated she wasn't happy.

Giving a few subtle taps on the microphone, he waited until the crowd quieted and their collective gazes swung to the podium.

"Great to see such a good turnout today." He held up his hand in a friendly wave. "Amazing what the promise of free food will do."

"Hey," Don yelled from behind the counter. "That's a lie."

Everyone laughed as Caden had intended. "Sorry, Don—a little Monday morning bad humor. Now that we've established that everyone's going to order big and pay up, I'd like to thank you all for coming."

He clasped the microphone tight, surprised to find that the nerves that had made his gut churn on the drive over had vanished.

He'd made his decision and it had been surprisingly easy once he'd removed all the extraneous obstacles. But as he glanced across the room and met Rose's disapproving glare, he knew he had to hurdle the biggest obstacle yet.

"We know this is about your campaign for mayor, so hurry it along," someone yelled from the back of the crowd. "We have your back and whatever you want, we'll support you."

Unexpected emotion clogged Caden's throat. He'd spent most of his life in this town, quirky folk and all, and to have such unconditional support was flattering. Maybe they wouldn't be so accepting when they heard what he had to say.

"Thanks, I've appreciated everyone's support. But my plans have changed." He glanced at the small media contingent, a photographer and a reporter from the local paper. "I'd like to formally announce that I'm withdrawing from the mayor's race."

Collective gasps gave way to mutterings, but all Caden cared about was Rose's reaction. She stared at him in open-mouthed shock, wrapping her arms around her middle like she had a stomach-ache.

"The other candidates are all upstanding people who have Redemption's best interests at heart, and I can personally vouch for each of them." He waited for some of the murmurings to subside before he continued. "And while I can't endorse a specific runner in the mayor's race, I'll be cheering for them all."

Applause filtered through the crowd and grew louder, accompanied by a few foot stomps.

"At this stage, I'm not sure whether I'll be staying around in town—"

"Why not?" the reporter called out.

"Because my living situation depends on the lovely lady over there."

He gestured toward the counter and Rose visibly cringed as heads turned.

Caden took a deep breath and blew it out. What he was about to say would be the most important speech of his life.

"Rose, I'm sorry for doubting you. I've been a fool but that's what love does to a schmuck like me. I'm crazy about you.

Having you in my life has been amazing and I'd like to make the arrangement more permanent."

Silence, eerie after the cacophony a minute ago, was broken by heartfelt sighs from a few women. But he was only interested in the reaction of one woman, who currently stared at him in wide-eyed horror.

"Wherever you want to live, I want to be by your side. To cherish you. To support you in whatever you want to do. And to be the best dad I can for Olly." His eyes burned and he blinked before he made more of a fool of himself than he already had. "Rose, I love you. Thank you for rescuing me. Will you marry me?"

This time, the silence was broken by an anguished cry. It came from the woman he loved as he watched her run out the side door as fast as she could.

32.

Rose couldn't breathe. A giant, invisible weight pressed down on her chest, making the simple act of forcing air into her lungs impossible.

She had to be hallucinating. High on the fumes of peanut oil and ketchup. Because no way in hell could that have just happened.

Caden had proposed to her in front of half the town.

Worse, he'd given up his dream and walked away from his future to do it.

Tears stung her eyes and she stumbled outside, gasping in great lungfuls of air to banish the spots dancing before her vision.

It didn't work, and she swooned a little, increasingly light-headed as she found the nearest object, an overturned crate, and sank onto it. Dropping her head between her legs, she waited for the wooziness to pass. When she finally felt strong enough to raise her head, she locked gazes with Caden, who'd burst through the door, his expression so distraught she couldn't breathe again.

"Are you okay?" He sank to his haunches in front of her, bracing himself with his hands on the crate, either side of her legs. Effectively pinning her.

"What do you think?" She wanted to shove his hands away and push past him, but she wasn't sure if her legs were steady enough yet. "How could you do that? Tell the whole town our business."

The tears she'd been trying so hard to suppress burned and when they trickled down her cheeks, she didn't care. "It was humiliating."

He stiffened, the concern on his face replaced by wariness. "You found me declaring my love in front of everyone so you would finally take me seriously, humiliating?"

Damn, she'd hurt him.

Then again, wasn't that the whole point? To drive a wedge between them once and for all?

Granted, the marriage proposal had come from left field, as unexpected as the depth of her feelings for this incredible man. But she'd stick to her plan and do the right thing. She could fix this. She'd politely refuse him and ensure he rejoined the mayor's campaign.

Easy.

The part where a sharp pain cleaved her heart in two, making rational thinking impossible, wasn't so easy.

"What do you expect me to say?"

"I expect you to say yes, dammit!" He stood so quickly he rocked the crate and she almost lost her balance and tipped off. "I expect you to be honest with me for once and not hide behind some bullshit story about your past and why you can't commit." He stalked a few feet away and whirled to face her again. "Don't you get it? I'm not some asshole like your father and uncle. I'm nothing like Olly's father, who screwed around on you then abandoned you through pure selfishness." He thumped his chest. "I'm nothing like them."

His audible anguish mirrored hers but she couldn't let him go without telling him the truth.

All of it.

She owed him that much.

Maybe then he could live with her refusal and move on, to find the kind of woman he deserved. A woman as perfect as him. A woman like Tully.

"I know you're nothing like them," she said, pushing into a standing position, feeling one hundred years old. Every bone in her body ached, every muscle cramped. Probably the aftereffects of her adrenaline surge in fleeing the diner as fast as possible. "That's what makes this so difficult."

"You're going to say no," he said, his tone deathly calm and laced with derision. "Even now, when I've handed you my heart, you don't want it."

"It's not that," she said, instantly regretting her instinctive response when hope flickered in his eyes. "But you need to know something to understand why I can't be with you."

He studied her with infinite patience, the way he had when they were kids and he'd sit there in his backyard, waiting for her to speak. Or not. Depending on her mood.

This time, she had a feeling he wouldn't be so understanding when he heard what she had to say.

"Do you know why I've held you at bay all this time?"

He nodded, puzzlement narrowing his eyes a little. "Because of Olly."

His tone held censure, like he couldn't believe she wouldn't trust him not to hurt her—and her son—after how close they'd grown.

"Olly's not the only reason. It's mainly because of you and the type of man you are."

She waited, watching his gaze turn from curious to wary.

"You expect perfection."

"That's bullshit—"

"Hear me out." She took a deep breath and blew it out. "Every aspect of your life is perfect. You returned to the town you grew up in. You bought your childhood home. You run a respectable accountancy firm. You ran for mayor. Heck, you even have the perfect wife waiting in the wings."

His lips flattened. "You're still doubting me about Tully?"

She shook her head. "No, I'm doubting that you can't see what's right for you, even when it's in front of your nose."

His eyes flashed with anger. "I feel nothing for Tully, so your theory's seriously flawed."

"Then why didn't you tell me about Effie?"

"Because she has nothing to do with us," he said, his voice rising. "Just like Dyson has nothing to do with us."

"That's where you're wrong." Glad he'd given her the perfect opening to finally reveal the truth, she sighed. "My relationship with Dyson is indicative of how I cope with every single thing in my life and is still affecting me to this day."

He didn't speak, his glower intimidating, but she continued.

"You know a bit about my dad but you don't know the half of it. He may never have raised his fists to me like he did Jake, but he battered my self-esteem to the point I don't trust my own judgment anymore. And I never did."

She took a deep breath. "Until recently, I even blamed myself for his death."

When Caden appeared ready to interject, she held up her hand. "Jake made me see sense, that it was just an accident, but I think I used the guilt I felt over his death as an excuse for everything I did after that."

She gnawed on her bottom lip. "Thanks to my dad's appalling treatment, I've been seeking affection my whole life. It's why I fell for Dyson, when he was obviously the wrong guy. It's why I kept Olly when I got pregnant, thinking it would bind Dyson to me and ensure he loved me, even when everyone around me insisted the sensible thing to do as a teen would be to have an abortion. It's why I sought comfort in alcohol when things got tough, because I wanted to feel good . . ."

She searched his eyes for judgment, especially after articulating some of her deepest secrets. But all she saw was pity, and that was almost as bad.

"And that's why we can't be together." She pressed her fingertips into her eyes before continuing. "Because I'll never be sure if you want me for me and are not just pandering to your lifelong rescue complex. And I'll never know if I'm just using you as yet another stopgap measure to make me feel good for however long it lasts. Heck, you couldn't even trust me enough to think I wouldn't start drinking again, and after what I've been through, I *need* someone to believe in me, always."

Horror darkened his eyes and a hysterical giggle bubbled up from within her and escaped, making her sound heartless. "Don't you see? As long as we're together, neither of us will ever be sure of how the other really feels. If we're just using each other for comfort or if it's the real thing . . ."

She trailed off, relief washing over her. She'd told him the truth and the sky hadn't fallen in and lightning hadn't struck her. It felt good. Like an invisible weight had shifted.

"First you think I'm too perfect to have someone like you in my life. Then you think I'm just rescuing you. Or you're using me as some kind of security blanket. So which is it?" Incredulous, he crossed the short distance between them to grab her arms. "Which of your wacky, psychobabble, bullshit theories is the one you'll ultimately cling to in order to drive me away for good?"

She gaped and broke his grip, annoyed by his cavalier attitude toward her revelation. "Can't you see the slightest glimmer of sense in what I've just said?"

"God, Rose, you really don't know me at all." He pinched the bridge of his nose, his expression pained. "Don't you get it? Nothing you could say or do will change how I feel about you."

He huffed out a breath. "I'm sorry I screwed up. I should've trusted you, not accused you. But when I saw those bottles, something inside me snapped. Losing Effie gutted me, but discovering her lies almost killed me. The thought you were lying to me too . . .

crazy, considering you hadn't given me any reason to doubt you. In fact, you proved your feelings by walking away from our relationship when you thought it would affect my becoming mayor."

Emotion tightened his throat but he continued. "And you're right about me needing to help others to feel good. Maybe being an only child living under the constant high expectations of doting parents screwed me up, but when I care for things, I like being depended on. Effie was a by-product of my rescue complex, but not you. You don't need to be rescued because you've done that all by yourself. You've faced your demons and come out on the other side."

Tears stung his eyes and he blinked them away. "I know you don't need me, but damn, I need you. I've shut myself off from everyone and thrown myself into a campaign that means little beyond a way to get over my grief, and then you come along."

He swallowed, in danger of blubbering. "*You* rescued *me*. And I'll do whatever it takes to make you believe it."

Before she could move he snagged her hand and pressed it against his heart, which pounded like a wild thing beneath her palm. "I love you. Wherever you want to go, whatever you want to do, I'll be beside you."

His rueful smile made her choke up. "The only way you can get rid of me is by getting Tully to join us for a threesome."

"You're making a joke about that?" Which actually impressed her, though she wouldn't let him know it.

He had disarmed her in a way she couldn't fight. She'd tried to drive him away with her innermost secrets yet he still stood in front of her, staring at her in that unique way he had of making her feel cherished and loved.

"Look, I get it. You've got self-esteem issues. And you've let it eat away at you all these years and erode your confidence." He shook his head. "I've done it too, to an extent. Though in my case, it was guilt. I thought I caused my parents to have a nervous breakdown one night when I tried to sneak out." He grimaced. "Turns out they'd both been sleeping around and I happened to stumble on a confessional moment I shouldn't have."

"Your mom had an affair?"

The thought of prim and proper Penny stepping out on her husband ranked right up there with her accepting Caden's proposal for improbability.

"Dad had the affair. She had a one-night stand as payback." He rolled his eyes. "Dad told me everything yesterday. He apologized for going along with Mom all these years, for making me feel guilty and using that guilt to control me."

"How?"

"Guess it was more me wanting to be the model son and not giving them any more reason to stress." He patted his chest. "I did that, not them. But they played up Dad's heart attack when I'd finished college and that's what ultimately made me return here." He scowled. "Mom berated me for getting involved with Effie, and when she died and the truth came out, she guilted me again. I entered the mayor's campaign because of that guilt. A real dumbass move."

Feeling strangely magnanimous now she'd unburdened her own secrets, she said, "You're their only child. They obviously love you. Guess they did whatever it took to keep you close."

"I don't like being manipulated," he said, his eyes narrowing. "Mom's to blame. None of it would have happened if it weren't for her."

"You should cut her some slack." Rose chuckled, sheepish. "She called me over yesterday. Apologized for sending that email. Gave me insight into your rescue complex."

Caden's lopsided grin twanged her heart. "Don't you get it?" he said. "You never needed to be rescued. You breezed into town, in charge of your future. I was the idiot who needed rescuing from wallowing in my past and you did that, sweetheart, in spades."

He hesitated. "So now you've told me all that private stuff you thought would drive me away, is there anything else keeping us apart?"

"Tell me about Effie," she said, needing to hear the truth from him rather than his biased mother.

Caden's eyes clouded. "She was wrong for me on so many levels but she also embodied everything I couldn't be. Free. Nomadic. No responsibilities. So we started something, she moved into the apartment and six months later, she was dead of an overdose. Had been hooked on painkillers. When I cleaned out the apartment, I found her stash . . ." The pain of remembrance darkened his eyes. "That's why I flipped last night, thinking you were hiding your alcohol addiction from me."

"I would never do that," Rose said, her heart aching for the pain he must've gone through with his last girlfriend. "I face up to my problems. I own them."

"I know you do and that's why I was damn mad at myself for foisting my hangups on you and wrecking us in the process." He eyeballed her, every potent feeling for her radiating in a blaze of emotion. "I'll never do that again, Rose. If you need my support, if you need me for anything, I'll be there. No questions asked. Trusting you. So can you please put me out of my misery and say yes?"

Damned if she could think of anything more to keep them apart, but she still wasn't sure that eventually this incredible man wouldn't tire of her, faults and all, and move on, leaving her broken-hearted.

"What about being mayor? You have no reason not to run now."

He shrugged. "I'm not interested. Yet another example of me being a people-pleaser."

"Guess that's one thing we have in common."

He stepped forward, invading her personal space. "The only person I want to please now is you."

Rose stared into his clear blue eyes, clear out of excuses. Now that he knew everything—her brush with alcoholism, her thirst for approval, her neediness, her average financial situation—she had no reason to hold him at bay.

But she gave him one last chance to back out of a lifetime commitment.

"We don't have to get married, you know. I'm more than happy to try a relationship, live in sin, whatever—"

He let out a loud whoop before crushing his mouth to hers in a kiss that stole her breath and sealed her fate.

When they finally came up for air, he cupped her face, the elation in his steady gaze making her feel more loved than she ever had in her entire life.

"I don't need a trial. I know what I want." He brushed a soft, tender kiss across her lips. "And that's you. By my side. Forever."

Rose couldn't think of anything better, so she nodded. "In that case, of course I'll marry you."

He laughed, a loud, joyous sound that startled some nearby crows into flight, as he picked her up and whirled her around until she was dizzy.

When he finally put her down and she staggered a little, she reached for his hands and said, "Considering I've just publicly humiliated you, perhaps we should head back into the diner and make the announcement?"

"I don't care what everyone thinks." He squeezed her hands. "Especially if you want to move?"

Touched he'd go to such lengths as leaving his hometown for her, she shook her head. "I'm not going anywhere. Olly's thriving here and in case you haven't noticed, I seem to be doing pretty darn well too."

His hands skimmed over her curves, lingering on her waist. "I noticed."

She laughed and playfully slapped him away. "Come on, I think we should go tell everyone."

"Only if you promise to play hooky and come home with me to celebrate?" He wiggled his eyebrows, leaving her in little doubt as to exactly how he wanted to celebrate.

"Don's short-staffed today. I doubt he'll let me leave—"

"Then quit." He kissed her again. "Besides, your food's too good for the diner."

"But that food pays my bills."

"Whatever you need, all you have to do is ask." His sincerity made her feel safer than she ever had. "I'd never presume to tell you how to live now we're a couple, but just know that I'm here for you in every way. Emotionally. Financially. Whatever. Okay?"

"You're incredible," she said, flinging her arms around his neck and burying her face in the crook of his shoulder. "I love you so much."

"Right back at you, sweetheart." He eased away, his eyes glistening. "Now let's go tell the town our good news."

She didn't have to be asked twice.

33.

The next evening, the Mathieson family and their significant others gathered for supper at Cilla's place.

For Rose, who'd never felt part of a family, it solidified what she already knew: she'd made one of the best decisions of her life when she'd chosen Redemption to settle.

"This is pretty cool, huh?" Tam leaned over to murmur. "First real family get-together I can ever remember."

"Yeah, it's great." Rose glanced around the outdoor table set for a late-night barbecue, feeling blessed to have each person here in her life.

Cilla and Bryce headed the table, with Sara and Jake opposite, Tam to Rose's right, Olly to her left and Caden on the end.

Her family.

Something she'd never thought she'd have considering her past. She'd never felt so blessed.

"I'm glad to see you and Mr. Handsome worked it all out." Tam winked. "He's divine, so if you hadn't snapped him up, I might have."

"Don't think he's your type," Rose said. "He's too young for you."

Tam's brow crinkled in confusion. "What's that supposed to mean?"

"Maybe you prefer older men these days?" Rose nudged her. "You're staying at the winery and the owner's rather charming. Has he showed you his barrels yet?"

"That's gross." Tam elbowed her, hard, her eyes twinkling with amusement.

Rose tapped her bottom lip, pretending to think. "You're single. He's single. Why not?"

"I'm not interested in a fling." Tam shrugged. "Though he is rather dishy, but since I've arrived, I rarely see him around. He showed me to my cottage when I checked in and left. That's it."

"You're in town for another few weeks; you never know what might happen," Rose said, giving Tam's shoulders a quick squeeze.

"Certainly not that." Tam pointed to the ornate Celtic engagement ring on Rose's left hand. "A winemaker who prefers hiding out in his cellar and a bona fide city girl will never get together."

"Famous last words," Rose murmured, wishing she could do something to make Tam as happy as she was.

Tam snorted and turned to answer something Bryce had asked, leaving Rose to focus on Sara.

She wanted to ask her sister-in-law how things were going with the baby but hadn't had an opportunity. Fortuitously, Jake chose that moment to go turn the steaks on the grill, and with Caden playing tic-tac-toe on a napkin with Olly, that gave Rose an in.

"You okay?" she mouthed to Sara, who nodded, looking more relaxed than Rose had seen her in weeks.

Sara leaned forward and Rose did the same.

"The spotting has stopped," Sara said, so softly Rose barely heard. "My obstetrician is happy with the baby's progress."

"That's great." Rose reached out and squeezed Sara's hand. "I'm so happy for you and Jake."

Sara's tremulous smile tugged at her heartstrings. "We're not out of the woods yet and I won't be truly relieved 'til this baby is born, but for now, we're breathing easier."

"So you should," Rose said. "Cherish every moment of this pregnancy."

Sara rested her hand on her stomach. "I will, now that the morning sickness has stopped." She wrinkled her nose. "It was the pits."

"Should be called all-day sickness," Rose said, remembering her own bouts, as she glanced over at Olly. "But it's so worth it."

"Absolutely." Sara's eyes glazed over slightly, as if lost in precious memories of her dead daughter, and Rose sent a silent prayer heavenward that everything would be fine with this next child.

"Mom, guess what?" Olly tugged on her sleeve. "Caden's real bad at tic-tac-toe."

He brandished the napkin. "I beat him five times."

"That's because you're too good, champ, and I'm too tired," Caden said, his gaze meeting hers over Olly's head, as Rose remembered exactly what had made him so tired.

Heat flushed her cheeks as Caden's gorgeous mouth curved into a knowing grin.

"Don't worry, Caden. You'll have plenty of time to get better at it once you marry my mom and we move in, because we can play all the time." Olly's head swiveled between them, happiness making him glow. "I think you'll be a great dad."

Caden cleared his throat. "Thanks."

He ruffled Olly's hair and it was Rose's turn for her throat to clog with emotion as she watched her son lean into Caden like it was the most natural thing in the world.

"I love you," she mouthed at Caden.

"Ditto," he replied, as she leaned over to hug Olly tight between them.

She might have had a lousy childhood but thanks to this beautiful man, she could ensure Olly had a spectacular one. Filled with love and hope and memories.

"I'd like to propose a toast." Cilla clinked a fork against her glass at the head of the table. "Thank you all for coming tonight." She glanced around the table, making sustained eye contact with everyone. "Every person here has had a huge impact on my life lately. I spent a long time on my own and thought I was happy that way. But now, I can't imagine my life without you."

She took a sip of her chardonnay and focused on Bryce. "This incredible man came into my life when I least expected it. He's put up with my moodiness and old habits, yet he's stuck around anyway. And I'm thrilled to announce he's accepted a permanent position at Redemption General."

Everyone cheered as Cilla leaned down to kiss him, a resounding lip-smacker that made Olly mutter, "Gross."

Next, Cilla's gaze moved to Rose, Olly and Caden. "Rose, I'm so glad you and your delightful son are staying in Redemption." Cilla beamed at Caden. "I have you to thank for that, young man."

Caden smiled and nodded as Cilla's eyes narrowed. "But you look after them. Otherwise you'll have me to answer to."

"And me," Jake piped up, shooting Caden a mock glare.

Rose laughed, knowing Jake couldn't be happier for her and Caden. He'd said as much when they'd told him the good news yesterday.

Cilla continued around the table. "Sara and Jake, I'm thrilled you're going to be adding to our family soon. Your baby will be loved and cherished as much as I love you both."

Sara dabbed at her eyes while Jake swallowed several times.

Cilla's gaze fell on Tam and she teared up. "Last but not least, I can't begin to describe how happy I am to have my baby girl back." She blew Tam a kiss, who captured it and pressed her palm to her cheek. "I love you, Tam. And I'm looking forward to making up for lost time over the next few weeks."

Tamsin blinked several times before replying, "Love you too, Mom."

"So I'd like to toast the Mathieson family," Cilla said, raising her glass. "And that includes each and every one of you."

"Hear, hear," everyone murmured, raising their glasses before sipping at their drinks.

"Now, let's eat," Cilla said, throwing her arms wide at the feast laid before them. "Rose, what do we have here?"

Excited to hear feedback from her family on some of the newest recipes she'd been experimenting with, she pointed at the various dishes.

"Sugar-cured salmon on a chive potato salad. Smoked trout with avocado and a mustard vinaigrette. Lightly-crumbed eggplant with basil pesto. Saffron rice balls. Quinoa with squash, chia and garlic. Crispy softshell crab with guacamole. Fried zucchini flowers with mozzarella. Asparagus with wild arugula, garlic aioli and pickled onions. And a ravioli salad with chilies and capers."

"Yummo," Olly said, rubbing his tummy, and there were general mutters of agreement from the rest of the table.

"I'll get the steaks and shrimp skewers." Rose stood to head off to the grill and Caden said, "I'll help."

When they reached the grill, Caden slipped an arm around her waist and hugged her tight. "I've had a brainwave."

"You love me and want to marry me?" She gazed up at him and batted her eyelashes.

He chuckled as he squeezed her tighter. "That too. But you know you're the best chef around here, right?"

"Tell me something I don't know." She bumped him gently with her hip. "If you're buttering me up to make more of my key lime pie, don't worry. We're having it for dessert."

His eyes twinkled. "As much as I'd like to keep your gourmet fare to myself, maybe you should open your own restaurant? Or café?" He gestured at the table. "Seriously, what you whip up for family is beyond comparison with anything in Redemption. Any place you open would be packed with satisfied diners."

"It's always been my dream, I guess, but I could never afford the investment."

He squared his shoulders, wearing a proud grin. "We could do it together. I'd be your silent partner and you could run it. A trendy new café is exactly what this place needs."

"Whoa." She held up her hand, unable to quell the flame of excitement he'd lit within her. "Where is all this coming from?"

"I want you to be as happy as you've made me," he said, his gaze burning with so much love she felt unworthy of it. Before banishing the thought. She'd wasted enough of her life feeling worthless. Time to accept the love of an amazing man and acknowledge she deserved it.

"You adore cooking," he continued. "You should be allowed to flourish."

Stunned, Rose tried to absorb the idea, while Caden's enthusiasm knew no bounds. "This could be an amazing opportunity. You're the best there is, babe—why not show it off to the world?"

"Is this your subtle way of boosting my self-esteem—because you know all there is to know about me now?"

"Nothing subtle about it," he said, kissing her until she could barely breathe. "You're incredible, Rose. I know it. Your family knows it. Time for Redemption to know it too."

Heartened by his belief in her, and feeling blessed beyond belief that she'd be spending the rest of her life with this man, she nodded. "Okay. Let's do it."

"That's my girl." This time, his kiss grazed her lips, soft and sweet. "In the meantime, let's go feed the hungry horde."

As they piled the meat and seafood on platters and took them back to the table, Rose marveled at how far she'd come.

Redemption had been good for her in so many ways. Especially after she'd wasted too much time dwelling on the past and letting it affect her.

Time to start living her future.

She could hardly wait.

ACKNOWLEDGMENTS

Writing a series is exciting, when characters from the first book demand their own story and I must acquiesce.

But it also presents challenges. Ensuring continuity, evolving character arcs and giving in to the plain stubbornness of some characters that can't be silenced no matter how hard I try.

Creating the Redemption series has been a fast, wild ride and several fabulous people have been along for the thrill. So thanks to the following folks:

Sammia Hamer, editor extraordinaire, it's super exciting for an author when an editor "gets" me, and I'm so lucky to have you. Your support of my burgeoning career at Amazon means so much.

Katie Green, insightful editor, your suggestions during the editing process really helped to bring out the best in this book. Thank you for putting in the hard yards.

Jen McIntyre, for LOL at my characters and telling me so.

Soraya Lane, fellow Lake Union author and fab friend. Your output as a writer never ceases to amaze me and your support as a friend is invaluable.

Natalie Anderson, life is way too busy for us and we don't chat as often as we'd like but I value your support always.

My street team, Nic's Super Novas, for their collective support and love of all things literary.

My amazing boys, you are the loves of my life. Every single book I write is for you. You make every single day brighter with your smiles and hugs. Love you.

My hubby, for being my number one cheerleader and for providing the laughs.

My parents, for their unswerving support.

And last but not least, my readers. Thanks for your loyalty, your fan mail and for buying my books. I hope you have as much fun reading my Redemption women's fiction series as I did writing it.

ABOUT THE AUTHOR

Nicola Marsh is a bestselling, multiaward-winning author, who has sold more than six million copies worldwide. Her first mainstream romance, *Busted in Bollywood*, was nominated for Romantic Book of the Year 2012. Her first indie romance, *Crazy Love*, was a 2012 ARRA finalist. Her debut young adult novel, the supernatural thriller *Banish*, was released in 2013, and her YA urban fantasy *Scion of the Sun* won the 2014 National Readers' Choice Award for Best Young Adult Novel. Marsh is a *USA Today*, Bookscan, and Barnes & Noble bestseller, and a 2013 RBY (Romantic Book of the Year) and National Readers' Choice Award winner. She has also won several CataRomance Reviewers' Choice Awards, and been a finalist for a number of awards, including the Romantic Times Reviewers' Choice Award. A former physiotherapist, she now writes full-time. Her other loves are raising her two little heroes, sharing fine food with family and friends, and her favorite: curling up with a good book!

Printed in Germany
by Amazon Distribution
GmbH, Leipzig